# MURDER AT FONTAINEBLEAU

### AN ELIZABETHAN MYSTERY

## AMANDA CARMACK

AN OBSIDIAN MYSTERY

OBSIDIAN
Published by New American Library,
an imprint of Penguin Random House LLC
375 Hudson Street, New York, New York 10014

This book is an original publication of New American Library.

First Printing, June 2016

For more information about Penguin Random House, visit penguinrandomhouse.com.

ISBN 978-0-451-47570-1

Printed in the United States of America
10  9  8  7  6  5  4  3  2  1

Penguin
Random
House

# PRAISE FOR
# THE ELIZABETHAN MYSTERIES

"Meticulously researched and expertly told . . . paints a vivid picture of Tudor England. . . . Amanda Carmack's talent for creating a richly drawn setting, populating it with fully realized characters, and giving them a tight and engaging narrative is unparalleled. An evocative and intelligent read."
—*New York Times* bestselling author Tasha Alexander

"This dramatic period is filled with intrigue, religious conflict, betrayal, and danger, which [Carmack's] writing brings out brilliantly."
—*RT Book Reviews* (4½ stars, top pick)

"Deliciously detailed." —*Publishers Weekly*

"Carmack truly delivers on fascinating period details, along with intriguing danger and vivid characters . . . a true reading pleasure!" —Fresh Fiction

"A very vivid and impressive picture of the time, the places, the people and the conditions . . . a fun read with a solid mystery and a determined and likable heroine."
—Historical Novel Society

"Stellar . . . flowing descriptions, wonderful historic and fictional characters, and an intriguing mystery."
—Open Book Society

"Another nail-biting, intoxicating ride . . . that had me wanting the next book immediately. . . . Buy two copies: one for you and one for a friend."
—Mysteries and My Musings

"Rich descriptions and [a] lively and interesting cast of personable characters. . . . This is going to be a great series." —Sharon's Garden of Book Reviews

## ALSO BY AMANDA CARMACK

**The Elizabethan Mystery Series**

*Murder at Westminster Abbey*

*Murder at Hatfield House*

*Murder in the Queen's Garden*

*Murder at Whitehall*

To my favorite city in the world,
*ma belle* Paris

# CHAPTER ONE

*January 1561*
*England*

HERE LYETH MATTHEW HAYWOOD, D. DECEMBER 1560. "SING AND MAKE MUSIC IN YOUR HEART TO THE LORD."

Kate Haywood watched, shivering, as the stonemason's men slid the newly carved slab into place in the floor of the church aisle. She felt so numb, frozen in place. The moment seemed to stand perfectly still, caught in the grayish ray of light that fell through the window over the altar. And yet it also seemed to rush forward too quickly, pushing her over a cliff into something she was not ready for. A world without her beloved father.

The scrape of the stone echoing in the empty church, felt even more final than the day Kate had tucked a sprig of dried rosemary and a locket containing a curl of her long-dead mother's hair into her father's cold hand, and then watched as the pallbearers lowered his coffin into the vault.

That day, there had been people surrounding her—her friend Lady Violet Green; her father's friends, the Parks, who had once played music with him at the court of Queen Catherine Parr; Lady Mary Sidney and her small son—all sent by Queen Elizabeth herself to lay a wreath and condole with Kate. There had been music, composed by her father, soaring majestically to the old rafters of the solid, square Norman church. There had been stories of her father's life around the fireside afterward, tales of his great love for her mother, of the kings and queens he had served, the brilliant music he had brought into the world.

Now she was alone. She had sent everyone back to their homes, with many tears and fond embraces, in the days after the funeral. She had wanted the quiet days of waiting for the stone to be carved, wanted the time to pack her father's music and think on what she would do now.

She'd done little of that, though. The books and manuscripts were still piled by the trunks, her father's chair still by the fire. She had played her lute, stared into the flames—tried to fight away the numbness. There was truly no question of what she would do now. She would go back to court to serve Queen Elizabeth with her own music—and with other, more secret matters when the queen was in danger. That was her life now, a life she loved, a life where she was needed and that had great purpose.

If only she could shake away the cold and *move*.

"How does it look, Mistress Haywood?" the stonemason asked. His voice was quiet, respectful, yet it still startled Kate from her icy trance.

She looked down to see that the workmen had finished laying the stone in place. It fit perfectly into the flagstones of the aisle, barely any line around its edge at all. The words were deep carved and crisp now, but she knew soon enough they would fade, mellowed by all the footsteps that would cover them.

"It is very fine indeed," she said. "Thank you."

The stonemason nodded. He twisted his cap in his hand as he studied the stone with her. "He was a fine gentleman, your father. He even taught my daughter some music on his lute; said she had a natural ear for a song. He will be missed here."

"That is most kind of you," Kate answered, making a note in her mind to send some of his music to the daughter. "I know he was most content in his home here."

And that was true. After a long life of turmoil and trouble, of being always on the move as monarch followed monarch on the unsteady Tudor throne, of losing his beloved wife and bringing up a daughter alone, Matthew Haywood had found great peace by his cottage fireside. His gout kept him confined at the last, but his letters to Kate at court had been full of his work, the music he finally had time to write down, and his new friends.

That comforted her now, as did the knowledge that he was with her mother again at last. Surely they would both watch her and help her now.

Kate slowly turned and made her way out of the

church. Even though it was a cloudy day threatening rain, the pale light after the gloom of the church blinded her for a moment. The cold wind caught at her skirts. She drew the dark silk veil down from her small peaked cap and turned along the churchyard path toward the gate.

On such a chilly day, everyone in the village was tucked up by their own firesides, and she met no one in the frozen lane that led through the center of the community. She could smell the tang of woodsmoke in the air, the scent of the promised rain. After her months at the queen's court, moving from palace to palace amid the crowds and the schemes, such quiet still caught her by surprise. She could see why her father had liked it at the last, but she found she missed the noise, the company.

At the end of the lane, she reached the low stone wall that bounded her father's small garden. She laid her gloved hand on the gate latch, yet somehow she could not make herself push it open. Once she stepped inside that empty cottage, she would know her father was truly gone and was not coming back. Somehow seeing his name carved in cold, hard stone had shown her what was truly happening. She was alone in the world.

"Kate!"

For a moment, she was sure she had imagined the sound of that voice calling her name. It was an illusion of a lonely moment and grief, mayhap, of too many sleepless nights. Rob Cartman would not be here in this little village. He would be with the queen's cousin Lord Hunsdon, the patron of Rob's acting troupe. His rare letters had told her of all the masques and plays he had been writing and the stately manors they had visited.

She closed her eyes and shook her head.

"Kate!" But there it was again. Half daring to hope, Kate spun around and saw Rob hurrying toward her down the lane, leading his horse. He looked travel stained with winter mud on his high boots, his short woolen cloak wrapped high around him. Yet he was still, as always, gloriously handsome, with his golden hair beneath a lavishly plumed cap, his smile flashing brightly through the dark day. He raised his hand and waved.

Suddenly feeling lighter, Kate ran to meet him and flung her arms around his neck. He lifted her off her feet, laughing in surprise.

"Oh, Rob," she said, trying not to break into sobs. She was a sophisticated lady of the court now—she could not show every emotion. But, oh, it felt so good to feel the warmth of a friend nearby again. An anchor in the world—even if an actor like Rob was the furthest thing from a solid foundation. His work took him from town to town, estate to estate, just as hers did. But she had missed him.

And his arms were comforting as he held her close. "If I had known I could expect such a fine welcome, I would have traveled faster," he said with a laugh.

Kate drew back to study his face. Aye, he was as handsome as ever, yet he seemed rather tired, with shadows beneath his eyes and new lines bracketing his smile. She saw he had grown a beard, close-cropped and golden, and he wore a pearl drop earring in one ear, which had been the new fashion set by Robert Dudley when she left court.

"You look as if you have been traveling long as it is," she said. "Were you not meant to be with Lord Hunsdon at his estate at Eastwick?" Rob's acting troupe had been employed by the queen's cousin Lord Hunsdon for many months, entertaining the court under his auspices. It was a high place, with the promise of greater to come.

"So I was, organizing his lordship's Christmas revels. He went to the queen at Whitehall after New Year's, and that was when I heard you had left court. Lord Hunsdon gave me leave to depart right away. My poor, sweet Kate. Why did you not write me directly of Master Haywood's death?"

"I did not wish to take you from your work, not now. And I—" She broke off, shaking her head. How could she explain how much she had wanted to see him, but how she was afraid of it at the same time? How lost she had been of late?

Rob stooped down, not letting her look away from him. "Kate, have we not been good friends for a long time now? Have we not seen much together? A queen's coronation, traitors, and murderers? Actors of a much lesser caliber than my fair self?"

Kate had to laugh. *Friends?* They had been that, and sometimes with the tiniest, diamond-bright promise of more. "Aye, we have known each other more than a year now. And truly, I am happier than I can say to see you. I just . . ." She did not know what to say, so she laughed and answered, "You have a new beard, I see. Most fashionable."

He rubbed his hand over his jaw. "I am told it is quite dashing. Mayhap it makes me look more serious."

"Serious? You? Never!" Another cold gust of wind snatched at her cloak and threatened to carry away Rob's plumed cap. "I am a poor hostess indeed to keep you standing here. There is a livery stable just along the lane. I shall make us some spiced wine while you see to your horse."

Rob gave her a small frown, as if he wanted to argue or ask her something more, but then he just smiled and took up the horse's lead.

Kate let herself into the cottage. When she left to walk to the church, it had felt cold and lonely, but now it seemed to welcome her again. She laid aside her cloak and veil and stirred the embers of the hearth back to life. As she poured the wine and mixed up the cinnamon and sugar, she thought of Rob. Surely he had brought news of the court, of Queen Elizabeth and her latest activities. There would be word of the outside world again. As the flames caught, they seemed to melt away her numbness, and she was interested in life again.

Was it Rob—or was it news of the excitement of the court—that made her feel thus? Queen Elizabeth declared that romance—marriage—was the ruin of a woman, and the single state was to be preferred above all others. One could not blame her for such a view after all she had seen in her twenty-seven years—her mother and stepmother beheaded under her father's orders, her young Grey cousins forced to the altar by their parents, untimely deaths in childbirth. The queen had her safety and independence at last, a throne all for herself. Yet Kate's own parents had been so happy in their brief time together, and she had seen other couples who made lives together and kept the coldness of the world at bay.

Kate rose from the hearth and turned to tidy the small table while the wine warmed. Her workbox sat open, spilling out thread and ribbons, along with books and slates she used to study codes and languages. Surely her confused thoughts meant she was just feeling lonely, with her father gone and her work at court far away. She needed distraction to feel of use again.

She swept everything into an open case and shut the lid on it. She knelt down beside the fire and reached for the heated poker to use for the wine. As she finished, Rob came through the cottage door, bringing the cold wind of the day with him.

Kate pushed away her old melancholy, her jumbled thoughts, and smiled at him. "Come sit by the fire, Rob," she urged. She took his cloak and cap and hung them up next to her own. "Tell me all the news of court, every little bit." There were two chairs by the fire, her father's cushioned armchair and her own stool. She hesitated for an instant, then held out her father's chair for him.

It was good to see it filled again.

"I can do better than that," he said. He reached for his

saddlebags and took out a letter. As Kate took it from him, she noticed the queen's own seal pressed into the red wax, and her heart beat a little faster in excitement.

"Queen Elizabeth herself entrusted this to me, and said to give it into no hands but yours," he said, his voice full of pride and his own excitement. They were both making their place in a royal world.

Kate eagerly opened the message and scanned the neat lines of the queen's spiky handwriting and the precious signature at the bottom—*Elizabeth R.*

> *My dear Kate,*
> *How gloomy this Christmas season is without your music! I hope you were comforted by memories of your parents, as I have been of mine, and will return soon to court. I am in great need of friends I can trust now, and have an errand that I can put in few people's hands. I will not say more now, but please heed my wishes and return with all speed. My cousin Hunsdon has sent Master Cartman to escort you and see to your safety on the roads. Make all haste . . .*

Kate's curiosity was most piqued by the intriguing words. She glanced up to see that Rob sipped at his wine and looked into the fire as if to give her a private moment in the small sitting room. But she could tell from the glint in his eyes that he was as curious as she.

"Did the queen tell you about this letter?" she asked.

"Not at all. She merely commanded Lord Hunsdon

to give me leave from his household, and told me that once I found you I must hire a cart for your father's possessions and see that you returned to court as soon as could be."

Kate looked down at the paper in her hands, her thoughts racing. She had learned so much in the past few months, studying with agents of Sir William Cecil, learning the ways of foreign courts and the methods of codes. She had seen the plots and schemes that seemed to lurk around every corner, just beyond sight, always there.

Was Queen Elizabeth in danger now? Could Kate's services be of some small use to her again? The frozen sadness of the past few days was still there, clutching at her heart, but at last it was not the only thing she felt. There was the anticipation of work, the excitement of moving back into the world and being of real use.

Perhaps *that* was really why the queen herself was so hesitant to marry. Few women were given the chance to be a person in their own right, to forge their own path. It was a heady prospect.

"Tell me more of what is happening at court," she said. "I was sorry to miss the Christmas revels."

"They say the music was decidedly of poorer quality without you," Rob answered. "And the queen's masques were a great shambles with none to direct them. The glittering reputation of the royal entertainments will only suffer more if you do not come and rescue them."

Kate laughed. She knew it was not true—the queen had an entire Office of the Revels to make sure everything was lavish and perfect. Yet it still made her happy to think she was needed. "Such fustian. They have *you* now, do they not? I have heard that Lord Hunsdon boasts of the fine quality of his troupe of players."

"He is a fine employer indeed. He loves a fine play and is most appreciative and generous. To have the queen's cousin as a patron is higher than my uncle could have dreamed."

"He would have been proud of you." Kate poured them more wine. "And what else do they speak of at court besides the shabby quality of the revels?"

"Sir Robert Dudley seems back in favor, though not at the great heights he knew before his . . . unfortunate bereavement," Rob said, talking of the mysterious death of Dudley's wife, Amy. She had fallen down the stairs of her distant country home in September, plunging the court into mourning and whispers of suspicion. The queen's favorite courtier had left court for a time, but Kate had heard that he returned after the coroner's jury declared the death an accident and cleared his name of wrongdoing. Yet he was not free of the gossip.

"The queen's comptroller, Sir Thomas Parry, died last month, and Dudley coveted his office of Master of the Court of Wards, but the queen has given it to Cecil. And she danced but once or twice with Dudley at the Christmas revels. Sir Christopher Hatton was much at her side," Rob said.

Kate nodded. The queen was fond of Dudley—mayhap more than fond. Everyone could see the glow in her eyes when he was near. But she was, above all, the queen. "Are his hopes of marrying the queen truly ended?"

"To all but himself, I think. Dudley doesn't seem a man to give up easily."

Kate laughed. "Nay, that he is not." She had worked with Sir Robert a time or two and rather liked him. His vitality and vivid sense of life was hard to resist, but his ambition was enormous.

"Nor should he, or any man, when he knows his heart's desire."

Surprised at the sudden serious tone of his voice, Kate glanced at him to find he watched her steadily. Flustered, she looked away into the fire.

Rob shifted in his chair as a silence stretched between them. Then he laughed and said, "They say Erik of Sweden wishes to come to England in person to press his suit. He sent the queen a fine pair of horses for a Christmas gift. There has also been talk of a new marriage for Lady Catherine Grey."

"Lady Catherine?" Kate said. She hoped that was true; Lady Catherine seemed so sad, so alone, a woman who truly wanted marriage, a family, and a home. Her royal blood, something so many coveted, held her away from such normal dreams. "With Lord Hertford?"

"Hertford? Nay, they say he will be sent to the Continent soon. A betrothal with the Earl of Arran, to thus unite the thrones of England and Scotland, though most think this is impossible. There are also whispers the queen will adopt Lady Catherine and make her heir, though Queen Elizabeth seems in no hurry to secure the succession."

"There are plenty of claimants if she was so inclined. Lady Catherine and her sister; Lady Lennox . . ."

"Most of the talk is of Mary, Queen of Scots."

Kate nodded. Queen Mary had been widowed in November, King Francis of France dying at the age of sixteen. No one knew what she would do now. Return to Scotland? Marry again? "What is the talk?"

"It's said she seeks a new marriage, of course, though it would be hard to match her first. There's whispers of Don Carlos of Spain."

"Indeed?" Kate gasped. Rumor said that Don Carlos, the only son of King Philip of Spain, was feeble-minded and violent, not to mention a hunchback. Mary's beauty and charm was legendary. But indeed, the throne of Spain was a glittering prize. "Anyone else?"

"The queen's other cousin, Lady Lennox, has sent her son, Lord Darnley, to carry the family's sympathies to Queen Mary, but few rate his chances high."

"It would be wrong to underestimate Lady Lennox, I think. A most determined woman."

"Also, there is an unfortunate new fashion for round collars of starched Antwerp lace. It makes everyone look like lions in the menagerie—it must be stopped. Along with the new style of yellowish green. Most bilious."

Kate laughed. Whether it was the wine, the company, or the news of the world, she felt much warmed and restored. "It sounds as if there is indeed much work to be done at court. We must leave at once."

# CHAPTER TWO

"Very nearly there now, Kate," Rob said. "See? Aldgate is just ahead."

Kate thought he sounded rather too cheerful. Her hands were numb from clinging too tightly to the horse's reins, and her backside was sore from the hours in the saddle, even through the layers of her woolen skirt and petticoats. She did not fear horses as she once had; riding constantly between royal palaces had taught her how to control them and understand them better, and they were surely far more comfortable than being bounced around in a rickety cart. But she would still prefer the solid ground under her feet.

She *was* very glad to be in London again, to leave the sad quiet and loneliness of the village cottage behind and slip into the stream of life once more. Strangely, away from her father's last home, his absence felt less sharp. It was as if she carried him with her into a new adventure.

And while the journey had passed swiftly, with Rob teaching her some new songs and telling her tales of his acting troupe, she was glad to see the gates of the city. Curiosity over the queen's letter had her about to burst.

She peered out at the gray day from beneath the narrow brim of her velvet riding hat. The hours on the road had indeed brought them into a different world. The crowded, bustling, noisy life of London surrounded them. As she and Rob passed through the gate, they joined the vast, flowing river of humanity, everyone in a hurry, intent on their own important business. Carts jolted over the muddy ruts of the lane, along with horses, mules, and people on foot with their parcels and market baskets. Even a few rare, expensive coaches rumbled past.

The random shouts and cries amid the clang of the wheels hitting cobblestones sounded like a rare song to her ears.

Rob reached out and caught her lead rein so they wouldn't be parted by the crowd. Their progress was slow through the narrow streets, the grayish winter light turned even dimmer by the press of the tall close-packed buildings. The peaked rooflines nearly touched high above their heads, as if they would fall if they didn't have each other's walls to hold them up.

The shop windows, at eye level, were still open, counters spread with an enticing array of bright ribbons and embroidered gloves, finely wrought gold brooches and silver rings, and leather-bound books. Their color and glimmer flashed through the frosty light as she hurried forward.

She had quite forgotten the city smell, though, after weeks in the country. Usually she didn't notice the London perfume at all, she had grown so used to it, but now it made her eyes water. The cold wind helped; it was nothing like the heavy, warm air when the queen and her court fled Whitehall for Greenwich or Richmond in the spring. The latrine ditch along the middle of the lane was almost frozen over, a noxious stew of frost, ice, and human waste from the buckets dumped from upper windows. It was nearly covered by the smells of roasted meats, apple cider, the sugary scents of a nearby bakery, and the smoke of dozens of chimneys.

Eventually, they left the thickest of the crowds behind and turned toward the queen's palace at Whitehall. It was much quieter there; the press of beggars vanished, and the road widened as it passed the gates of fine mansions.

Most of the vast, winding puzzle of the palace complex, where Kate had lost her way many a time, was hidden from view, tucked away behind thick walls and long, plain-fronted galleries that gave away nothing of what lay behind them. Kate knew what was beyond: grand banquet halls, all carved and gilded and draped in gold-threaded tapestries; palatial chambers where courtiers would play cards and music and whisper together in masked desperation as they waited to catch the queen's attention; beautiful gardens of mazes, fountains, and flower beds.

It was the royal court. Her only real home now.

She drew in a deep breath, suddenly nervous even when faced with a place she knew so well. She felt as if she floated free, anchorless in the world.

She opened her eyes to find Rob watching her, his bright blue eyes dark, the lines around his mouth tight. "Are you well, Kate?" he asked gently.

Kate made herself smile brightly. "Very well indeed. I can't wait to start working again."

Rob said nothing, but in his smile she could see the same twinge of sadness she felt in her own heart. He urged the horses forward again, and they made their way to the foot of a stone staircase that led from the narrow lane in St. James's Park up the queen's long privy gallery, shimmering with its gilded roof and many windows. The cold wind was blocked there, along with the sickly sweet, frosty smell of the river. Rob swung down from his horse and lifted her from her saddle. She swayed for a second, her legs weak from the hours of riding.

"You need your land legs back, Kate," he said with a laugh.

She smiled and reached up to try to smooth the stray strands of hair back into the knitted caul beneath her hat. She had just brushed at her skirt and the fur-trimmed sleeves of her riding doublet when she heard the hollow click of footsteps along the flagstone stairs. She glanced up to see the queen's Mistress of the Robes, Mistress Kat Ashley, coming toward her.

Mistress Ashley looked just as she had when Kate left court, her graying dark hair braided and pinned beneath a white cap; the lace at the edge of her dark green gown bright white; her eyes, deep-set in her lined face, watchful and serious. Her loyalty was to the queen, always and above all else; she had long been like a mother to Elizabeth. But Kate knew her to be kindhearted, perhaps even a secret romantic at heart.

"Mistress Haywood," Mistress Ashley said. "I have been set to watch for your arrival. I hope your journey was comfortable enough?"

"It was blessedly short. Thank you, Mistress Ashley."

Mistress Ashley nodded and gave her a small smile. "We will surely all miss your father here at court. His songs are among the finest I have ever heard. None have any but praise for him."

Kate blinked against the prickle of tears in her eyes. She could not cry again, not now. "Thank you. He will be missed."

Mistress Ashley nodded. "Her Grace is most eager to see you. I have orders to take you to her now."

"Now?" Kate squeaked. The queen was always most insistent on her orders being obeyed right away, or there would be that Tudor temper to contend with. Elizabeth was ever impatient. Yet Kate had still hoped she might be able to change into one of her nicer gowns before facing the court again.

She glanced back at Rob, who shrugged and gave her a reassuring smile.

"The queen has many concerns right now making demands on her time," Mistress Ashley said sternly. "She has been asking about your arrival all day."

"Of course, Mistress Ashley," Kate answered.

Mistress Ashley nodded. "Master Cartman, a groom is on the way to assist with your horses. Lord Hunsdon wishes you to attend on him right away, as well."

Kate exchanged one more glance with Rob before she hurried off after Mistress Ashley. The stone gallery was spare and silent, with only a few liveried servants rushing past on their errands. They crossed over the lane through the old crenellated towers of the elaborately carved Holbein Gate and were then in the palace itself.

New tall windows of diamondlike glass looked down onto an empty, snow-dusted tiltyard. A shining blue-and-gold ceiling arched overhead, glowing like summer in the gray day, and a rare, thickly woven carpet muffled the footsteps of the well-shod crowd around them.

The queen's courtiers—clusters and pairs of people clad in brilliant satins and lustrous velvets—stood near the frost-dusted windows, talking and laughing, whispering intently. They watched Kate with curious eyes as she hurried past.

But she had no time to look in return, to stop and greet the people she knew well or to make curtsies. There was no time, either, to glance at the treasures on display, the paintings and tapestries, the crystals and cameos and clocks, the portraits of the queen's father, brother, and stepmothers that watched everyone walking past. They hurried down various corridors, up and down stairs, until they reached the queen's own apartments.

The Privy Chamber was crowded with those waiting to petition the queen, and many tried to stop Mistress Ashley, knowing her great influence. She waved Kate ahead when she stopped to talk with one of them, through the Presence Chamber and the small dining closet, to the queen's sanctum, the bedchamber.

It was crowded, as it always was, but the atmosphere was lighter, the chatter free of the strained quality in the rooms outside, where no one was guaranteed a moment in the royal presence. Ladies-in-waiting and maids of honor in their pale shimmering silks gathered on cushions and low stools scattered over the floor and around the warmth of the large fireplace, giggling over their sewing, feeding tidbits to their little dogs.

Queen Elizabeth sat by herself next to the single window, at a table covered with documents and books. The grayish sunlight filtered hazily through the panes of glass, turning the red-gold loops of her braided hair into a fiery halo and making her pale skin glow. She wore a loose robe of crimson figured velvet trimmed with white fur, with rubies adorning her long fingers and a band of creamy pearls around her hair.

She looked every inch the Queen of the Sun that had been the subject of her most recent masque, a role she grew into more with each passing month of her reign. Yet Kate could see the shadows beneath Elizabeth's dark eyes, which always meant the queen was not sleeping well, and her narrow lips were set in a tight line. Kate thought of the courtly gossip Rob had told her, of the scandals and worries that plagued the queen.

But Elizabeth smiled when she glanced up to find Kate waiting. "Mistress Haywood! You have returned at last."

Kate curtsied and made her way closer to the window. Elizabeth tapped her long, pale fingers on the papers, her rings sparkling. There was an ink smudge on her thumb.

"I am glad to see you again," the queen said. "I trust your father had a dignified and proper funeral?"

"He did indeed, Your Grace, and I thank you for sending mourners and the wreath. My father would have been most honored."

"To lose a parent is a sad thing. But you must know always he loved you and was proud of you, aye?"

Kate couldn't help but think that the queen had no such reassurances about her own father. Kate felt a cold touch of sadness. "I will always know that. My father will surely always be with me in that way. But I am glad to be back at court, Your Grace."

"You may not be so happy when you hear my task for you, Kate," Elizabeth said. "Please, sit. Talk with me quietly for a moment."

A page leaped forward with a stool at the queen's gesture, and Kate sank down onto it gratefully. She found she was still tired from the ride, yet her nerves hummed with curiosity.

Elizabeth glanced across the room as if to be sure her ladies were otherwise occupied before she said quietly, "As you surely know, Kate, my cousin Mary of Scotland was widowed in November."

Kate nodded. Rob had said that was the main subject of courtly gossip over Christmas, and she had heard talk of it even in her quiet country days. Mary had been Queen of France for only a little over a year when the young King Francis died of an infected ear after hunting in a winter storm. Queen Mary—and her influential, fanatically Catholic Guise uncles—had been a great thorn in Elizabeth's side ever since her own ascension to the throne.

It was said that Mary and her late husband, while always loudly proclaiming a great affection for their dearest cousin and sister-queen, still quartered the arms of England with those of Scotland and France, thus declaring themselves the *real* rulers of England.

"I had heard that, Your Grace," Kate answered. "They say Queen Mary has gone on retreat to a convent to mourn, yes? A time away from the French court and her mother-in-law, Queen Catherine?"

"Mourn?" Elizabeth said with a humorless little laugh. "She went into isolation for forty days when King Francis died, as all French queens do, but her time in a convent now is surely not for weeping. My ambassador in France, Sir Nicholas Throckmorton, says her Guise uncles are not content to lose their power at the Paris court now there is a ten-year-old king, the late king's brother, under the control of his mother, Queen Catherine de Medici. Queen Catherine has allied with the Guise before because she had no choice, but she is no true friend of theirs."

"Nor is she a true friend to her daughter-in-law Queen Mary?" Kate asked.

Elizabeth shrugged. "Queen Catherine is a sly one indeed, a Florentine to her core, but she is no fool." There was a note of grudging respect in the queen's voice. Queen Catherine was a devout Catholic, one who, it was said, had made jokes at Elizabeth's rumored betrothal to Dudley, her horse master, but Elizabeth knew a fine political mind when she heard one. "She has bowed to Queen Mary for a long time. She will no longer. Her day has come. Sir Nicholas says she immediately dismissed the idea that Mary might now wed the new king Charles and seized the regency for herself. I think Queen Catherine would like to see Mary gone from France—but not as the wife of Don Carlos of Spain, as they say the Guise are desperate to see happen."

"Don Carlos?" Rob had told her that was the gossip, but she hadn't quite believed it, not if the sad state of Don Carlos's health was true. "Would she really want that?"

"Exactly so. They say he is a cruel, hunchbacked idiot. Yet a Spanish crown could make so many unappealing qualities quite vanish to one as ambitious as my cousin. I have heard that King Philip is not enthusiastic, as he has just married Queen Catherine's own daughter, Princess Elisabeth, and one connection to

France is surely enough for him. But Mary will have plenty of other suitors. A queen with her own throne is always an attractive mate, as I have seen myself. And she may indeed return to Scotland and try to rule there herself."

What changes would a Catholic queen bring to England's northern borders? Elizabeth and above all Cecil had worked so hard to further England's own interests there, sending aid to the Protestant lords. "What of the Treaty of Edinburgh, Your Grace?"

Elizabeth frowned. "She has still not ratified the terms, and Throckmorton writes that she says she will not until she can consult with her Scottish lords, since she is now sadly deprived of her husband's counsel and she followed him in all things." Her scoffing tone said what she thought of *that* excuse. "This displeases me greatly. She must be made to ratify the treaty before anything else can go forward."

Elizabeth suddenly slammed her hand down on the table, rattling the ink pots and sending books clattering to the floor. Her ladies went silent and glanced her way, wide-eyed at the fear of another Tudor temper storm.

Kate knew to just sit and wait, for Elizabeth's mood would change again in a moment. She thought of what little she knew of the Treaty of Edinburgh, which had been signed after Elizabeth's forces defeated those of the Queen Regent, Queen Mary's mother, Marie of Guise, many months before. It had been mostly Cecil's work, a way to bring Queen Mary's pretensions to the

English throne to an end, and Kate knew Sir William considered it of vital importance. France was forced to recognize Elizabeth as the rightful Queen of England; Mary and Francis's claims were to be dropped immediately and the quartering of the arms to cease. French forces were to be removed from Scotland. A council of Protestant nobles under Lord James Stewart, Mary's illegitimate half brother, was to rule Scotland in Mary's absence. If Mary and Francis did not ratify the terms, England had the right to intervene in Scotland whenever it was thought necessary to protect Protestant interests.

Yet Queen Mary had long brushed aside the treaty, claiming she had no part in the negotiations at all.

"This is why I have called you back to court, Kate," Elizabeth said, calm once again. The ladies went back to their whispering.

Kate was puzzled. Queen Mary was an intriguing topic indeed, but she couldn't see where her part could be in the Scots queen's tale. "Am I to force Queen Mary to ratify the treaty at the point of my lute?"

Elizabeth laughed. "I wager if anyone at my court could do such a thing, it would be you. Your quiet sweetness can lull people into confessing much."

Kate was secretly pleased at the queen's words. She did not mean to convey quiet sweetness. She often wished she were more skilled at changing masks at will, as so many courtiers were, putting on the appropriate character for every situation, changing in a lightning flash. She was quiet because that was the way to learn the most. When people forgot someone was there, they spoke more freely, let their masks slip.

As for "sweet"—she knew her father would have laughed at such an idea, for she had often been a willful child. Yet she knew her heart was sometimes too soft for courtly life. Her mother had secretly been a Boleyn, but everyone who knew Eleanor Haywood said she had been calm and serene. Not very Boleyn-like at all.

"Nay, don't look so uncertain, Kate," Elizabeth said. "You have often served me well, and you know it. You can go where most ladies cannot, and you know the art of waiting and listening. You know people, as if they were characters in a play. And, for so many reasons, I know you are loyal to me. Loyal to England."

Kate nodded. She was indeed loyal to Elizabeth. Not only were they secretly family, but Kate knew that Elizabeth was the only hope for a peaceful, united kingdom. She had seen too many storms, too much danger growing up under King Edward and Queen Mary to think otherwise. "I will always serve Your Grace however I can."

"Good. Because I need you to go to France as soon as possible."

Kate had heard some rather strange requests from Elizabeth before, but she had not expected *that*. To go to France—she, who had never been farther from London than Nonsuch?

It was frightening, the thought of venturing across the sea to a new land. Yet also most intriguing. Kate had read so much of France, but she had never thought to see it for herself.

"You will not go alone, of course," Elizabeth said. "I am sending a small party to offer condolences to my cousin, and perhaps bring some small cheer to her in such a doleful time. I will leave the hard-hearted politics to Cecil. Or so it will appear. I need someone I can trust there, someone who knows how to watch and listen, who knows the workings of people's hearts. A musician, mayhap."

Knew people's hearts? Kate often wished she did know such things. But she would do anything for the queen. "Whom would I travel with, Your Grace?"

"I have not assembled everyone yet, but Sir Henry Barnett has agreed to go, along with his wife, Jane, who was once a Percy. Perhaps you know them?"

Kate nodded. She had met the Barnetts, though she did not know them well. Sir Henry had long worked in royal diplomatic circles and was known to be a hard but fair man, and much liked by his servants. Lady Barnett was pretty, and said to be proud of her maiden name, though she had come from an impoverished branch of that ancient family. Kate knew little else.

"Lady Barnett once served at the French court, at the same time as my mother, when they were only girls," Elizabeth said. The words were spoken casually, carelessly, but her tone sharpened when she mentioned her mother. Kate nodded, remembering that Anne Boleyn had spent many years at the French court when she was young, acquiring the Parisian polish and style that made her so distinctive. "I think that might have been where she met Sir Henry, for they married very young. They have no children, but Lady Barnett's niece, Amelia Wrightsman, will go with them. Mistress Wrightsman was recently in France herself. Sir Henry is dull but steady. You will be able to rely on him for help."

Kate nodded. "Who else, Your Grace?"

"A kinsman to Ambassador Throckmorton, Master Charles Throckmorton, is going to join Sir Nicholas's household. He will travel with you. Cecil will add others." She glanced down at the papers on her desk, seeming to hesitate. "Also, our cousin Lord Hunsdon has agreed to send some of his company of actors to assist you in creating entertainments for Queen Mary. Your friend Master Cartman will be one of them."

Kate was surprised again—and pleased. Surely France could not be so frightening with Rob to share it with her! To make her laugh. "Rob Cartman, Your Grace?"

"Aye. Rob, as you say. I have heard that Queen Mary much enjoys the company of handsome young men, and plays and music give her much pleasure. The game of courtly love is strong at the French court." Elizabeth frowned disapprovingly, as if she herself did not fully take advantage of such courtly-love masquerades, playing her suitors against one another, reveling in poetry and gifts. "Though they also say that young men are even more susceptible to *her*. That she is very beautiful indeed."

"Rob is most loyal to you, Your Grace, and to England."

"So Lord Hunsdon says, and I do trust both of you.

If this Master Cartman will be of help to you, then he may go." She paused and leveled a stern glance at Kate, one that made her cheeks turn warm, though she did not know why. "Kate, you know I caution my ladies against any thoughts of marriage."

Kate nodded slowly. She did indeed know that. Was not Lady Catherine Grey pining away for love? She had been sent to the Tower for marrying Lord Hertford in secret and bearing his child. More ladies than her had been banished for the crime of wishing to marry and have their own families. The queen had to be the center of all her courtiers' lives. "I know."

"Very well, then, Kate. You may go now. Rest for now; you have your old room, and warm water and refreshments will be delivered there. I will also send my tailor to you; you will need new gowns for the French court. Tonight I will dine with you and the others who are to go to France."

"Thank you, Your Grace. I shall do my best for you," Kate said. She rose from her stool and curtsied as the queen waved her away and turned back to her papers.

"I know you will, Kate," Elizabeth whispered. "I also know you will be most careful. The French court is not like my own. You must be ever vigilant there."

Kate nodded and made her way out of the royal apartments. Her own room was along a distant corridor, far from the grand royal apartments and the lodgings of favored courtiers, but she was glad of the quiet there, the moment to think. A fire was laid in the grate, and her familiar bed and chair were waiting. Her box of books was already laid on her small table, along with a tray of wine and cakes. *I am to go to France!* She could hardly absorb the thought. What would it be like there? Not like England, certainly, but Elizabeth was wrong if she thought vigilance was something that would only be needed in Paris. Watching and listening constantly was the only way to even hope to stay out of danger in any royal court. Kate knew she had much to learn, but she had also come a long way since her days at Hatfield with Princess Elizabeth.

She reached for the box of books, thinking to start studying right away, only to find a note tucked on its lid. *Mistress Haywood, welcome back to Whitehall. If you would please to attend me as soon as possible? Sir W. Cecil.*

Kate laughed. It seemed there were to be few quiet moments after all.

# CHAPTER THREE

The chamber Sir William Cecil used for his office was not a large one, and every table and chest was covered with documents. The papers seemed to teeter and lean precariously, but Kate knew each one was carefully noted and placed. Three clerks sat near the window, using the waning light to decipher the letters before them. The only sound was the scratch of their quill pens across parchment, the slight rustle of their black clerks' robes. The air, warmed by a crackling fire occasionally fed by more papers, smelled of dust and ink.

Sir William sat by the fire, next to a small writing table. Like his secretaries, he wore black, but his was glossy silk trimmed with fur. He was not an old man, merely in his early forties, but his task of guiding the often-stubborn queen and keeping England secure had aged him. His shoulders seemed stooped from constantly looking over papers, his eyes red-rimmed, his brown beard flecked with gray.

Kate had come to respect him greatly. He worked

even longer hours than the queen, got little sleep, and would never give up when it came to ensuring the queen's safety. She was grateful to him for the lessons he gave her as well, having some of his men help her with code breaking, lock picking, and even a bit of swordplay.

"Ah, Mistress Haywood, there you are," Cecil said, not even looking up from his writing. "'Tis good to see you at court again."

"'Tis good to be back, Sir William," she answered.

"Of course it is. There is no need for your fine music in the country, I would warrant." He waved her to a stool across from him and offered a silver pitcher of wine. "And I do not have enough people to help me here these days."

Kate took a sip of the wine and studied the secretaries bent over their papers. "Does not half the court work for you, Sir William?"

"Ha! That they do—unless they work for that fool Dudley. And they will see the light soon enough." Cecil laid down his pen and sat back in his cushioned chair. "I would wager you do not work for either of us, Mistress Haywood."

"I serve Queen Elizabeth however I can."

"As do we all. Without her we are all lost." Cecil sighed. "If I could just persuade her to do what she must, to marry and give England a son at last . . ."

"If only there was the right bridegroom to father that son . . ." Kate said with a laugh, and thought of Elizabeth's attitude toward marriage. She thought Cecil would be waiting long for a king consort.

"Only that would put an end to the Queen of Scots' demands to be acknowledged as heir," Cecil said severely. "She must be brought into place. She and her plague of Guise uncles have paraded their arrogance before the world long enough."

"Thus this journey to France?"

Cecil nodded. "My friend Nicholas Throckmorton, the ambassador to France, wishes greatly to return to England, but Queen Elizabeth insists he shall not leave Paris until Queen Mary has ratified the Treaty of Edinburgh. Nick is a fine man, a loyal one, but even he seems susceptible to Mary's reputed charms. He needs some assistance in this endeavor."

"Queen Elizabeth says Mary will not ratify because she insists she needs counsel from her Scots lords, that she was not consulted in the terms."

A flash of anger, a rare show of emotion, crossed Cecil's bearded face. "Queen Mary is a viper, waiting to strike at England at every opportunity. She thinks the English throne will fall into her hands. This refusal is yet another of her hostile acts. It is a refusal to recognize Elizabeth as rightful Queen of England, and no honeyed words will disguise that. She will always conspire to overthrow her cousin and bring Catholicism back to England. She must be watched most carefully at all times."

It sounded like an enormous task, and for an

instant Kate felt lost. How could she be of any help in a scheme so big? She drank the last of her wine. "And you think I can be of assistance in such a matter?"

"I know you can, Mistress Haywood. Queen Mary loves her entertainments above all, music and dance and such." His tone clearly showed his doubt in such a thing. Cecil would attend royal plays and masques if needed, but he much preferred his own desk to amusements. But he would always utilize whatever might get the task done. "She is always on her guard with Throckmorton, always dissembling. My friend the Earl of Bedford, too, has gone to France to deliver Queen Elizabeth's condolence letters to Mary, but I fear he lacks a certain . . . patience. He presses Queen Mary too insistently, and she will not give him an audience. A young lady who can bring music to Queen Mary in her more private moments, who speaks fluent French and knows the art of watchfulness—aye, you can be of much assistance."

"What must I do?"

"Only what you do already. Play music, watch the dancing. Listen to Queen Mary speak in private to her ladies and her family. If you could persuade her that Queen Elizabeth is truly her friend and ally, that ratifying the treaty would be the only thing that could ensure her a place in the English succession, all the better."

Kate nodded. She could indeed do that, at least the music and listening part. She had learned how to notice so many things in the last months. But to persuade a queen . . .

That she would certainly have to practice.

"I also need you to deliver these." Cecil handed her a small bundle of letters carefully sealed with plain wax. "For Nicholas Throckmorton and Lord Bedford, as well as a few other friends. They are in cipher, of course, but it would be best if they did not fall into Guise hands. Or into those of Lord James Stewart, for that matter."

"Queen Mary's illegitimate half brother?"

"Aye. He poses as our ally, writing me asking for support for the Lords of the Congregation if his sister returns to Scotland, declaring his staunch adherence to the Protestant church. But I know he plays a double game. He has also written to the King of Navarre in France and to Spain. He is with his sister in France now, no doubt giving her the same honeyed words of support. He was regent of Scotland with her gone from her kingdom. He wants only to keep that power in his own hands."

"I will guard these letters most carefully, Sir William." Kate carefully tucked the letters into the purse at her waist.

"I know you shall. These also came for you while you were away." He passed her more letters, his expression impassive.

The seals appeared unbroken, but Kate knew that was no sign of privacy. She had been taught how to steam them open and reseal them, making them look perfectly intact. Before she could study them, the door opened and a young man entered the chamber. She slid the letters into her purse with the others.

"Ah, Toby. There you are," Cecil said. "Come and meet Mistress Haywood, who will be accompanying you and the Barnetts to France. Mistress Haywood, you know Master Toby Ridley? He is recently returned from a journey on the queen's business to Venice, and was in Paris before that."

Kate gave him a smile. She knew him by sight, though she had never actually met him. He was one of those young men who hovered at the edges of the royal court, though she had heard that many of the ladies liked him.

Master Ridley gave a bow, and when he faced them again, Kate saw he had a wide, merry smile, one that surely made everyone else want to smile as well. Though he was too plain-faced to be really handsome, with freckles across a flat nose and curling brown hair to match his brown eyes, that smile was one of rare charm.

He was also very fashionably dressed, which set him aside from the somber Cecil and his secretaries. Master Ridley's purple velvet doublet, the sleeves slashed and pinked in gold, and the gold embroidery on his short satin cloak shimmered.

"I am glad to see you have given me a much more beauteous travel companion this time, Sir William," Master Ridley said teasingly. "All those hatchet-faced Puritans have made for some dull journeys."

Much to Kate's surprise, Cecil actually chuckled. Surely no one else dared speak to the dour chief secretary like that! Except for his wife, Mildred, everyone was most careful and circumspect around him. She studied Master Ridley with even more interest.

"Do you care for music, Master Ridley?" she asked.

"I fear I have an ear of lead, Mistress Haywood," he answered cheerfully. "Perhaps you could give me lessons on the lute during our voyage? I have heard you play for the queen's dancing, and it is like hearing angels' songs. Such a talent might be of much use in wooing the fair ladies."

Kate burst out laughing. She couldn't help herself; he looked so mischievous. "I have the feeling you need little help on *that* errand, Master Ridley. But I am always happy to bring more acolytes to Euterpe."

"Ah, I knew you two would work together well," Cecil said. "Now take yourselves off to walk in the garden and speak more of these French matters. I must finish my work here."

Master Ridley offered his arm to Kate and led her out of Cecil's office and through the gallery. Courtiers still gathered there, gossiping and laughing together, and Toby Ridley stopped to greet several of them. Kate noticed everyone seemed glad to see him, and he had an easy, convivial way of speaking to them.

"It must be very interesting to visit so many foreign lands," Kate said as they went down the stone steps of the gallery.

His open, merry face turned more somber of expression when they were out in the quiet garden. It was too cold for very many people to be outside as they would be on warmer afternoons. The trees were bare, their brown branches stark against the gray sky, and the gravel paths wound past sleeping flower beds.

"You have not been to France before, have you, Mistress Haywood?"

"Nay, I have never been farther from London than Nonsuch," she answered. "I have scarcely had time to become accustomed to the idea of such a journey, but I confess I'm rather excited by the prospect. They say France is most beautiful."

"And so it is. The palaces are beyond compare, decorated by the finest artists from Florence and Venice, with the most exquisite gardens. The fashions are as beautiful as the ladies who wear them. Everything has a lightness and grace to it we do not see so often in England."

Kate was intrigued. "You have been to France many times, then, Master Ridley?"

"Aye, but not since before I was in Venice. At my last visit, for the marriage of Princess Elisabeth by proxy to King Philip of Spain, I saw the joust where King Henri was killed."

His voice was quiet, but Kate saw the tightness of his jaw as he said those words, the way he closed his eyes for a moment. She could only imagine the horror of that scene, when the late French king—Mary, Queen of Scots' father-in-law—was killed when a lance splintered and pierced his brain, with all his family and courtiers watching.

"I am sorry, Master Ridley," she said.

He nodded. "And now the boy who became king on that day is dead himself. King Francis was surely never destined to be a great king. He was ill and feverish all the time, obsessed with hunting, never attending his own council meetings. And he was much shorter than his wife, Queen Mary."

"But now France has a king who is only nine years old."

"And the Guise brothers competing with the Bourbons for power. They are all ruthless and will not give up even a shred of authority without a very fierce fight." He stopped on the graveled path and turned to face her. He looked like a different person than the one who had laughed with the courtiers in the gallery, his plain face older. "Never forget, Mistress Haywood. The beauty of France conceals naught but a vipers' pit. No one is ever what they seem."

Kate thought surely the same could be said of the English court. She had learned long ago to look deeper, look beyond charming smiles and sweet words, for so many people had proved false to her in the past. Yet Master Ridley looked so intent, so eager to make sure she understood his warning, she could only nod. "I will be most careful—I promise, Master Ridley."

His taut expression relaxed into a smile. "I know Sir William would never send you to France if he did not know that to be true. He is never wrong about people."

Kate hoped that was true, for she was trusting Cecil— and the queen—to send her off on a long voyage with a party of people she barely knew.

"Master Throckmorton!" Toby suddenly called, turning from Kate to wave to a man who was passing them on a parallel path. "I understand you are to travel with us to France."

The man paused and made his way over to them. She studied him curiously, for he was surely Charles Throckmorton, whom Cecil said was also to be sent to France. He was handsome, with a dark, hawkish face, his hair and short-trimmed beard also dark. He was dressed more quietly than Toby, in brown velvet and wool, his cap unadorned with any beads or plumes. He did not glance at her, his gaze intent on Toby.

"I am to join my kinsman Sir Nicholas at his embassy," Master Throckmorton said. "I would prefer to stay here with my studies, but royal orders must be obeyed. I am happy *you* are going, Toby. At least there shall be one person to converse with on this journey."

"More than one, I am sure." Toby reached for Kate's arm and gently drew her forward. "This is Mistress Haywood, the queen's musician, who is also to journey to France. Sir William says she is fluent in French and will surely entertain Queen Mary. Mistress Haywood, may I present Master Charles Throckmorton? We have known each other since we were lads; we shared tutors and were pages in Sir William's household."

"I am glad to meet you, Mistress Haywood." Master Throckmorton gave her a bow, but he still did not look directly at her or seem very interested.

"What are your studies, Master Throckmorton?" Kate asked.

"I am interested in alchemy and astronomy."

"Indeed? I have had the honor of meeting Dr. John Dee at the queen's court. His studies are quite fascinating. Alchemy can be much like music, can it not? A means of exploring the interactions of the celestial forces," Kate said. She thought of that summer at Nonsuch Palace, of all the things she had seen there that could not be explained.

"Truly? How fascinating," Master Throckmorton said. "I have been reading his work on the Monas, the possibility that astronomical symbols, and maybe even musical notes, could be the keys to a lost universal language. . . ."

The sound of bells tolling from the royal chapel made her look up in surprise. The sky was darkening and the windows of the palace began glowing with new amber candlelight, one by one. Soon it would be time for the court to go to their supper, and for her own dinner with the queen.

"Perhaps we could more speak of this later, Mistress Haywood," Charles Throckmorton said. He looked livelier now, his thin features more animated.

"I shall look forward to it," Kate answered.

Master Ridley offered his arm to lead her back to the warmth of the palace. "Charles likes you as well, Mistress Haywood—I can tell. At least we shall all be able to trust one another in Paris."

Kate nodded, but she was not entirely sure she agreed. She did not yet know these men so well, and surely they carried secrets like everyone else at court.

In the corridor, she parted from Toby and made her

way up to her chamber. The tiny space gave her a precious moment of quiet and privacy. The fire had been built up and the trunks and chests from her father's cottage had been delivered. Her precious lute, which had once been her mother's, lay in its stand, yet there was no time to pick it up now, to find her usual comfort in the feel of its strings under her fingers, the flow of notes through her mind.

She took the letters from her purse and locked Cecil's messages away beneath the false bottom of her small jewel case. Her own letter she opened, and was pleased to see she had indeed recognized the handwriting—it was from her friend Anthony Elias.

*My dear Kate—*

*I have heard that you are at Whitehall with the queen, and I have also found myself in London for the time being. I am finishing my studies with Master Hardy and will soon be seeking my own clients, hopefully finding a home of my own one day. I hope you will have a few moments to say hello to an old friend, and allow him to tell you in person how very sorry he is for the loss of your honorable father. It has been too long since I saw you, and I have so many things I would like to say to you. Send me word, and I will meet you whenever you are able.*

*Your friend, Anthony E.*

Kate smiled and sat down to pen a reply, telling Anthony she would be happy to see him before she departed for France. She longed to hear more about his planned life, his hopes, and to ask him about what he or Master Hardy might know about the situation in France.

But what could she write to him now? She would have to think about it most carefully. For a time, she had been alone in the country, lost in memories of her father, but now she had to think about the present. Rob and Anthony had both made appearances in her life again, and she found she needed both of them, in their own very different ways.

She went to her small window, pushed it open, and looked down at the garden below. It was not one of the grand royal promenades, but a simple kitchen garden. In the summer it would provide perfumed herbs for the queen's table. Now it seemed to slumber under a thin, pale layer of frost.

Yet it was not entirely deserted. A couple walked slowly along the narrow path, their heads together as if they whispered secrets. Kate was surprised to see Master Ridley's elaborate gold-embroidered cloak.

Next to him walked a lady with lovely silver-blond hair, bound with a twist of pearls and sapphires that matched her blue gown. He whispered in her ear, his face tense, not as open and merry as it had been when he'd talked with Kate and Charles Throckmorton. The lady shook her head and laughed. She turned as if to leave, but Master Ridley caught her arm. She merely shook him off and hurried away as he stared after her.

So Master Ridley was thwarted in romance, as so many at Elizabeth's court were? Kate couldn't help but feel sorry for him. It would be a long journey to France, but mayhap it could help him forget, as she hoped it would do for her. Her father was gone, and she had to learn to live her life on her own terms. Perhaps that would be easier in a completely new place.

# CHAPTER FOUR

When Kate made her way to the queen's small privy dining chamber later that evening, she found several people already gathered there. They stood around the oblong table, which was already spread with gleaming silver plate and goblets. Master Ridley was there, talking with Charles Throckmorton, and they both gave her bows. An older gentleman stood near the fireplace, half-turned away from her, and she assumed he must be Sir Henry Barnett. He was a stout man in a fine velvet robe of subdued gray, which matched his beard. Rob waved at her as she lingered in the doorway. Everyone was silent, gazing around with slightly confused expressions.

Kate shared their puzzlement. The queen's dining chamber was usually used only by Elizabeth herself, on evenings when there was no grand banquet or masque. She would be served by her senior ladies-in-waiting, taking the small portions of vegetables and broiled game she preferred. Sometimes she would dine with a favored courtier, such as Robert Dudley. Tonight, they seemed a motley collection whose chief connection was the upcoming voyage to France.

The queen was not there yet, nor were Sir Henry's wife and niece. Kate found a quiet corner and surreptitiously smoothed her hair beneath her small embroidered cap and adjusted the skirt of her blue silk gown. She had feared she would be late and had rushed through her toilette, but luckily she seemed rather early.

Rob came to stand beside her. Unlike her, he did not seem to have rushed through his change of clothes, for he looked almost gleaming in his scarlet satin and black velvet in the torchlight.

"Well, Kate," he said quietly in her ear. "Are you looking forward to our voyage?"

"Mayhap not the voyage itself," she admitted. "I have heard little encouraging about a Channel crossing in winter. But to see France—aye, I *do* look forward to that. They say it is most beautiful, and surely Queen Catherine de Medici has brought the newest Italian plays and songs there, long before they will appear in London."

Rob smiled. "They say there is an Italian troupe at the Queen Mother's court that allows a woman on their stage."

"Nay!" Kate gasped, shocked.

"Aye. I suppose we shall see for ourselves. Mayhap you will even run off to join them?"

She laughed. "It does sound tempting. I look forward to seeing it."

Rob crossed his arms, studying the room in a seemingly casual way. "Did you know Thomas is also to go with us?"

"Your apprentice?" Kate was surprised. Out of all the men in Rob's troupe, men who had traveled much and performed many roles for many different types of people, Thomas seemed an odd choice. He was young and in the past had been susceptible to romantic misadventures.

But those things could also work in his favor. Robust, and handsome, he was surely eager for adventure. He was loyal to Rob, who had given him a good place in his acting troupe. And they did say Queen Mary had a keen eye for a fine-faced young man.

*She will have a good many choices of faces among this little group,* Kate thought as she studied the gathering around her. Master Ridley and Master Throckmorton were both appealing in their very different ways, and Rob was one of the most handsome men she had met.

"Someone must assist with the entertainments, and Lord Hunsdon says Thomas has no family or sweetheart here to pine for," Rob said. "Thomas does seem excited by the prospect. Do you think he will elope with a pretty mademoiselle as soon as we arrive?"

"He very well might," Kate said with a laugh. "He does seem to enjoy swooning for love at every opportunity, and a whole new kingdom full of ladies seems a rare opportunity."

The door to the dining chamber flew open and three

ladies rushed inside, a blur of bright satins, jewels, and fluttering ribbons.

Kate studied them carefully. Sir Henry Barnett took the arm of the eldest lady and whispered in her ear, his bearded, lined face thunderous. Kate thought the woman must be Lady Barnett, and she did not seem in the slightest abashed by her husband's scolding. She laughed and tapped his sleeve with the peacock feather fan that dangled from the silver-and-pearl chain at her waist.

She must have once been a rare beauty, and she was still lovely and delicate, with an oval face painted lightly with white lead and cerise, and bright blue eyes echoed by the blue-and-green-satin gown trimmed with silver ribbon. The hair swept up in elaborate curls and braids beneath a silver headdress was still sunny blond, barely touched with gray.

The young lady who stood beside her had to be her niece, Amelia Wrightsman, Kate thought, for they looked as near alike as sisters. If Lady Barnett was beginning to fade, Mistress Wrightsman was like the sunrise. Her cheeks glowed a natural peachy color against her pink silk dress and the loops of her pearl necklace. More pearls wound through her pale hair, which smelled of sweet violet perfume.

Toby Ridley drifted to her side as if pulled there by an invisible chain, his plain, expressive face written with an infatuated smile. For a man of Cecil's, Master Ridley seemed shockingly poor at dissembling.

*Mayhap* too *poor?* Kate wondered. The man she had talked with in the garden seemed most sensible. But she suddenly realized she was not the only lady he walked with in the twilight. It was Mistress Wrightsman's blond head that had been close to Toby's as Kate watched them from her window.

As he whispered now to Mistress Wrightsman, who blushed the same pink as her bodice and giggled behind her beringed fingers, Kate studied the third woman. Perhaps she was a servant of sorts, for she was much more plainly dressed, in a black overskirt and bodice with tawny-striped sleeves and skirt forepart. The bit of hair that could be seen at the front of her old-fashioned headdress was plain brown, liberally frosted with gray. Her face was heavy, lined, but her eyes were bright blue.

She leaned toward Mistress Wrightsman and said something quietly, intently, to her, much as Sir Henry had done with his wife. Mistress Wrightsman took as little notice as her aunt, brushing the woman away and taking Master Ridley's arm. He led her across the room, where they could talk quietly together in the corner opposite Kate's.

Kate noticed that Charles Throckmorton did not look happy at this progress of events. He watched Toby and Mistress Wrightsman with a frown.

But there was no time to puzzle over the people around her any further, for the door that led to the queen's bedchamber opened, and Elizabeth appeared with Cecil at her side, followed by Mistress Ashley. The queen had changed from her loose robe into a gown of black-and-white velvet trimmed with ermine, not as elaborate a garb as she would have worn at a banquet, where her courtiers and foreign ambassadors would see her.

She swept to her seat, the only armchair at the table, and gathered everyone else to the stools around her. Cecil sat beside her as Mistress Ashley hurried to place a cushion beneath Elizabeth's velvet slippers and behind her back.

"I am glad all of you are here," Elizabeth said merrily, obviously in one of her good moods. "You must be eager to hear all the details of your journey. Have you all met?"

As servants brought in the first course of stews and salads and poured fine malmsey wine into the silver goblets, Cecil said, "Sir Henry Barnett and his wife, Lady Barnett . . ."

"Oh, I am to be Jane, surely!" Lady Barnett said with a laugh. She took a long drink of her wine and waved for more, even as her husband tried to catch her hand. She neatly evaded him. "We shall all be spending so much time together. Isn't that right, Amy, my dear? Oh, and this is my niece, Mistress Amelia Wrightsman, *naturellement*."

"We are so looking forward to seeing France again," Amelia chirped brightly. She really did seem like a little bird, bright and fluttering, alighting here and there on her cloud of violet perfume.

Sir Henry did not look quite as enthusiastic as his kinswomen. "We shall do our duty wherever we are sent."

"And you have served me very well, Sir Henry," Elizabeth said. "This lady is . . ." She gestured toward the woman in black and tawny with a puzzled frown.

"This is Brigit Berry, our companion," Lady Barnett said dismissively. "My health is not so robust, so I need her assistance at all times."

"I am sure the voyage will revive you, Lady Barnett," Elizabeth said.

"Oh, aye, Your Grace!" Lady Barnett cried. "We shall be forever grateful you are sending us on this important mission."

"And this is Master Ridley and Master Throckmorton, who will be joining his kinsman, our ambassador to France," the queen continued. "Also, my chief musician, Mistress Haywood, who is fluent in French and is to bring back to my court all the latest songs and dances. She will be assisted by my cousin Lord Hunsdon's man, Master Cartman. Ah, good, more wine!"

As more wine was poured and dishes of venison in apricot sauce and trout dressed in cherries were passed around, Master Ridley gave Kate a wink, but no one else seemed to pay the least attention to her and Rob. All the better for them to do their tasks unnoticed.

Except for Amelia Wrightsman. Kate caught her watching Rob, her bright smile momentarily dimmed. But then she laughed again, and that fleeting expression vanished. No one else seemed to see that instant of a mask slipping, but Kate wondered if she shouldn't keep a closer eye on Mistress Wrightsman.

"So, Sir Henry, tell us of the situation in France since King Francis's sad demise," the queen said.

Sir Henry shook his head. "France is in great disarray, I fear, Your Grace, as it has been ever since King Henri died. Under King Francis and Queen Mary, the Guise have reigned unchecked. They chased away Antoine de Bourbon, the King of Navarre, who should have been next in line to the throne. The public debt, thanks to their lavishness, is near forty million livres, while the royal tax revenue is only ten thousand per annum. Rebellion and religious conflict are always threatening, as it was at Amboise."

Elizabeth and Cecil nodded solemnly. The bloodbath at Amboise was notorious, and said to have been entirely engineered by the Guise to eliminate their enemies.

Elizabeth frowned. She surely knew what it was like to have such troubles in her own kingdom. She had inherited a throne beset with debt, thanks to Queen Mary's warfare abroad, and conflict over the religious settlement. There had been no open rebellion yet, thanks to the work of Cecil and his men.

"But the Guise have fallen now?" the queen said, popping a sugared wafer into her mouth.

Sir Henry smiled at last, and it made him look much younger, though still stout and jowly and gray. "Virtually overnight. Queen Catherine, whom everyone thought so quiet and complacent, struck quickly after King Francis died. She had herself declared regent and governor of the kingdom before anyone knew what was happening. Monsieur de L'Hôpital is her chancellor. He is said to be very wise and calm, and no friend to the Guise. She has summoned the Estates-General to help reform the royal finances, but there is no doubt she in charge. There is none now to stand in her way."

"It is too bad she is so very unattractive!" Lady Barnett cried. Her husband gave her a disapproving glance, but she just smiled and waved her fan to summon more wine. Amelia giggled. "So short and stout, and never wearing anything but black. Queen Mary made the court so fashionable."

"Oh, aye," Amelia said in disappointment. "I do recall one gown she wore, cloth of silver, trimmed with sapphires and pearls, with an ermine cloak. And her hair! Such a glorious auburn. She surely will be in mourning when we return, Aunt Jane."

"Yes—a shame," Queen Elizabeth snapped in a cold voice. "You must take the finest of our English fashions to *her*. Now, Master Throckmorton, what does your kinsman at my embassy write to you about these matters?"

As Charles and the queen talked, Kate looked up to find Rob watching her, his lips twitching as if he was about to laugh. That made her long to laugh as well, and she had to look away to keep from bursting out. Platters of sweet wafers and the queen's favorite, sticky fruit suckets, were brought in—a welcome distraction.

At least the voyage would not be dull with Rob beside her.

# CHAPTER FIVE

Kate stood on the narrow walkway of Gracechurch Street, studying the house across from her. It was the home of the lawyer Master Hardy and his wife, where Anthony had worked as an apprentice. Now he was on the edge of setting up a legal practice of his own, but he had asked her to meet him there, as it was an easy distance from the palace and in a respectably prosperous area.

And it was *respectable* indeed. Tall and narrow, but with expensive glass in all the windows, the tiny diamond-shaped panes glinting in the light like eyes that could see out but not let anything in. The plaster-work, so bright and new the last time she saw the house, had darkened in the city's smoke and fog, yet it was still finely done and spoke of a quiet prosperity.

Kate thought of Anthony and of how such a place suited him. When they first met, when Elizabeth was a mere princess at Hatfield and the future was so uncertain, Anthony had been a very junior law student working for Master Hardy, who, as a Protestant, was not favored by Queen Mary. After Elizabeth was crowned, all his noble clients returned and Anthony's studies progressed quickly. Now he was on the cusp of a fine career, a well-to-do independence, and she served the queen.

But the memory of their friendship, of Anthony's great kindness and steadiness, his lovely green eyes, never left her—even though their lives seemed destined to follow such different paths.

The black-painted front door opened as she walked the path to the house, and Anthony appeared with a market basket in hand. He wore the fine black wool garments of a young lawyer and a black-and-tawny cap on his glossy dark hair, an austere style that suited his classically carved features.

"Kate!" he called out happily. He hurried across the lane to her side. "I'm glad you could find time to meet me. It must be busy days at court."

Kate smiled up at him. He had such a simple, quietly happy way about him. She had forgotten how reassuring it could be after the drama and tension of court. "Not so much since Christmas is past." She gestured to his basket. "It looks as if you are on an errand, though."

Anthony laughed. "Mistress Hardy asked if I could fetch some vegetables and cinnamon from the market, since she saw I was going out, and I hoped to persuade you to walk there with me."

"Of course. 'Tis a fine day for marketing." The cold wind had ceased to race around the tall buildings and the sky was clearing, though the roads were still laced with frost. Anthony offered her his arm, keeping her to the more sheltered side of the walkway. As they strolled through the marketplace, they talked of Kate's father, of Anthony's widowed mother, who lived back in the village near Hatfield, of the Hardys, and how Anthony was soon to move out of their household and into his own lodgings.

They did not speak of Mistress Hardy's pretty niece, who had visited London last year, and whom Kate knew the Hardys had encouraged him to court. Anthony had not mentioned her in a long while, and Kate was not sure she really wanted to know what was happening with the matter.

After the provisions for Mistress Hardy were acquired, they turned to stroll along the river. Boats were thick on the water that day despite the chill, ferrying people from one bank to another, the boatmen and passengers calling out to each other.

"So, your note to me said you are to go to France," Anthony said, his tone now grown more serious.

"Aye, to carry Queen Elizabeth's messages to Queen Mary."

Anthony nodded, though his expression was doubtful. He knew something of her secret work for the queen; indeed, he had helped her on more than one occasion. He had access to records and archives she did not, and he had a lawyer's way of making people say things they meant to keep silent.

"My friend Tom Overbury is in Paris right now," he said. "Perhaps you remember him?"

Kate nodded. Master Overbury had assisted Anthony with looking through the dusty court records during the troubles at Nonsuch Palace. She remembered he had once been at school with Anthony. "He is studying to enter the Church, is he not?"

"Aye. His master, Bishop Grenfeld, sent a delegation to meet with the Huguenot King of Navarre, and Tom went with them."

"I hope I shall see him there, then. A familiar face would be a most welcome sight."

"I will write to him and ask him to look for you." Anthony paused at the edge of one of the stone-and-wood bridges that crossed the river. He looked down at her, his face very solemn under the brim of his black-and-tawny cap. "You mentioned in your note that Sir Henry Barnett and his wife and niece are to go with you?"

Kate nodded. Anthony and Master Hardy knew everyone at court and worked for many of them. "I do not know them well, and thought mayhap you or Master Hardy came across their names. They have been to France before."

"I have not done any work for them myself, but I have seen their names before. Or, rather, that of their niece. Mistress Wrightsman, is it not?"

"It is. I met her at a dinner in the queen's apartments. She is very pretty and vivacious."

Anthony laughed, a wry sound. "I am sure she is. When Tom Overbury was first in France last year, he sent me a letter that related the tale of a court scandal."

Kate frowned. "A scandal involving Mistress Wrightsman?"

"It seems several French chevaliers fell in love with her, and there were rumors she might even marry a certain Monsieur d'Emours, a kinsman to the Guise family."

"Mistress Wrightsman was to marry a Frenchman?" Kate wondered how likely that would be. Amelia's uncle seemed a very English sort of Englishman, and surely a member of the Guise family would be expected to marry a French fortune.

"There was no official betrothal. And it seems that one night, Mistress Wrightsman danced too many voltas with a certain Monsieur Mamou, kinsman to the Constable Montmorency, enemy to the Guise."

Kate nodded. It seemed the French court was just as complicated with alliances and betrayals as the English—probably much more so. "Then what happened?"

"Mistress Wrightsman disappeared with this fellow Mamou, and was found with him by Monsieur d'Emours in a cozy little garden alcove. D'Emours challenged Mamou to a duel."

"A duel!" Kate cried. It was like a romantic poem. Duels were forbidden by Queen Elizabeth at her court, though, of course, many happened in secret. Was it so very different in France?

"Aye. And it seems the Queen Mother has banned dueling, on pain of execution, but this one went forward."

"Was anyone hurt?"

"Monsieur d'Emours wounded Mamou, but he was not killed. D'Emours was declared the victor."

"But he did not claim his prize, the fair Mistress Wrightsman?"

"Perhaps he found she was not such a prize after all. Tom said she was immediately sent back to England in the care of her aunt, and d'Emours and Mamou are friends once again, though Mamou left court when his kinsman Montmorency retired. D'Emours is said to be of a crowd that is most fond of gambling and good wine, who enjoy making mischief both among the court ladies and country maids."

"How very strange," Kate murmured. If Amelia Wrightsman had instigated a duel, why would the queen and Cecil send her back to France now? It was a puzzle indeed. Kate knew very well she would not be told every part of Cecil's plan in France. Yet she hated feeling as if she were stumbling through a darkened room, unsure of what obstacles lay in wait with every step.

She and Anthony walked onward along the river. She could hear the cries of merchants selling hot cider and apple cakes, fried fish and fresh bread. The spires and roofs of London gleamed in the gray light from across the water, and London Bridge lay ahead, with its crowd of houses, its heads of traitors grinning down at the city from the pikes high overhead. London was both great and terrible, and she wondered when she would see it all again.

Anthony tossed a coin to one of the merchants, an old woman with a cart selling warm gingerbread, and he handed the treat to Kate. She nibbled at it, the warm spices and sugars familiar and reassuring, and she wondered if she should tell the queen she could not help her in France. Almost everything she knew was here. Yet France . . . it beckoned to her, with its unknown people and places, its promise of rare adventure.

"Kate," Anthony said intently, "I know you have been at the queen's court for many months now, and that you are a very clever lady. You know how to watch out for yourself. . . ."

She tried to give him a teasing smile. "Why, thank you, Anthony. I do try."

He gave her a stern look, as if he faced her in a law court, but she could see his lips twitch with a smile. "But you are also kindhearted. The French court will be very different from anything you know."

"Aye, I do see that. I have read much about it and heard tales from courtiers who have been there. Queen Mary is of constant interest to the court. But I must go where I am asked, where I can be of use."

He reached out and took her hand. Even through their gloves his touch was warm, grounding her to that moment, that place. Warm—and safe. "You can be of much use here. To me."

Surprised, Kate took a step back. "Anthony . . ."

"Please, Kate, hear me. We have been friends a long time now."

She nodded. "So we have, and I am glad of it."

"Then surely you must know my feelings for you are more than friendship. I am just starting my own law practice now, but I have many contacts. In a year or so, I know I could provide a fine home for a wife and family. You would be comfortable and protected always."

Kate swallowed hard, trying to make sense of the feelings that were tumbling through her. She was tempted, very much so. Anthony was so kind, steady, and handsome. But there was the queen and her work at court. She owed Elizabeth so very much, and she wanted to think that what she did was important. That in some small way, she could use her skills to help keep England a bit safer in a rocky world. "Anthony, I do not know what to say now . . ."

He gave her a reassuring smile and squeezed her hand before placing it on his arm again. "You needn't say anything now. I know you feel you must go to France for the queen. Just think about what I have said while you are there."

Kate nodded. "I will think about it, aye."

"And write to me, so I know you are safe."

"Of course I will write." She squeezed his arm. Her throat was tight with all the emotions rising in her. All the emotions that usually only found an outlet in music. "I care about you as well, Anthony. Please know that."

He nodded. "Then I will be content with that—for now. Come. We should take Mistress Hardy her provisions, or supper will never be finished."

He drew her close to his side again, and they pushed

their way through the crowd back toward the street. He said nothing more of love or marriage or of what might wait for her in France, but they talked of inconsequential things such as the new apprentices in Master Hardy's office and new styles at court.

When they parted at the gates of Whitehall, Anthony took her hand and bowed over it for a long moment. "Don't forget me while you're gone."

Kate shook her head, her throat thick with tears she knew she could never shed. "I could not do that. I will write to you very soon."

She spun around and hurried up the steps into the palace. In her quiet chamber, Kate laid aside her cloak and went to peer out the window at the garden below. She would miss Anthony, aye, but surely this time in France would be a good thing. She would have the space to think about her own life and where she wanted it to go now that her father was gone. Did she want to stay at court? Did she want a different home, a place of quiet and respectable comfort? She had never known that. Or would a life of adventure be best, with a man who could understand her love of music and her need of the challenge of courtly life? A man like Rob.

Kate shook her head. If only—if only—she could somehow have both . . .

Anthony sat down at his desk in his small chamber at the top of the Hardys' house. He meant to write to Tom Overbury in France, to ask his friend to help Kate and look after her, as he could not. But he found himself staring out over the chimneys of Gracechurch Street, unable to forget the way Kate had looked when they parted.

The Hardys had wanted him to marry Mistress Hardy's niece, and it would have been an excellent match. She was a kind girl and a pretty one, who knew how to run a prosperous household and assist with a husband's law career. Yet something—or someone—had held him back, and Anthony knew it was Kate. They had been friends for a long time, and at certain moments he had been sure it was more than that. Yet he knew she had work to do, just as he had, important work for the queen, and she was reluctant to leave it behind.

Just as he was reluctant to ask her. Now she was going to France, beyond where he could persuade her, and all he could do was hope she would come back to England in a different set of mind.

He took out pen and paper and sat down to write to his friend Overbury. If Kate insisted on running away on this errand, he would do all he could to help her—and would pray for her safe return.

# CHAPTER SIX

Kate sat on a coil of rope in a quiet corner of the ship's deck, watching as the very last glimpse of England's shores faded from view. In an instant, there was only the gray sky meeting the edge of the gray water to be seen. She felt tossed out into a strange new world, unable to find her bearings, and yet there was excitement in her heart as well. Here, on the endless-seeming sea, real life was postponed for a while. Grief was left behind, and something completely new was ahead.

As the ship lurched farther out to sea, the wind grew sharper and colder. Kate drew the fur-lined hood of her cloak closer and watched the white-foamed waves surge around the prow. The sails whipped over her head, and she could smell the salt spray. She could see why most of their party had retired to their cabins, claiming seasickness. She herself didn't feel queasy yet, but her legs did feel rather unsteady, her head light.

She thought of the ginger tea infusion Brigit Berry had given to the others, and she knew she could go inside to her own berth and sip some of the brew to warm her bones and steady her stomach, but she didn't want to leave the open view just yet. The sea, the changeable colors of the waves, the wheeling, shrieking birds overhead, were too fascinating.

"Mistress Haywood, are you not too chilled out here?" she heard Toby Ridley say.

She shrugged back her hood and turned to see that Toby had been strolling around the railings of the deck, wrapped in his own fashionable black cloak elaborately embroidered with gold, which made him stand out like a torch in the gray day. With him was a man she recognized as being from a small group that joined the ship when they paused at Dover. He was not quite handsome, but was most striking, with a red-brown beard and lively dark eyes.

"I think I prefer the fresh air for the moment, Master Ridley," she answered. "Everyone belowdecks is ill, I am afraid." Except for Brigit Berry, whom she shared a cabin with for the voyage. But Mistress Berry was buried in a book, and seemed not to want to be disturbed.

"Do you not feel the sea yourself?" he said.

"Not yet, thankfully. Nor, would it seem, do you." Kate thought the voyage seemed to agree with him, for his eyes glowed with new energy, and the pale strain she had seen on his face at Whitehall was gone.

He laughed heartily. "Nay, but I have traveled by ship often before. It usually takes people longer to find their sea legs the first time."

"This is your first voyage, then, mademoiselle?"

the other man said, his voice touched with the musical lilt of a French accent.

"Forgive me—you have not yet met," Toby said, his laughter fading. "Mistress Kate Haywood, may I present Monsieur Claude Domville? He has lately been in England on business for his father, the comte Domville, and is returning home."

So the newcomers to the ship were a group of Frenchmen returning from England. She wondered what the comte's business had been. "I am pleased to meet you, Monsieur Domville."

Monsieur Domville took her hand and bowed over it gallantly. His smile was wide and white, full of delight. "The journey has become much less tedious in this moment, Mademoiselle Haywood! My old friend Toby did not tell me how lovely his travel companion was."

Kate laughed, wondering if all Frenchmen were tutored in flirtations. They said the queen's mother, Anne Boleyn, had learned much of flattery and disguise in her own time in France, as well as the management of men and their passions. Perhaps it was the same vice versa, men to women. "You knew Master Ridley before, then, monsieur?"

"I did indeed. We met the last time he came to Paris, and he was able to do some small favors for my father. I hope to repay the debt very soon."

The two men exchanged a strange glance that Kate could not read. She gave him a smile, one she hoped was quite oblivious. "I would so enjoy hearing more about your country, monsieur. I am told it holds so many rare beauties."

"And so it does. But I have found England to be just as enticing as my homeland," Monsieur Domville answered. "Perhaps we could all dine together tonight, those of us who remain in good health? I can tell you of France, and you can tell me more of England—and of your fair self."

Kate agreed with a laugh, and the two men bowed to her once more. As they walked away, their heads bent close as they talked quietly, Kate made her way back to the railing. She was alone for a moment, the crew on the other side of the ship, the gentlemen vanished. She stared down at the gray waves that broke around the ship far below, their white foam soaring and cresting. The sky was growing darker as night began to close in, and she heard the distant shouts and laughter of the sailors. For a moment, it seemed she stood alone on the very edge of the world.

Suddenly, she heard a running footstep, a boot on the wooden planks of the deck, heavy and quick. Afraid she was in the way, Kate started to turn. Her hood fell forward, obscuring her view so she could see nothing. In the instant it took her to reach up and push it back, she felt a rough hand grab her arm. She was yanked backward, almost off her feet, and cold fear shot through her veins.

It happened almost in dream motion, her shock slowing her thoughts and making it seem as if she were watching it all happen from above. She remembered what one of Cecil's men had taught her of fighting, to let the opponent's own weight and movements defeat him. There was no time to get her dagger loose from its sheath beneath her sleeve, and her cloak wrapped around her, hindering her movements. She instinctively kicked back and her foot, encased in its sturdy traveling boot, connected with a shin.

Her assailant let out a groan, too low for her to tell if it was male or female, and the iron grip tightened on her arm.

Kate tried to spin around to drive her fist into her attacker's eyes, but he was obviously skilled in stealth fighting. One hand tore the purse from her belt, and the other gave her a hard shove forward. She heard footsteps running away.

In a rush of raw fear, Kate tumbled over the railing. It hit her high on her torso, stealing her breath, and she flipped over, her ankle wrenching painfully beneath her. Her cloak suffocated her as she hung off the side of the boat in midair, the horrible cold waves beneath her.

"Help!" she screamed. She caught the railing with both hands. It was damp and slippery, the splinters of the wood digging painfully into her palms. Still she clung on, screaming as loudly as she could.

Luckily, in an instant there were sailors clustering on the deck above her, shouting and cursing as they pulled her up to safety. She collapsed onto the wooden planks, out of breath and shaking.

"Mademoiselle Haywood! What happened? Are you hurt?" Claude Domville knelt beside her, taking one of her trembling hands.

Kate shook back her hood. She looked up at Monsieur Domville, whose handsome, dark face looked gray and shocked. Toby hovered behind him, his hand on the hilt of his sword. Kate couldn't help but glance down at their feet; they were both wearing tall, heavy boots.

"Did you see anyone running away from here?' she demanded. "Anyone nearby?"

Claude shook his head. "We were speaking with the captain on the other side of the deck. There were crewmen around everywhere. Did one of them . . ."

"Nay, I doubt it. I think—" Kate suddenly broke off her words, shivering hard. It felt as if a cold wave crashed down on her all at once as she realized that someone had stolen her purse, had tried to push her overboard. That she was not safe.

She studied the men clustered around her, Claude and Toby confused and concerned, the sailors unsure. She knew she couldn't tell them she had been pushed. They wouldn't believe her, would say she was just a nervous young lady on her first ship voyage. And what if one of them had done it? She did not want them to know she was suspicious of them, of everyone. Perhaps it was better if they all *did* think her a nervous, anxious young woman, prone to swooning. If her assailant thought she wasn't sure what had really happened, he might become careless, give himself away.

She had to be cautious at every moment, suspicious

of everyone around her. It was a lesson she would not forget on this journey.

Kate touched the place at her belt where her purse had once been tied. There would be a fine bruise there in the morning, and her twisted ankle would probably swell as well. She would have to be even more vigilant at every moment. And she was very glad she had hidden Cecil's letters and her own documents away instead of carrying them on her person. Though how could she know if they were after the papers or just a bit of coin?

"Did you slip?" Monsieur Domville asked. "The decks can be most treacherous. We should not have left you. Should we, Toby?"

Kate made herself laugh. "I must have slipped, aye. So careless of me. You and Master Ridley cannot be my nursemaids at every moment, though."

The ship's captain, a grizzled, weather-beaten old Welshman, nodded sagely. He did not look terribly surprised by what had happened. Perhaps such things occurred on every voyage. He handed her a pewter flask, which she found was filled with strong port wine. She took a long gulp.

"Aye. I saw a man swept overboard just last month by a wave when he tried to use the privy," the captain said. "Best to have a care, mistress. Most ladies keep to their berths for the voyage. Long skirts and velvet slippers are dangerous aboard ship."

Kate nodded, thinking it best not to point out that she wore breeches under her plain wool skirts and sturdy boots.

"Shall I escort you to your cabin, Mademoiselle Haywood?" Monsieur Domville asked. Kate nodded and let him help her to her feet. Her legs shook, and she held on to his arm to keep from falling.

She glanced back over her shoulder at the surging gray waves and shivered.

Monsieur Domville fetched her cloak from where she had dropped it to the deck and carefully wrapped it over her shoulders. She noticed he exchanged a long glance with Toby over her head, and the Englishman hurried away. "The journey is not long, mademoiselle, but it can be a miserable one. I promise it will be worth it when you see France."

"I have certainly heard that your country has many charms," Kate said. She let him guide her to the narrow wooden stairs that led down to the cabins. It was dark there, the air warm and stuffy, smelling of salt and brandy and people. It was strangely reassuring after the open freedom of the dangerous sea. She could see all around her belowdecks.

"Indeed it does. The forests, the palaces . . ." As he chattered on, leading her along the corridor, Kate was glad of the distraction, the freedom from the need to talk. "The clothes! No one dresses like a Frenchwoman—or Frenchman."

They found her cabin, a tiny space she shared with Brigit Berry at the end of the corridor. She opened the door to find their trunks and boxes piled up in every available space, half hiding the narrow berths tucked against the damp wood walls.

Mistress Berry was not there as Kate sat down care-fully on her berth, and Monsieur Domville poured her some ale from a pitcher left on the small washstand, which was fastened to the floor. But the maid came rushing in only a moment later.

Mistress Berry was usually so tidy, even on their long journey, but now her gray-streaked brown hair was haphazardly tucked beneath a fine white cap with tendrils escaping. Her short cloak wrapped closely around her, concealing her gown. She set down a basin on the washstand and brushed off her gloved hands.

"Mistress Haywood!" she said. "Are you well? We heard you slipped on the deck."

News did travel fast aboard ship. "Indeed I did. It was most foolish of me, Mistress Berry. I am well enough now, aside from a swollen ankle and a bit of bruising." Kate surreptitiously glanced at Brigit's feet. She wore stout, worn boots, carefully polished, and the hem of her black wool skirt was damp. "I see there are no secrets on a ship."

"I was with Mistress Wrightsman next door. She hears all the news immediately, almost as if she was one of Dr. Dee's clairvoyants." Brigit studied Kate care-fully, her eyes narrowed, and gave Monsieur Domville a suspicious glare.

"Let me fetch you a better wine, Mademoiselle Hay-wood," he said. "That rough ale will do no one any good. You need a good Alsatian, which restores the spirits remarkably."

"*Merci*, monsieur. You have been very kind," Kate said.

He gave her a low bow before he ducked out the narrow doorway. As soon as the creaking door closed behind him, Mistress Berry let out a loud harrumph. "Frenchmen. Such flatterers all."

Kate bit her lip to keep from laughing. "You do not approve of Frenchmen, Mistress Berry?"

"They are well enough, I suppose, in their place."

"And what is their place?"

Mistress Berry shrugged. "I met many of them when I was last in Paris with Mistress Wrightsman, and I am told my own mother had some French blood, God rest her soul. The Frenchmen seem to do well enough with dancing and hunting. And their clothes are fine, I will grant you that. They are a grander sight than the men of Queen Elizabeth's court. But if you want them for some serious purpose—pft."

Kate laughed aloud. "Then an Englishman would serve better in that case?"

"No man would be better for any serious purpose, Mistress Haywood. They just get in the way."

Kate nodded, wondering about Mistress Berry's past. She knew so little of the woman beyond the fact that she was a kinswoman of sorts to Lady Barnett and served her. If Mistress Berry had some French blood, did Lady Barnett as well? "Have you been in the Barnetts' service for long?"

"Long enough, to be sure." Mistress Berry opened her trunk and sorted through a variety of small pots and bottles, all stored in specially fitted little slots. "As you know, I am a distant kinswoman to Lady Barnett, and she needed someone she could trust to wait on Mistress Wrightsman in France. I thought seeing a different country, one that my mother once knew, would be better than slowly moldering in some country cottage."

"And is it better?"

Brigit shrugged. "About equal, I would say. At least I have been able to see France again."

"You were there before?"

"Many years ago." Brigit held out a small white pottery jar. "If there is bruising, you will feel the ache of it tomorrow, Mistress Haywood. This salve should help."

Kate took out the stopper and gave a cautious sniff. She smelled the sweet scents of chamomile and lavender, along with something more sharp and medicinal. "What is it?"

"Merely a salve of herbs. It helps with bruising and aches. I made it myself and have found it most useful."

Kate nodded toward the bottles in their little slots. "You seem to know a great deal of herbs and cures, Mistress Berry."

The woman shrugged again. "Enough. I have found such knowledge most helpful in travels. One never knows what one may face on the road."

"Would you teach me some of your recipes?"

"If you like. They are not complicated."

Kate longed to ask her more about France, about herbs, about her work with Mistress Wrightsman and the Barnetts. A woman's perspective was often sharper and clearer, especially that of a woman who was quiet and intelligent, as Mistress Berry seemed to be, yet was considered only a servant by the people around her. But it seemed Brigit was done talking for the moment. She sat down on her berth and took a pile of mending from her workbox. Her white cap bent low over it, and she hummed a soft tune as she worked, her hands quick and neat with the stitches.

Kate turned to her own trunk, hoping to glance through it before Monsieur Domville returned with the promised wine. She spread out her damp cloak over a stool and reached for a warm knitted shawl. As she smoothed back her folded garments in the trunk, she noticed some of them were out of place, slightly mussed, and the books and musical manuscripts that lined the bottom were not in the same order. It was as if someone had gone through it while she was on deck.

She locked the trunk and turned to her lute case. Her mother's fine instrument was unharmed, thankfully, but there was a small tear in the silk lining of the case she had not noticed before.

Kate sat back on her berth and settled her skirts carefully around her. She felt the weight of the small secret pocket she had sewn beneath her petticoats, where Cecil's letters were safely tucked away. She vowed to herself to keep them there for the rest of the journey.

# CHAPTER SEVEN

"**. . .** And I cannot say I find the new style of sleeve at all flattering! Do you, Mistress Haywood?"

Kate shook her head with a smile as Amelia Wrightsman talked on, comparing the old, closer-fitting sleeve to the new puffs. Amelia could certainly talk a great deal without requiring any answers, which suited Kate very well as they rode slowly forward across the French countryside, up the slight hills and along steep riverbanks.

She was becoming weary of travel, and her mind drifted away too often to focus on serious conversation, so she was glad Amelia had fallen in beside her on the road.

The lady also knew all the best gossipy tidbits about French courtiers they would soon meet, which would surely be most useful later.

Kate glanced back over her shoulder. Mistress Berry rode behind them, grim-faced under the broad brim of her hat. She had been quiet on the rest of their ship's voyage, and now, on the road, she kept close to Amelia.

She had taught Kate some of her herbal knowledge, and one evening showed her how to mix a calming tisane she often gave to Lady Barnett, but other than that had kept much to herself.

Behind her were Rob and his apprentice, Thomas. Rob gave her a merry wave, but she saw how watchful he was, as he had been ever since she told him of what had happened on the ship. Thomas stared, wide-eyed and rapt, at Amelia, as he was so often wont to do. As so many men did when they were near her.

There was no room on the narrow, rutted, muddy lane to travel more than two across, so their party stretched long both back and ahead. When they arrived in Paris, they found the Louvre Palace almost deserted. Queen Catherine had taken the young king and the rest of the court to Fontainebleau until Easter, to take the fresh air and hunt in the forest.

Queen Mary, who had been on retreat at the convent of St. Pierre, where her aunt Renée de Guise was abbess, was meant to join them there. There was no word yet on what the young widowed queen had decided to do— marry again, stay in France as a wealthy dowager, or go back to Scotland.

The slow journey from Paris to Fontainebleau made it feel even more as if they were all trapped in a strange limbo, neither in one place nor another, unsure of what lay ahead.

They were warned in Paris that there had been some unrest in the countryside. Anger was still high over the bloody events in Amboise the autumn before, the gruesome executions under the orders of the Guise brothers and the imprisonment of the dashing Huguenot leader the Prince de Conde. Protestants had pillaged Catholic churches, while bands of Guise supporters roamed villages and farms, killing any Huguenots they found in retaliation.

Their small party had hired guards and outriders to keep them safe on their journey, as well as several pack mules to carry their considerable luggage. Mistress Wrightsman and Lady Barnett alone had many gowns, shoes, and jewels, and there were also gifts for the queens. They looked like an important group as they traveled, and outlaws had certainly not harried them, but they were not fast enough to outrun evildoers if any appeared.

Kate had not minded the slower pace. It gave her time to study the country around them. Paris had been crowded, with narrow lanes and smoking chimneys much like London, but the countryside, even in the damp, cold gray winter, was beautiful. They had passed lovely châteaux, all built of gleaming pale stone with steep slate roofs, surrounded by moats and set amid carefully laid-out gardens that would surely be like vivid jewel boxes in the summer. The villages, too, had been clean and pretty, with cottages and shops glinting with candlelight, all quiet under the thin layer of new snow.

But now she wasn't sure where they were at all. It had been hours since they stopped at the last inn for a quick meal and short rest. The dour-faced landlord there had served them thin wine and a few oatcakes, and directed them tersely on a shorter route to the main road that would lead them to the edge of the famous forest that surrounded the palace at Fontainebleau.

Yet this did not seem *shorter* at all. The lane was only getting rougher and even narrower. Their horses had to slow to a crawling pace to keep from tripping in the ruts.

Kate peered ahead. Sir Henry Barnett, his wife beside him, led the party behind some of the guards. Like Amelia, Lady Barnett had been full of chatter earlier, but now even she was quiet. Charles Throckmorton and Toby Ridley rode behind them, just ahead of Kate and Amelia, and she noticed Toby stayed as close to Amelia as he could, watching Monsieur Domville, who rode just to the side of Amelia with narrowed eyes.

Amelia's words about sleeves trailed away, and she glanced back at Mistress Berry. Brigit gave her a grim smile, which strangely seemed to reassure her. She straightened in the saddle and stared ahead, unblinking.

"I do wonder what we will find at court," Amelia said.

"It will be quieter," Brigit answered. "They are in mourning, you know."

Amelia tossed her head, the white plumes in her black velvet hat dancing in the cold breeze. The feathers carried the scent of her violet perfume. "Surely not everything will be silent! There will be hunting, at least. Cards. Perhaps some archery contests or music . . ."

"You wish to see all your old admirers again, *oui*,

Mademoiselle Wrightsman?" Monsieur Domville said teasingly.

Amelia laughed. "I have not so very many admirers, monsieur. Not as many as Queen Mary's Scottish Maries, I would say, or as Comtesse Villiers. Or as Queen Mary herself, who is surely the most beautiful of all."

"*Non?* I had heard you had five proposals of marriage before you last left Paris," Monsieur Domville said, still giving her that teasing smile. "My friend Monsieur d'Emours has been missing you a very great deal."

Amelia bit her lip and turned away from him to fuss with her reins. Kate noticed that her cheeks had turned bright pink, and she remembered the tale of the duel d'Emours, the kinsman to the Guise family, had fought over her. Or so the story went.

"I doubt he noticed I was gone at all," Amelia said. "Surely he is not even back at court."

"Ah, but he is," Monsieur Domville said. Kate had the distinct sense he took a mischievous delight in teasing Amelia, but a duel seemed a strange thing to tease about. "He has been back since the autumn, before King Francis died."

Amelia's blush deepened, and she tossed her head again. "Surely only to find a young mademoiselle with a fine Loire estate for a dowry. I care not for you Frenchmen and your forgetful ways. I have heard there are many rather ruggedly handsome Scotsmen at court right now. I wonder what *their* manners will be like?"

"Not at all to your liking, I am sure, Mademoiselle Wrightsman. They cannot dance, for one thing, except to kick and fling themselves about." Monsieur Domville gave Kate a smile and a wink. "Nor would Mademoiselle Haywood like them. They know naught of music, except for a strange, wheezing sort of pipe that sounds like a stable cat in distress."

Kate laughed. "I assure you, Monsieur Domville, I am interested in *all* kinds of music—especially instruments I have not seen before."

Monsieur Domville gave an exaggerated wince. "You will not like this, I can assure you, *chère mademoiselle*. These Scots have no—how do you English say?—refinement."

"I think manly strength is surely better than mere refinement," Amelia said angrily. Her hands tightened on her reins, making her horse shy. "I cannot wait to meet them. I shall make them teach me their kicking dances!"

"You should have a care, mistress," Mistress Berry said. "After last time . . ."

"Oh, hush, Brigit! What do you know about it?" Amelia cried. "You have never loved at all. You are just a—"

"Be silent!" Sir Henry called. He held up his hand, and their slow procession drew to a halt.

For a moment, Kate was confused by the sudden call for silence. Then she smelled it—the sharp, metallic smell of smoke on the clear, cold breeze. At first it was a mere whiff, as if from the chimneys of a village nearby. But it grew heavier, too thick, tinged with something darker.

Her throat tightened, and she froze.

Sir Henry and the guards at the front dashed ahead, and Monsieur Domville and Toby Ridley edged around the ladies to ride after them, then drew their swords. Kate instinctively followed, shaking her dagger from its sheath under her sleeve until she could grasp the twisted steel hilt.

The narrow lane turned a sharp corner into a clearing, which had been hidden and blocked by the thick curtain of trees. Kate gasped, her gloved hand pressed to her mouth, at what they found there.

It was a farmhouse, or once had been. It was now a charred, smoking ruin, the roof collapsed, the walls blackened. There was no sign of life, not even a chicken or milk cow. Only a crudely drawn cross of Lorraine in red on the one still partially standing wall, along with the outline of a lion. The emblem of the Guise.

Amelia, who had come up beside Kate, screamed, and Kate whipped around to reach for her hand.

She saw what had made Amelia scream, and nearly cried out herself. Two men were hanged from the bare, skeletal branches of a tall tree at the edge of the clearing. A rough sign dangled from one of them with large black letters that spelled out HERETIC. She remembered what they had heard at the inn, about Catholic churches pillaged and Protestants killed in punishment. It made her glad to be English, with a queen who cared not to open windows in men's souls, as Elizabeth often said.

She looked back to Amelia and wondered if the flighty, frivolous lady was going to faint. But Mistress

Wrightsman did not look on the edge of hysterics at all. Her delicate jaw was set in a hard line, her eyes cold and angry.

"Come. We must be away from this place," Sir Henry said. He spurred his horse around and galloped back to the lane, where the others waited. Lady Barnett was tearful, demanding to know what was happening, but her husband ignored her. Mistress Berry offered her a vial of smelling salts.

"Are you quite well, Mistress Wrightsman?" Kate asked quietly.

Amelia gave her a hard, bright smile. "I am, Mistress Haywood. You will have to learn that things like this happen all the time in France. But we must keep moving forward, must we not?"

She jerked her own horse around to follow her uncle, and Kate rode to catch up with her.

"It is a sad thing indeed," Monsieur Domville said solemnly. "But surely they were breaking the law of the land. These Huguenots think they can do as they like, but they must learn to keep the peace. It is a very dangerous thing to make enemies of the Guise and their friends."

"*Oui*, they were Huguenots," the landlady at the inn said with a scowl. She waved to a maidservant to continue pouring ale into the traveling party's pottery cups. The maid sniffled; her eyes were red, her plump cheeks blotched, as if tears were a common thing with her. She stopped only when the landlady gave her a stern glance.

Mistress Berry, calm and expressionless, handed Lady Barnett a vial. Lady Barnett had been crying as well, and Mistress Wrightsman's cold anger had quickly faded once they were on the road again, and she had almost fainted in new hysterics. Her swoon had led them to find an inn to rest for a time. The ladies looked a bit restored now beside a warm fire, with spiced ale and a hearty stew to warm them. It was a prosperous establishment, clean and well furnished, with an elaborate cross prominently displayed on the whitewashed wall.

Kate took a sip of her drink, but she felt restless, watching everyone around her.

"We had heard in England that things were much more settled now since the death of King Francis," Sir Henry said.

The landlady gave a snort. "'Tis the Duc de Guise and his family. They've become desperate; everyone knows that. Queen Catherine will rule now, and she is no true friend to them. She seeks peace with the King of Navarre and the Huguenots—so they say. Such leniency can never hold, not in a Godly kingdom."

"Can it not?" Toby Ridley said tightly. "Surely a peaceful realm is a laudable aim?"

"In this district, monsieur, monks have been killed, an ancient statue of the Blessed Virgin destroyed by a Huguenot mob they say was emboldened by Queen

Catherine's mild words to them," the landlady said, crossing herself. "How can there be peace thus?"

The woman suddenly seemed aware she had perhaps said too much to foreign strangers. She bobbed a hasty curtsy and left the small sitting room, shooing the sniffling maid ahead of her. "I will send in more ale, monsieur."

For a long moment, silence fell heavily over the English group crowded into the little room. Kate sipped at her ale and studied everyone around her. Lady Barnett and her niece reclined on the cushioned settee by the fire. The men gathered around a round table, all of them looking grim. Rob and Thomas stayed near Kate, and she was glad of their presence. They made her feel not quite so alone in a strange land.

"It would do these people well to listen to Queen Catherine," Lady Barnett said, tearful and angry. Kate was surprised—Jane Barnett had never shown even a flash of such seriousness before. "She is a very clever lady. What is the use of losing everything over such trifles?"

Sir Henry brought his fist down on the table before him, rattling pitchers and goblets. Amelia burst into tears all over again, and even Kate was startled enough to jump a bit. Everyone's nerves seemed terribly on edge.

"Be quiet, woman, about matters you have no knowledge of!" he roared, his bearded face red. "Queen Catherine is a Florentine to her very bones, and one day her Italian ways will bring France down with her. Kingdoms need strong kings, and one faith to unify them. I should have left you and your silly niece in London.

Matters are much too delicate and vital to have such ridiculousness to deal with."

Lady Barnett let out a wail before she buried her face in her hands. Sir Henry slumped back in his chair, as if wearied by his outburst, something that seemed a common occurrence between the married couple. Everyone else went still and silent, which only made Lady Barnett's sobs sound louder.

Amelia took her aunt's arm and helped her to her feet. The two ladies limped out of the room. "I will take her to rest," Amelia said as the door closed behind them.

"Women," Sir Henry muttered as he raised his goblet for another long drink. "They understand naught."

Mistress Berry scowled down at him.

Kate slipped out of the room and into the cool quiet of a narrow corridor. She could hear Lady Barnett crying from somewhere in the shadows. Mistress Berry came out of the sitting room as well, and hurried past Kate with a basin in her hands.

"Is anything the matter, Mistress Berry? Can I help?" Kate asked.

"Mistress Haywood, I did not see you there," Mistress Berry said. "Aye, follow me, if you like. I fear Lady Barnett often has such fits. 'Tis only to be expected."

Kate wondered what she meant by that. *Only to be expected because of the way Lady Barnett's husband dismissed her? Because things are so uncertain there in France?*

"I thought Lady Barnett enjoyed her last time in France," Kate said, watching as Mistress Berry took a vial from her valise and shook a drop into the basin.

The scent of lavender filled the air. "I suppose things have changed a great deal since then."

"So they have, I fear," Mistress Berry said. "In other ways, though, they haven't changed at all. The Catholics and the Huguenots have been at each other's throats for years, and men like the Guise brothers only make it worse. With King Henri's strong hand, it was different. None dared defy him. Now . . ."

"Now there is only a dead king, a sickly boy to take his place, and Queen Catherine?"

Mistress Berry shrugged. "Queen Catherine, the Duc de Guise. Who knows? Is there any difference? But Lady Barnett was quite friendly with the queen when last we were here. She would sit and embroider and whisper with Queen Catherine for hours. I daresay the Queen Mother will have no time for such things now."

Kate nodded. "Did Mistress Wrightsman like the queen as well?"

Mistress Berry laughed. "She liked Queen *Mary* right enough. The two of them would laugh and dance together at every banquet. I daresay Queen Catherine could have found great use for Mistress Wrightsman, though, if there was a thought of more than silks and jewels in her head."

Kate thought of that cold, still look in Amelia's eyes at the farmhouse. "What do you mean?"

Brigit gave her a strange smile. "What do you know of the French court, Mistress Haywood?"

"Not as much as I think I will soon need to," Kate

said cautiously. "They say Queen Catherine is eager to wield her power on behalf of her children now."

"Queen Catherine is not a pretty lady, to be sure, and never has been, in a court that prizes beauty above all else. But she is a clever woman," Brigit said. "Almost as clever as our own Queen Elizabeth, mayhap. I am sure she learned much in her Italian youth, and one of those lessons is the great use a clever person can put beauty to, when it is needed."

Kate frowned. "I do not quite see your meaning, Mistress Berry."

"You will find that Queen Catherine surrounds herself with ladies who are fair indeed. And they are most loyal to her. That is all." Brigit held out a small bottle. "Would you carry that for me, Mistress Haywood?"

"Of course." Kate followed Brigit as she took up the basin again and made her way into a small bedchamber.

Lady Barnett lay on a narrow bedstead while Amelia knelt beside her, pressing a damp cloth to her aunt's pale brow. "I am sure my uncle is just worried, Aunt Jane," she was saying in a beseeching voice. "He has much to concern him."

"And his wife is not one of those matters, as always!" Lady Barnett cried. "I have worries as well. What awaits us at Fontainebleau . . ."

"I have brought your tisane, Lady Barnett," Brigit said. "And Mistress Haywood has come to help. We shall be on our way again in no time at all."

Lady Barnett sat up with Amelia's help. She did indeed

look pale under the edge of her lace cap, her eyes red from crying, but she tried to smile cheerfully. "Thank you, Brigit. I do not know what I would do without your help. And Mistress Haywood! What must you think of us? I promise I am not usually such a watering pot."

"Not at all, Lady Barnett," Kate said. "It has been a most trying day for everyone. Surely it will be better once you can rest at our destination."

"Of course," said Lady Barnett, sipping at the herbal tisane Brigit had mixed up for her. "There is no place more luxurious than Fontainebleau! Wait until you see it."

She and Amelia talked on of the beauties of the palace, the rare comforts of hot water from spigots and brocade blankets on every bed, and Kate nodded. But she could not help but wonder, as Lady Barnett had, *What exactly awaits us at Fontainebleau?*

# CHAPTER EIGHT

Kate shivered at the silence that wrapped around them as they made their way through the forest of Fontainebleau, hopefully in the direction of the palace. It was an eerie quiet, almost absolute, like being muffled in a feather blanket. There was no whisper of the wind through the towering trees, no call of birds—no word from the people around her, who had been quiet and tense ever since they left the inn, since the quarrel between the Barnetts.

*It is probably the mist muffling every sound,* Kate thought with another shiver. It had descended on the countryside in the night, and hadn't lifted even when they mounted their horses at the innyard early that morning. Lady Barnett and Amelia had protested, but Sir Henry insisted they had to leave. So they had all ridden forth, carefully close together, launched into a half-hidden world.

The mist was thick, a shimmering white-silver that seemed to catch on the treetops and around the underbrush piled at the sides of the path. A deer suddenly leaped past between the thick curtain of trees before vanishing, making Kate gasp.

Rob, who rode close at her side, gave her a reassuring smile. He looked at ease, making quiet jokes with her as they rode, sometimes turning to say a quiet word to Thomas at his other side, but even Rob's fine acting skills could not quite make her feel comfortable. Perhaps the forest was under an enchantment.

"Surely we will be there soon, Kate," he said.

"I cannot wait to be next to a warm fire," Lady Barnett, just ahead of them, said with a sob. "I vow that I shall not stir from the hearthside for a week!"

"You will change your mind soon enough, Lady Barnett, once you hear the dance music," Mistress Berry said drily.

"I shall not! I won't feel like dancing again for a very long time after this appalling journey," Lady Barnett protested.

"We have been on worse journeys, to be sure," Mistress Berry muttered.

"Will there really be dancing, do you think? Even if it is just in privy chambers?" Amelia said wistfully.

"If there is, will you be my partner, Mistress Wrightsman?" Toby asked.

Kate couldn't help wincing at the sheer eagerness in his voice. Master Ridley seemed to be such a nice gentleman, always cheerful through the trials of travel, always most considerate. And, if Cecil trusted him, he had to be a loyal Englishman as well. Yet his infatuation with Amelia, who never took much notice of him at all, was all too clear. During their voyage, he had lost no chance to be close to her, to speak to her, to bring her small comforts such a sweetmeats and cushions.

Amelia, though, would just smile at him and thank him, patting his hand as if he were a loyal lapdog, and then send him on his way. Perhaps she still thought of Monsieur d'Emours.

Kate noticed Charles Throckmorton, who rode on Toby's other side, give his friend a sad glance and a small shake of his head. He, too, seemed to wish to warn Toby away from Amelia.

"Of course I shall dance with you, Master Ridley," Amelia said with a careless laugh. "But you may have to stand in line!"

"Or mayhap *you* shall have to wait, Mistress Wrightsman," Brigit said. "Master Ridley will surely have his choice of Queen Catherine's lovely ladies-in-waiting."

"What do you know of such things, Brigit?" Amelia snapped. "You are always in the corner with your nose in your herbs and tinctures! You know nothing of dance partners."

"Very true," Brigit said.

"Be quiet, all of you," Sir Henry shouted. "There is no time for such nonsense now. We have a great deal of work ahead of us."

Everyone fell silent again, and Kate glanced at Rob. He gave her another smile, but his jaw was tight, his eyes taking in the forest around them. Toby rode ahead of them, and the intricate gold embroidery of his fashionable cloak gleamed like the only beacon in the mist.

Suddenly, the narrow path widened and flowed out into a clearing. The mist was still thick and white, but with no trees to cling to, it seemed to drift in lost wisps around a graveled lane, catching on the tall spikes of a metal gate.

It was not just any gate, though. The elaborate iron-work was gilded, sparkling even in the fog, and to either side rose tall stone pillars topped with carved lions, rearing as if to roar out fiercely. It was surmounted by the coat of arms of France, fleur-de-lis in gold.

"I am Sir Henry Barnett, delegate of the Queen of England, come to join Sir Nicholas Throckmorton's embassy," Sir Henry called to the guards in their blue-and-gold livery. They swung open the gates, and Sir Henry led them through.

When the gates shut again with a metallic clatter, Kate seemed to enter yet another new world. She was reminded of romantic poems of the fairy realm, or of masques where mortals found themselves tumbling into the kingdom of the gods. She could only stare, astonished, until Rob nudged her to move forward.

A long graveled pathway led in an arrow-straight line. Elaborately shaped trees and large square flower beds bordered the path on either side. The plants slept now for the winter, overlaid with a thin, sparkling layer of frost, but Kate could see that in summer tumbles of color would spill over green velvet grass.

To their right was a long palace wing made of mellowed red brick with white stone pillars, a steep gray slate roof, and a forest of brick chimneys looming above, which sent plumes of thick, fragrant smoke to join with the mist. From the many windows that sparkled there, Kate thought she could see clusters of pale faces peering out curiously.

Yet it was the wing straight ahead of the path that caught her attention. It looked like a fairy castle indeed. All gleaming white stone, it stretched across the length of five symmetrical pavilions like an enchanted princess's towers. At its center, leading to carved double doors, was a gray stone staircase that swept upward in a double horseshoe shape.

At the foot of the stairs, servants hurried forward to take their horses. Rob helped Kate from the saddle, and she was glad of his arm to hold on to as she found her feet on the ground again.

Up close, Fontainebleau was even more beautiful than at first sight. It seemed all of one piece. Its white stone and brick, its pillars and towers, could have sprung up all at once under a fairy wand, instead of growing up wing by wing from a small hunting lodge. It was most unlike the jumble of Whitehall.

She thought of all the lovely châteaux they had passed on their journey, white and pale gray and elegant, and the long expanses of vineyards and orchards that in the summer would be bursting with the color and fragrance of sweet fruits. She remembered the well-dressed people who lived in those fine homes, their scarlet, lavender, and pale blue silks; snow-white lace; and pearls and diamonds. All of that had made France seem a fairy realm indeed, overseen by this enchanted palace.

But the image of the burned farmhouse suddenly appeared in Kate's mind. The suspicious innkeepers and quiet people on the sides of the lanes watched them ride by. With a country where the people were at one another's throats, surely nothing was as it seemed.

The doors opened and a lady appeared. She seemed to fit very well in this fairy poem of a palace, for she was tiny and delicate, pale brown curls piled high beneath a small lacy cap that frothed and frilled around an elfin face. She wore a plain Spanish-style surcoat of dark gray satin and black sleeves, but even those somber colors couldn't dim her smile.

"Amelia, *mon amie*!" she cried. "You have returned."

"Celeste!" Amelia cried in return. She dashed up the curving stairs to hug the fair lady.

The rest of them followed at a slower pace, with Lady Barnett leaning on Charles's arm. Her husband seemed to take no notice of her fatigue. Kate watched everything with great curiosity.

"That is Mademoiselle Celeste Renard," Brigit said quietly to Kate. "She once served Princess Elisabeth, until she went to Spain. Now she is lady-in-waiting to Queen Catherine. She and Mistress Wrightsman were great friends when we were here before. Two chattering magpies in the same tree."

Kate could certainly see how happy the two ladies were to see each other again, but surely they could not be called anything as plain as magpies. Their plumage was too handsome.

Celeste held out her tiny hand to Toby and Charles

and laughed with them. Even Sir Henry smiled as she greeted him with a teasing exuberance. Kate remembered what Brigit had told her of Catherine de Medici, the plain queen who surrounded herself with beautiful ladies. For beauty had a power of its own.

"But come inside quickly, quickly," Celeste said, clapping her hands. Kate noticed she wore a ring on her smallest finger, a black cameo set in gold, but she couldn't make out the carved image. "This fog is horribly chilling. The Queen Mother waits to greet you most eagerly. And Queen Mary, *naturellement*. She does so pine for word from her cousin queen."

"How fares Queen Mary?" Kate heard Amelia ask. "We heard she went on retreat to her aunt's convent."

"And so she did," Amelia said, leading them through a small, cold stone foyer and along a corridor. "But our young dowager queen could never be happy among nuns and silence for long! Her grief for poor King Francis was so great and she fell most ill for a time, as she often does in difficult days. But her spirits are recovering."

"Recovering enough for a dance?" Amelia said hopefully.

Celeste laughed. "Or for a play. The Christmas season was a dark one; everyone will want to laugh a bit now." She glanced back over her shoulder and gave Kate a quick smile. Or perhaps it was a smile for Rob, who gave a small bow in answer. "We heard you were bringing actors with you."

"Only two actors, Mademoiselle Renard," Sir Henry

answered. "And one of Queen Elizabeth's own musicians." He gestured toward Kate and Rob, with Thomas peeking eagerly from behind them. "This is Mistress Haywood, and Master Cartman, who is head of the queen's cousin Lord Hunsdon's troupe. And he brought an apprentice with him."

"Mademoiselle Haywood? We have heard of you," Celeste said. She looked at Kate again, her blue eyes wide. "Do you not compose your own music? You must be very clever."

Celeste looked at her so intently, Kate wondered if her words held some strange message. But she could read nothing else there. "When I have time to write, which I fear is not often. Usually I organize the rest of the queen's musicians for her revels."

"It sounds a most fearsome task! The royal musicians here would not care to be organized—they all think *they* are the finest performer at court—but they play well enough when it comes to it. Queen Catherine is most particular about her music. She is entertained now by an Italian theater troupe she brought from Florence. They are most amusing." Celeste's gaze flickered over Rob, and her smile widened. "And you, Master Cartman. You will be *most* welcome, I am sure."

Rob gave her a low bow. "France is full of so many beauties already. How can anyone help but be inspired in his art?"

Kate tugged hard at his arm, and he gave her an innocent look. Celeste laughed merrily, and Kate had to push away a pang of something that felt horribly like jealousy.

They came to an imposing set of doors guarded by two men in the royal blue-and-gold livery, but Celeste did not lead them through those. She turned toward a narrow, winding staircase hidden behind a tapestry.

"I will show you to your rooms, and refreshments will be brought. There will be a reception tomorrow, but Queen Mary asks if you will dine quietly with her this evening," Celeste said, leading them up the stairs. "As I said, she longs to hear all the news from England."

Sir Henry and Lady Barnett exchanged a long glance. Kate had sometimes noticed on their journey that despite the Barnetts' many quarrels and very different personalities, they seemed to be able to communicate with a look or a nod. Many long-married couples did such, like the queen's cousin Lady Knollys and her husband, and even the fearsome Lady Lennox and her Scottish husband. It was an enviable thing and also a strange one.

"We would be most happy to dine with Queen Mary at any time, Mademoiselle Renard," Sir Henry said carefully. "But should we not pay our greetings to King Charles and his mother?"

Celeste laughed, a sound like tiny silver bells. Kate wondered if she practiced it. "Oh, Sir Henry, you needn't worry about that! King Charles is still at the day's lessons with his younger siblings, and Queen Catherine will greet you at tomorrow's official reception. But she always knows all that happens within these walls."

She turned up another staircase and along a narrow corridor lined with tapestries that muffled sound and kept out any hint of draft. "Here are your rooms," she said. "I hope they will suit. I fear court is most crowded at the moment. You are near Sir Nicholas Throckmorton and his household, though, and Queen Mary's Scots family is just along the next gallery."

Kate's room was most suitable indeed, she thought as Celeste showed it to her after she led the Barnetts to their spacious bedchamber and sitting room. Kate's room was a small one, more of a closet, just off Amelia's chamber, but she had it to herself, a rare luxury at court. It was slightly round, as if in a tower, and furnished with a narrow bed with plain but fine dark blue hangings and coverlet, a cushioned stool by the small fireplace, and a writing table under the tiny window. It was much like her room at Whitehall.

Her traveling cases and lute were already there, and Kate quickly searched through her belongings, sorting through the clothes and books and pages of music. It did not look as if anyone had been through them again. She carefully examined the lock on her small jewel case and reminded herself to find a new box with a stronger lock. The letters were safe enough now in her secret pocket, but they needed a better hiding spot soon.

She closed the trunk and went to open the little window set high in the curved stone wall. She found herself looking down on an exquisite garden, all carefully symmetrical flower beds and trees in silver pots, along with another wing of the palace. In the distance she glimpsed a pond, as smooth and silvery as glass, with a beautiful little summerhouse set on an island at its center. How she wished her father could have seen it; she was sure he would have been inspired to compose a lovely song.

There was a knock at the door, interrupting her bittersweet musings, and servants brought in pitchers of water for washing and a goblet of fresh wine. They also brought a note from Charles Throckmorton, asking if he could escort her to meet with his kinsman Sir Nicholas as soon as possible.

There was work to be done.

*Where is he?*

Amelia Wrightsman paced along the path winding beside the decorative pond in the palace gardens, anxiously scanning the horizon. She barely noticed the mud clinging to her satin hem, or the cold wind that tugged her hair loose from her headdress. It would be full dark soon, and she was expected to help her aunt retire.

But she couldn't leave until she talked to him. Surely he knew she was here now; he knew she would wait for him here, in their old place.

She swung around and stared across the rippling water to the marble pavilion set on an island at the pond's center. It was a shimmering white in the gathering dusk, and for an instant she thought she saw a light flash in one of its windows. She had a wild thought of finding a boat, of rowing herself across the pond to hide in those stone rooms. She laughed at herself even as she desperately wished she *could* run away.

There was nowhere to run. She had made her choice long ago, and she had to finish it.

A fallen branch crackled somewhere in the trees beyond the pond path. Her heart pounding, Amelia whirled around. A bird took off from a skeletal-bare branch.

"Only a bird," she whispered.

She started pacing again, twisting her hands together. Surely he wasn't coming now; it was too late. Too late for so many things. She would have to find another way.

As she neared the turn of the path that would take her back to the palace, she heard another sound, this one softer, lighter. A man stepped out from behind the trees, but it was not who she was expecting.

She had not even an instant to smooth her expression into her usual mask of female frivolity, the mask that always served her very well. Who would ever suspect a silly young lady who thought only of gowns and dances? She flashed a flirtatious smile, but feared it was too late for cover.

"Were you expecting someone else, Mistress Wrightsman?" Charles Throckmorton asked, his dark brow arched.

Amelia did not like Charles. He always seemed to see too much, know too much, and say far too little. "I was merely taking a bit of fresh air, Master Throckmorton," she said with a laugh. "Mayhap you have a rendezvous here? I was just leaving, so you will have the gardens all to yourself for your wooing. A fair Frenchwoman, perhaps? One of Queen Catherine's ladies? They are renowned for their great charm."

She knew her words were only teasing, though, and she saw they found their mark as his jaw tightened and his eyes narrowed. Charles was a handsome man, but, like his uncle, he was a serious one. Always intent on work and studies. She wasn't sure he even liked women. He was not easy to read, as most men were. Not easy to fool.

She had to be wary of him.

"You should leave him alone, Mistress Wrightsman," he said quietly.

Him? Did Charles know? *Nay*, she assured herself, *he couldn't possibly know*. But she shivered with a cold feeling of doubt. "Whoever do you mean?"

"Toby, of course. You can only hurt him."

Amelia laughed. So he did *not* know. He was only trying to protect his friend. Toby Ridley was a sweet man, so earnest and attentive. She feared she hurt him just by being, but there could be no help for that. Not now. "I would never hurt him. He is a kind man, and they are a rare breed in this world."

"Indeed he is. That is why I would beseech you to leave him alone. I know you could never care for him as he does you."

Charles was right about that. Amelia had only ever cared for one man, cared too deeply, too passionately.

And look at the trouble it had brought her. Jacques d'Emours had been like poison, and she had yet to find the antidote.

Suddenly angry, she whirled away from Charles and started toward the palace. "You must speak to your friend, then, Master Throckmorton, not me. I cannot be responsible if others are so foolish as to leave their hearts open."

"Just think on what I have said, Mistress Wrightsman," he called after her. "I know you have a heart, too, hidden there somewhere. There is much you do not show to the world."

Amelia didn't answer him. She felt confused, frightened even, but she couldn't let Charles Throckmorton see that. She lifted the mud-stained hem of her gown and ran toward the reassuring lights of the palace.

Her messages would have to wait for another day.

She hurried up the winding staircase that led to her aunt's chamber, hoping she might have a moment to compose herself before Aunt Jane called for her. Yet she found she was not alone as she turned along the corridor. The musician, Mistress Haywood, was there, walking along with her lute in her hands.

"Mistress Wrightsman," she said. She looked as startled to find someone else in the corridor as Amelia was herself. "Are you well? You look flushed."

Amelia nodded. She did envy Mistress Haywood, with her quiet composure, her calm watchfulness. Her work as a court musician, work that was all her own. How lovely such a life would be, dependent on no one.

Free to love as one chose. "I am very well. Thank you, Mistress Haywood. I was just taking a walk in the gardens and hurried back when I realized how late it was."

"The gardens here are so very beautiful," Mistress Haywood agreed. She studied Amelia's face carefully and said hesitantly, "Mistress Wrightsman, if you wish to tell me something—if you need assistance with anything . . ."

For an instant, Amelia wished she *could* confide in Kate Haywood. To share her secrets would be like a great burden lifted. But it was too dangerous. She had no one she could trust now.

She laughed lightly and turned toward her aunt's door. She could hear Aunt Jane now, arguing with Brigit. "La, Mistress Haywood, but surely you know a lady must always have a few secrets! It is part of her rare allure. I bid you good night."

"Good night, Mistress Wrightsman."

Amelia could feel the musician watching her carefully, and she made herself smile even brighter and wave as she slipped through the door. *There is nowhere to be alone in this world at all*, she thought with a sigh.

# CHAPTER NINE

Kate could hear the echo of music as they made their way along the wide corridor that led to Queen Mary's apartments, though she could not recognize the song. *"Mignonne allons voir si la rose,"* a lady sang, high, sweet, and clear.

Ahead of her walked the Barnetts and Mistress Wrightsman, trailed by Mistress Berry. Lady Barnett chattered happily to her husband, but Amelia seemed preoccupied, as if her thoughts were far away. Toby Ridley and Charles Throckmorton followed them, and once Toby tried to take Amelia's arm, to speak to her, but she shook him away. Kate remembered how Amelia had looked when she encountered her in the corridor last night, her face flushed, hair mussed, out of breath. She had looked a bit upset, unhappy, before she covered it in a bright smile. That smile was still in place today.

Kate brought up the end of their little procession with Rob and Thomas. She studied the gold-and-white-paneled walls, glittering and elegant, and she felt a nervous flutter deep inside. Rob grinned down at her, and she smiled back, glad she was not alone there.

Liveried servants opened a set of double doors to usher them through. A steward announced, "Sir Henry Barnett of the court of England, *pour la reine.*"

Sir Henry bowed, and Lady Barnett and Amelia dipped into low, elegant curtsies. Kate hastened to follow them, studying the chamber from beneath her lashes. At the end of the room was a raised dais that displayed an ornately carved chair softened with velvet cushions. It was surmounted by a canopy of state: crimson velvet embroidered with thistles, fleur-de-lis, and the rose of England. A few ladies sat on the carpeted steps of the dais, but no one was in the chair.

"Sir Henry! Lady Barnett, *chère* Amelia," a musical voice called from the crowd. "You have returned at last. I have been so eager to hear all the news from my English cousin."

"We bring messages of great condolence from Her Majesty, Your Grace's own cousin, as well as from many of her courtiers in this sad time," Sir Henry said with a low bow.

The thick knot of people parted to allow a lady to pass through. Kate glimpsed a beautiful set of virginals near one of the tall windows, a beautifully painted instrument even finer than the set Queen Elizabeth had inherited from her mother, Queen Anne.

But the beauty of the instrument was imminently suited to the lady who had been playing on its keys and now stood before them. Kate realized it could be none other than Queen Mary herself, and the rumors of her loveliness had not been exaggerated.

Queen Mary was surpassing tall, perhaps even taller than Rob, who was the tallest man Kate knew. She was as slim as a willow wand in a white silk gown. Kate remembered that French queens were meant to wear white in mourning, the *deuil blanc*, and that Queen Mary was said to have brought bad fortune by wearing the color at her wedding to King Francis a year and a half ago.

This gown was unadorned by any embroidery or fine jewels, as the wedding gown had been described, but was plainly styled and untouched by any color except a sable around her shoulders for warmth.

The style suited her slim figure and marblelike skin perfectly, and Kate wondered if perhaps that was why Queen Mary clung to the white when it was said Queen Catherine would only wear black, in the Italian style. Queen Mary's pale skin was set off by curls of red hair, dark auburn rather than Queen Elizabeth's red-gold. They were clustered in ringlets around her high forehead and drawn back beneath a small white cap draped with a sheer veil.

Her long, straight nose and small rosebud mouth looked much like Queen Elizabeth's, surely a Tudor inheritance from their grandmother Queen Margaret. She smiled as she held out her hand to Sir Henry, and for an instant the whole room hushed, as if her smile dazzled like a sudden burst of sun.

Kate, too, found that she could not look away from

the queen. Her royal smile seemed to draw everyone in, making them feel as if they fell into a secret world where all was beautiful. It was quite an astonishing quality.

Kate realized that she had to be on her guard with this queen if her charm was exactly as rumored.

Sir Henry cleared his throat. "If Her Grace will permit me to speak the words her royal cousin has entrusted to me . . ."

"No more of these formalities, I beg you, Sir Henry," Queen Mary said in English, her voice low and sweet, full of laughter. "We are old friends now, are we not? I want to hear all your news! And of my cousin—everything."

Queen Mary raised Lady Barnett and Amelia, kissing them on each cheek and exclaiming over their gowns. Mistress Berry hovered behind them and leaned over to whisper something short in Toby's ear. He shook his head, frowning.

"We are all in mourning, as you see," Queen Mary said, gesturing to her crowd of courtiers in their sea of black, gray, and violet. "But you shall make us cheerful again!" Her gaze swept over the rest of the English party, her smile widening with an expression of perfect delight, as if she had been waiting days to see each of them. "I do not know all your friends, my dear Sir Henry. Though of course I do remember the handsome Monsieur Ridley."

The queen laughed and reached out to tap Toby's

arm lightly with her black feather fan. He smiled, his freckled cheeks turning red, and Amelia scowled.

Sir Henry set about making the introductions. When he came to Kate, she dipped into a low curtsy as Lady Barnett and Amelia had. As she glanced up, she noticed that Queen Mary's eyes, which seemed focused now directly on her, were an extraordinary sparkling amber-brown. She held out her hand for Kate to kiss and waved for her to rise.

"You play music for my cousin queen, Mademoiselle Haywood?" Queen Mary asked.

Kate nodded, suddenly struck mute. The queen's smile was dazzling indeed, her tone most interested. "I do, Your Grace."

"I want so much to know her favorite songs! Does she play the virginals? The lute? Does she sing?"

Kate nodded. "She plays both, Your Grace, but she rarely sings. I would be honored to perform a few English songs for you, and to learn the fashionable music here in France to take back to Queen Elizabeth."

Mary beamed. "There is surely no better means of communication between two human spirits than music! I long to meet my cousin in person. As two queens in one isle, we would have much to discuss. For now, I suppose I must content myself with asking questions of those who know her."

"I was also charged by Queen Elizabeth to pass on a message of deepest condolences to Your Grace," Kate said. She glanced past the queen to see her courtiers watching them with curious eyes and whispers of speculation. Surely they wondered why the queen was speaking with her, an unknown at their court, for so long.

But Kate was accustomed to such glances, such whispers. She knew she had to pay them no heed and go on about her own business, Queen Elizabeth's business.

Tears shimmered in Queen Mary's eyes, and she raised a lacy handkerchief to dab at them. "She is most kind. It has been a grievous loss. And so soon after my dearest *maman* died, too! I knew my poor husband since we were children. We have been sweethearts for so long. I am lost without him." She turned and held out her hand to a man who stood at the edge of the crowd. "I am most fortunate to have my family with me at such a dark hour. Sir Henry, have you met my brother, Lord James Stewart?"

Kate studied the man with great interest. She didn't know how she could have missed him before. Like his half sister, Lord James would stand out in any gathering. He was a large man, tall, broad-shouldered, with a bright red beard. He was dressed expensively in purple velvet striped in black and gold. His manner as he greeted Sir Henry was bluff and hearty, most friendly, but Kate remembered what Cecil had said about him. He played the game from every side.

"You shall play for us later, Mademoiselle Haywood?" Queen Mary said as she turned to lead Sir Henry and Lady Barnett away. "A favorite song of my dear English cousin?"

"Of course, Your Grace," Kate said with another curtsy.

"All of you must try the wine—it is from my own vineyard at Joinville." On her brother's arm, Mary led the Barnetts to her dais, where she settled herself in her fine chair to talk with them quietly.

The French crowd quickly took up their talk again, watching the new English arrivals with curious eyes. Rob took two goblets of the golden wine from a page and handed one to Kate.

"What do you think of the Scots queen, then, Kate?" he said, studying the room over the edge of his own goblet.

"She is as charming as they say," Kate answered cautiously. She watched Queen Mary as she talked to the Barnetts, her lovely marble-white face intent, her beguiling smile flashing. "And as beautiful."

"Beautiful," Rob said wryly. "Aye, she is that."

Kate studied him curiously. He did not seem infatuated with the queen as everyone else was. "Do you not like Queen Mary?"

"I do not know her to say I like or dislike," Rob answered. "She is a queen and seems a different one from Queen Elizabeth. Surely we know from our plays that there is more than one way to rule a country."

Kate studied Queen Mary again, turning his words and those of Cecil over in her mind. Queen Mary *did* have a different air about her from Queen Elizabeth. Queen Mary had been a queen since she was a newborn, raised in these luxurious French palaces, cossetted, petted, pleased—and learning to please in return. She had a comfort in her fine and sophisticated surroundings, a sort of regal informality that could come only from always knowing exactly where she belonged, knowing her high worth to everyone around her.

Elizabeth had never known such a life. Since her mother was executed when she was three, she had been in danger and desperation, with only her education to sustain her. Queen Mary, even now with her cushioned life thrown into uncertainty and chaos, the French throne she had been bred for gone, seemed most self-assured.

"France is certainly most interesting," Kate said. "I am happy you're here, Rob. I should hate to be alone."

He looked down at her with a smile. Rob's smiles were many—charming, cajoling, persuading, drawing people to him from the stage. This smile was surprised—hopeful. "If it was up to me, Kate, you would never be alone at all."

Kate felt her cheeks turn warm at his words. But she had too much to watch now, too much to be wary about, to try to decipher Rob's meaning. She took a sip of her wine and studied the crowd again. Many of the French ladies watched Rob in turn.

Toby and Amelia were standing together across the room, Toby whispering intently in her ear. Amelia laughed and turned away from him, and a spasm of anger passed over his face before he erased it and smiled. Amelia drifted away in a cloud of blue satin skirts to giggle with Celeste.

"You will perhaps change your mind about an English wren like me when you meet more of these French court ladies," Kate said, trying to be light, teasing. "How can they make their hair look so very perfect? Their elegance seems effortless."

"Pomade of rose petals and beeswax with a bit of lemon juice, I should think, Mistress Haywood," Brigit Berry said as she came to stand next to them. Her dark skirts and plain cap, her watchful expression, made her stand apart from the glittering crowd. "Mistress Wrightsman has tried it before, though I did warn her that sometimes lemon juice can make hair fall out."

"I shall not try it, then, Mistress Berry," Kate answered with a smile. "Mistress Wrightsman does seem happy to be back in France, with or without her hair pomade."

Brigit studied Amelia across the room, a half-smile on her lips. "Poor Master Ridley. He has long courted her, but I fear his is a lost cause. I do feel for him, for he seems good-hearted. He deserves a wife who is equally kind."

Kate nodded and glanced behind her at Rob's apprentice, Thomas, who watched Amelia with infatuation written on his face for all to see. She wondered if he would make a good actor after all, he seemed so little good at hiding his emotions.

"I think I must warn Thomas," Rob whispered to her. "I knew it would be futile to tell him not to fall in love here in France, but there must be a safer target for his affections somewhere in this palace."

Kate laughed, remembering Thomas's infatuations every time he went to court.

Rob turned to Brigit and gave her one of his charming smiles. It made even that stern lady smile in return. "What of you, Mistress Berry? Have you fallen in love here at the French court?"

"Certainly not, Master Cartman!" Brigit said with a laugh. "My days of infatuation with handsome faces are long past, and I learned my lesson in my youth. You men are naught but a nuisance."

Rob pressed his hand over his heart as if wounded. "Mistress Berry! You do pierce me to the core with such unjust words."

"Mayhap *you* can be excluded from my judgment, Master Cartman," Mistress Berry said, still laughing. She looked younger, prettier, with such a smile on her face, her cheeks pink. She looked indeed like Lady Barnett. "You do recite a pretty poem exceedingly well. But these Frenchmen—pah." She waved her hand dismissively at the crowd.

"You do not care for Frenchmen, then, Mistress Berry?" Kate asked.

"None here now, I daresay. When I was a girl . . ."

"You were in France when you were a girl?" Rob asked.

"For a time, aye, and have returned a few times since, as I am now in my kinswoman Lady Barnett's service and must go where she does. Under the old King Francis, there was such glamour here. Now . . ." Her words trailed away.

"Now?" Rob said gently.

Brigit took a sip of wine, her eyes downcast. Her expression pinched and closed off again, as if she feared she had said too much, though it seemed she had said nothing at all. Kate found she wanted to know more.

"Now it is dull," Brigit said shortly. "You must excuse me. I think Lady Barnett requires my services."

She hurried away, though Kate noticed Lady Barnett still sat with Queen Mary, deep in conversation. She didn't appear to need any attendance at all.

Kate glimpsed Amelia's friend Celeste Renard making her way to them from across the room, her embroidered skirts sparkling.

"Ah, Mademoiselle Haywood! How pleased I am to see you here tonight," Celeste said. She turned her dazzling smile onto Rob and held out her hand to him. "And you, of course, Monsieur Cartman. Amelia was telling me earlier of some of the plays you have presented for Queen Elizabeth. You did not tell me of your great fame."

Kate pursed her lips as she watched Rob laugh and bow low over Celeste's bejeweled hand.

"I am a court performer, mademoiselle, with none who know my name at all," he said humbly. Kate nearly snorted aloud.

"Court performer—yes, as we all are," Celeste answered. "Yet I would certainly wager far more people know of you than you realize. Especially the ladies, *non*?" *We are all court performers indeed*, Kate thought, *some more than others*. She remembered the rumors of

Queen Catherine's beautiful ladies, and none she had seen yet at Fontainebleau were as pretty as Celeste. "You are lady-in-waiting to Queen Catherine, are you not, Mademoiselle Renard? Are your services not required by her tonight?"

"The Queen Mother bade me come to Queen Mary's rooms this evening, as she is spending the night in quiet contemplation and prayer, as she often does." Celeste glanced around the room, her attention landing lightly on each group in turn before she smiled at Kate again. "These small gatherings are always the most interesting, don't you agree, Mademoiselle Haywood? There are fewer places for people to hide. They are all arranged like characters on a stage."

Kate nodded. She could not quite decide whether she liked Celeste Renard or not, but she certainly did not trust her. She was pretty and charming, just like Queen Mary herself, but there was something behind her easy smile. She looked as if she expected Kate to say something in particular, but for once Kate had no idea about her own role on the stage. "I suppose if one wanted to hide in here, there would be room behind the tapestries. But only if a person were very slender indeed."

Celeste laughed. "I do like you, Mademoiselle Haywood. We must speak more later. I have the feeling we have much in common."

Kate was not so very sure of that. Yet she also wanted to talk more with Celeste; she had the sense there was much to learn there. The lady surely knew more about what happened beneath the elegant surface of Fontainebleau.

Before she could answer, she felt a gentle touch on her sleeve and turned to find Claude Domville smiling down at her. She was glad to see a familiar face, especially as Celeste had engaged Rob in laughing conversation and he seemed quite distracted. Monsieur Domville had changed into his own court garb, black velvet and satin trimmed with pearls, his dark hair and beard neatly trimmed. He looked very much a part of the courtly gathering around them.

"Mademoiselle Haywood. I am so happy to see you again so soon after our arrival," he said, bowing over her hand. "How are you finding my homeland thus far?"

Kate sensed Rob and Celeste watching them, and she smiled up at Claude. "Your descriptions of the beauties of France were entirely correct, Monsieur Domville. Fontainebleau is like a palace in a fairy story. And the fashions are exquisite. I shall need to order a new gown or two, at the least, while I am here."

"I can assist you with that," Celeste said. "I know all the best tailors and embroiderers, and all the milliners Queen Mary herself uses. You are so tiny, Mademoiselle Haywood—like a delicate little bird singing high in a tree. We shall soon have you looking like the most elegant Frenchwoman, just like my friend Amelia."

*Or like Queen Anne Boleyn?* Kate thought of the tales of Queen Elizabeth's mother when she returned from her own time at the French court as a girl, of the elegance and sophistication she brought back with her. Kate's own mother might have been Queen Anne's secret half sister and passed down the dark Boleyn hair, but Kate thought she would have a great deal to learn to even begin to emulate them.

Yet she certainly wouldn't turn away a skirt cut in that new tulip-shaped fashion so many of the ladies were wearing. It was pretty indeed.

"I doubt any dressmaker would have such transformative magic, Mademoiselle Renard, but I confess I am eager to see their wares," Kate said.

The doors to Queen Mary's chamber opened, and a large party appeared there. They froze for a moment, framed between two large gold-threaded tapestries, as if they did indeed pose for a play. And their audience obliged. The room fell silent as everyone turned to stare at them. Kate, too, found herself watching in astonishment, for they were a beautiful spectacle.

The man at their head was tall and strongly built, with wide shoulders in his white-and-silver doublet. A red-gold beard framed a face that was scarred on both cheeks, and his gray eyes were hard and cold as he took in the gathering. Beside him was a much smaller, plumper lady, smiling in dark red velvet, and gathered behind them was a train of beautifully dressed attendants.

"'Tis the Duc de Guise and his household," Celeste whispered. "See his wife, Duchesse Anne, in the red? She is great friends with Queen Catherine, thanks to their shared Italian families, but Queen Mary has long loved her aunt and uncle like her own parents."

Beside Kate, Claude stiffened, and when she glanced up she caught him frowning. He quickly erased his expression and put on a bland smile like everyone else, but Kate recalled that he was kinsman to Constable Montmorency, who had been pushed from power when the Guise came in with their queenly niece. She feared she would never be able to remember who was allied to whom here at Fontainebleau.

The crowd suddenly surged into motion again, parting to let Queen Mary sweep through. She was smiling, her pale face radiant, and Lady Barnett and Amelia followed close behind her.

"Uncle, Aunt!" Queen Mary cried. "How pleased I am you could join us tonight. I have missed you so very much." She hurried over to kiss the duc's and duchesse's cheeks.

As the rest of the Guise party made their obeisances to the queen, Kate noticed that Amelia, who stood so very near them, had gone pale as snow. She swayed a bit as if she would faint, and her aunt grabbed her arm and whispered something in her ear that made her shoulders stiffen.

Puzzled, Kate followed the direction of Amelia's attention to find a man who stood on the edges of the glittering Guise group. She saw why he would catch any lady's rapt stare: He was the most beautiful man she had ever seen. Tall and elegantly slender but with powerful shoulders encased in silver satin, his hair and short beard were almost the same pale shade, shimmering and starlike. His eyes, though, were bright blue, almost a sky shade that seemed strangely familiar, though Kate could not quite recall why.

Yet his masculine beauty was of a distinctly wintry sort, as if he were a king in an ice palace, remote and austere. He stared back at Amelia, and for an instant Kate thought she saw shock on his face. But then it was wiped away and his chin tilted in a disdainful expression. He turned away in a slow, deliberate motion that almost made Kate shiver with its coldness.

"Who is that gentleman in the silver?" she whispered to Celeste.

Celeste glanced up and frowned. "Monsieur d'Emours. They said he would not be returning to court until the spring. What is he doing here now? *Pauvre* Amelia!"

Monsieur d'Emours—the man who had fought a duel over Amelia Wrightsman. Kate glanced back at Amelia and found she was more composed, though her hands shook. She clutched at her skirts to make them still.

Toby Ridley stepped to her side, touching her arm, but she shrugged him away and he stalked back into the crowd. Charles Throckmorton tried to speak to his friend, but Toby visibly pushed away his words of consolation. Charles shook his head sadly but did not try to speak again.

"Uncle, I have a rare treat for us tonight," Queen Mary said, her voice bright and almost childlike, as if she sought her uncle's praise. "A musician from my dear cousin Queen Elizabeth's court is actually here in France, and will play us some English songs before we dine. It will be almost as if my cousin has come to visit us in person!"

Before Kate could realize what was happening, Queen Mary took the duc's arm and led him toward Kate. She swiftly curtsied as low as she could, and as she rose he nodded, though he did not look very interested. Up close, his old scars were more noticeable, marring his high cheekbones and strong jaw. There were tales that he had gained them when he was young, in fierce battle with Huguenot rebels.

"English songs?" he said. "I am sure they cannot compare in beauty to our own songs of Lorraine."

"We shall be able to compare them ourselves, Uncle," Queen Mary said. "Please, Mademoiselle Haywood. If you would care to use my own virginals?"

Still feeling a bit nervous at having the eyes of Queen Mary and the Guise watching her, Kate seated herself carefully on the cushioned stool at the keyboard. It was a very beautiful instrument. Queen Elizabeth played a set of virginals that had belonged to her mother, Queen Anne Boleyn, but this one seemed even finer. The sleek, polished wood was inlaid with elaborate scenes of flowers and curling ribbons, and the keys gleamed a bright white.

The crowded chamber, filled with the Guise family and Queen Mary's noble attendants, seemed to melt away and there was only music. She thought about all the songs she knew, trying to decide which ones Queen Mary might most like to hear.

Something romantic, surely. Maybe even a little sad. She seemed to be the sentimental sort. Kate nodded and launched into the opening bars of "If Love Now Reigned," written by Queen Mary's uncle, King Henry himself. It was a song Kate knew well, so she could also study the crowd that swirled around her as she played.

To her relief, Queen Mary led her fearsome uncle the duc back to the chairs by the hearth, and her ladies flocked around them like bright birds. Servants passed trays of wine goblets and sweetmeats, and laughter was heavy in the air.

But Kate noticed that Amelia Wrightsman was not laughing. She stood near the doorway, her face as white as her gown, staring at Monsieur d'Emours as he stood behind the duc's chair. He carefully did *not* look at her, but Amelia seemed to be unable to turn away.

As Kate watched her, wondering if she should try to go to Mistress Wrightsman's side and assist her, Toby Ridley came up beside Amelia and gently touched her sleeve. She whirled on him, her cheeks turning pink, and said something to him. It must have been harsh, for he fell back a step and shook his head. Amelia rushed away and was quickly lost in the crowd.

Toby's jaw tightened, his usually kind face like a thundercloud, and he started toward d'Emours, only to be stopped by Charles. Toby tried to pull back from his friend, and Charles spoke in low tones near his ear.

Kate's shoulders grew tense, her fingers fumbling at the familiar notes, as she feared there might be some quarrel starting in the queen's own chamber. But Toby finally nodded and let Charles lead him away.

*One argument diverted,* Kate thought with a sigh as she fell back into the rhythm of the song. In public, anyway. Who knew happened behind closed doors at Fontainebleau?

# CHAPTER TEN

Kate was barely awake the next morning, after the long hours of music in Queen Mary's chambers, when a message came for her from Queen Elizabeth's ambassador Sir Nicholas Throckmorton. She had been summoned to meet with him after he broke his fast. Charles Throckmorton would arrive to escort her.

A maid of the French household arrived just as the winter sun peeked through the window, bringing warm water for washing. She pursed her lips at Kate's meager selection of gowns, her unfashionable English sleeves and petticoats, but Kate just had to shrug. There was little she could do about her garb at the moment, though she did wish for one of the lace-trimmed French bodices, or at least a more stylish neckline! She would have to hunt for some new fabric, she decided, and beg someone to help her sew, for she had little skill with the needle.

After she was ready, her hair dressed in a fashionable twisted braid by the French maid and her clothes as attractive as they could make them, there was little to do but wait. Sipping at her morning ale, she went to open the window and peer out at the gardens in the fresh new light.

In the daylight, there was none of the fairylike mystery of the pathways under the stars, but it had a freshness that made her want to run outside and take it all in, every sight and smell, every lovely inch. She wondered what she would find there, if the beauty would be as blinding and deceptive as that of the courtiers in Queen Mary's chambers last night. The Guise, Monsieur d'Emours, Queen Mary, Celeste Renard—what did they hide beneath their smiles and fine fashions?

Kate shuddered as she thought of the burned farm, the people so suspicious of each other. Elizabeth was right that something was here in France, behind the smiles and music. Perhaps Queen Mary herself was planning something. Kate knew only that she had to find out, and soon.

For just an instant, she thought of Anthony and the Hardys' pretty, respectable house. What would a life like that be like? She would be mistress of a fine household—safe, quiet. There would be no confusing palace corridors, no secrets, no fears. She smiled to think of Anthony's laughter, his kind eyes as he looked down at her.

It was a tempting idea indeed, to run away from kings and palaces and their dangers, to be normal and have an ordinary life. But it would be frightening in its own way, with no adventure, no Queen Elizabeth. She had to serve the queen now, be her eyes and ears in this palace in faraway France, no matter what dangers it brought. All other thoughts could wait.

"What did you think of Queen Mary, Mistress Haywood?" Charles asked as they made their way up the stairs.

"She is certainly as beautiful as they say," Kate answered carefully. "And most welcoming."

"Aye, her charm is renowned. It draws everyone to her, like a magical spell that only releases people when they are out of her sight."

Was he suggesting Queen Mary used true spells? Witchcraft was a dangerous accusation to make, even in jest. Such accusations had helped lead Elizabeth's mother Queen Anne to the block. "A spell?"

"One that can make men and women alike enthralled with her."

Kate carefully studied his expression, but as usual she could read nothing with him. He always looked most serious. Yet she knew his studies of alchemy were his particular interest. "Are you enthralled with her, Master Throckmorton?"

Charles gave a hoarse laugh. "Me? Nay, Mistress Haywood. I fear Queen Mary's feminine charms hold little attraction for me, except for a matter of interesting study. She and her friends are much too frivolous and flirtatious, even the English ladies in her circle. I look for other qualities altogether."

"Really? Such as what?"

Charles gave her a strange little smile. "Just not one

such as Queen Mary. Or her friend Amelia Wrightsman, for that matter."

Why would he think of Amelia in particular? Kate thought of Queen Mary's and Amelia's many admirers, and the adroit, affectionate, but rather careless way those ladies dealt with them. "There seem many who would not agree with you."

But there was no time for him to answer. They came to a halt at a door tucked at the end of a short corridor. Two maidservants hurried past, their arms laden with clean linens, but the rest of the wing seemed deserted. Charles knocked at the door.

"Enter!" a man's voice called.

The chamber was a large one and stuffed to the paneled walls with trunks and cases, along with stacks of books. Next to the fireplace was a small table where a tall, slender man was writing. Kate could see only a long reddish beard, a dark, close-fitting cap, and ink-stained fingers flying over the paper before him.

At last he looked up with an impatient frown. "So you are the girl who brings me Sir William Cecil's letters?"

"I am, Sir Nicholas," Kate answered with a quick curtsy, though she thought it had been several years since she could rightly be called a girl. She took the letters from her purse and passed them to him over the cluttered desk.

He glanced over them, still frowning. "I do wonder that my old friend chose a female as his messenger. Surely he has no shortage of reliable agents now?"

Kate felt her cheeks warm. She was certainly accustomed to such attitudes in England, and they actually served her well. People often underestimated a female, especially one who was rather young and petite. But sometimes they made her want to throw something and shout, just like the queen.

Before she could answer, Charles said, "Perhaps Sir William thought a lady would attract less attention on the journey. Mistress Haywood has proved herself to be a most discreet and observant traveler, Uncle. And Queen Mary did seem to like her very much last night."

Kate flashed him a smile, surprised and grateful for such a compliment. Charles smiled in return, and she suddenly realized that was something she had never seen before. He was such a solemn man.

Sir Nicholas glanced at her with a bit more interest. "Is that so?"

"They did tell me that Queen Mary is very fond of music," Kate answered. "I found her to be most welcoming, though still regal, as befits her station. She wishes to know a great deal about Queen Elizabeth."

Sir Nicholas's stern expression softened. "So she does. She asks many questions of Her Grace and our English ways. A lady of great charm, though one to be wary of. Hm. Perhaps William knows a bit of what he is doing, after all."

"Do you find Queen Mary so charming, Uncle?" Charles said. "You spoke of your great frustration that she still will not ratify the Treaty of Edinburgh, and that she has quartered the arms of England with those of France and Scotland. I noticed it was still on her canopy last night."

Sir Nicholas gave a deep sigh. "I am frustrated. It is my mandate from the queen to make Queen Mary ratify the treaty and explain the quartering. Without it, I have no hope of returning to England, which would be a better place for my wife's health. Anne does pine for home. But what can I do? Queen Mary insists she must have counsel from her Scots lords before she can decide, as she is now a lady alone in the world. She says it was her father-in-law's idea to quarter the arms of England, as a compliment to her cousin, and she could not say him nay. She has the soft heart of a female—content to be ruled by good counsel and wise men, as a lady should. I cannot help but feel for her."

"And does Mary consider you and Lord Bedford wise counsel?" Charles asked.

"'Tis true Bedford has no patience for diplomatic work," Sir Nicholas said. "He grows too angry. But Queen Mary has the company of her brother, Lord James Stewart, now. We shall see good results soon, I am sure."

Kate was not so sure of that. Lord James was in contact with Cecil, but also with the Guise. If Queen Mary returned to Scotland, he would lose his preeminent position. Which would Queen Elizabeth truly prefer: Mary in France or just over Elizabeth's own border?

"I must tell you, Sir Nicholas, that there may have been an attempt to steal those letters on our journey from England," Kate said.

Sir Nicholas gave her a startled glance. "What do you mean, Mistress Haywood?"

Kate quickly told him of how she was pushed overboard on the ship, her purse taken. "I have nothing else anyone could want," she said.

"Why did you not say something then, Mistress Haywood?" Charles asked. "We were told you merely lost your footing on the slippery deck."

"I did not want whoever it was to know I guessed what they were after," she said. "And I was not sure whom to fully trust."

She still did not. The more people she met at Fontainebleau, the more complicated things became. The letters seemed to be only a tiny part of matters she could not yet piece together. Yet Charles looked so shocked. If he were the thief, then he had missed his true calling as an actor.

"Do you know what is in these letters, Mistress Haywood?" Sir Nicholas said.

"Nay," Kate answered. "My skills with codes are not great enough yet, and Sir William entrusted them to me on behalf of Queen Elizabeth."

"Have you any idea who would want them?"

"I do not know who could read them if they are in code. The Barnetts were aboard, but they would not have to steal them, I am sure. And there was a French party who had just transferred to the ship to return home, led by Monsieur Domville."

"Perhaps there were French spies among the crew," Sir Nicholas said. "The Guise have eyes everywhere,

I fear. I will have my men decipher these this very morning. In the meantime, Mistress Haywood, just keep a watch among the ladies. They are far more likely to let careless words slip, even if they don't understand their true meaning." He sat back in his chair and rubbed wearily at his brow.

"Ah," Sir Nicholas sighed. "If only one of these two queens in the isle of Britain were a man, and could make a happy marriage to unite the countries into one. But that is beyond even Sir William's work. We can only hope Queen Elizabeth shall marry soon and have sons. Now, Mistress Haywood, if you would excuse Charles and myself, we have business to discuss which I am sure would not interest you."

*Interest me?* What, then, was the purpose of her coming all the way to France? Kate felt a burst of anger but she pushed it away. Her work there was secret; it was the only way she could discover any little tidbit that might help Queen Elizabeth. A man like Sir Nicholas would never understand. She curtsied and hurried out of the small office and made her way back to her own room, getting lost only twice.

To Kate's surprise, when she opened her door she did not find her chamber empty. Celeste Renard was there, piling a gleaming heap of silks and satins onto the bed.

"Mademoiselle Renard," Kate cried. "What are you doing here?"

Celeste looked up with one of her dazzling smiles. She sat on the edge of the bed, swinging her legs carelessly beneath her velvet skirts. "Mademoiselle Haywood, there you are! Queen Mary sent these to you. She thought you might like to wear some French fashions to the reception in the grand gallery later today."

"Queen Mary sent *me* clothes?" Kate said, amazed.

"Indeed. She is always most thoughtful." Celeste held up a satin bodice. "What do you think? I think this blue will suit you. Perhaps with these black-and-silver sleeves? The ribbons are the newest style . . ."

Kate studied the lustrous fabrics, the narrow-cut sleeves and lace-trimmed bodices. "They are very pretty indeed. I shall not feel at all like myself wearing them!"

Celeste laughed. "That is the point of fine fashions, is it not? An armor for us ladies to hide behind."

Kate glanced at Celeste's own gown, violet velvet and cream silk stripes with embroidered flowers. "Your own gown is the loveliest I have seen."

Celeste gave a little twirl. "Do you like it? My aunt sent me the fabric. She lives in Burgundy, where my family is from, and they have weavers renowned for their silks."

"Burgundy? How did you come to court?"

"My aunt once served Queen Eleanor, very long ago. When she heard Queen Catherine required new ladies, she got me the post through some of her old friends." Celeste's glance fell. It was merely a blink, but Kate had the sense that there was more to the story. Or perhaps a different story indeed. But she knew Celeste would not tell her anything yet.

"And you are friends with Queen Mary as well?"

"Queen Mary is the kindest of souls, as well as very

merry." Celeste held up a length of blue ribbon against Kate's hair. "Until she lost her husband, anyway, poor little queen. Now she has nothing."

"Nothing? Except palaces and servants . . ."

"Her power here in France is gone. Queen Catherine will see to that."

"Does she not care for her daughter-in-law? Everyone says Queen Mary came here so young, she remembers no other parents."

"Queen Catherine has her own children to see to now, and she will let nothing get in the way of those ambitions. Her children are everything to her. She was powerless for so many years, but now she is in charge." Celeste frowned. "And we all must remember that."

Kate feared she would never keep all the alliances and enemies at Fontainebleau straight. How could she know whom to trust? What was real? "Will Queen Catherine deal well with Elizabeth, then?"

Celeste laughed. "How could I know such a thing, Mademoiselle Haywood? I am merely a lady-in-waiting. Now, what do you think of this petticoat for tonight? The embroidery is so exquisite. You will be thought a true Frenchwoman."

# CHAPTER ELEVEN

As Kate followed Lady Barnett and Amelia into the grand gallery, she was glad Celeste had given her the French gown to wear, for the crowd gathered near the tall, gleaming windows was sparkling indeed.

Queen Elizabeth's courtiers thought themselves most fashionable, often spending the equivalent of a year's wages for a prosperous London artisan to try to impress the queen with their embroidered velvets and feathered hats, but most of them would look like mudhens beside the French. Even in their muted colors of mourning—black, gray, violet, and midnight blue—they were elegant beyond compare, their simple perfectly tailored lines and rich trimmings giving them an air of crisp, careless perfection. Though Kate was sure they must have spent hours dressing and choosing jewels, they looked as if they always woke up looking just that way.

They watched the English party as Kate and the others made their way past, their ceruse-painted lips smiling faintly, their eyes bright with curiosity. A few of the older courtiers showed their disdain plainly.

There were muted whispers behind fans of feathers and painted silk, but mostly there was only silence, strangely loud in the vast space around them.

And what an awe-inspiring space it was. Kate focused on the gallery rather than the stares of the French courtiers, and hoped she was not gaping like a country mouse. Elizabeth had some beautiful palaces—Nonsuch, Richmond, Greenwich, Whitehall—all of them filled with tapestries, portraits, porcelain, and silver plate. Yet Kate had never seen a room as perfectly proportioned, as graceful and opulent, as this one. It fit perfectly with the fairy tale she had seemed to be living in ever since they rode through the Fontainebleau gates.

From the stark vestibule where they had first entered the palace, carved doors had been thrown open to reveal a space that seemed all gleaming gilt and pure white alabaster. Beneath the sea of satin shoes and jeweled hems, the floor was of an inlaid pattern of light and dark woods in intricate triangles and diamonds, echoing the coffered ceiling above. Tall windows with deep embrasures lined the walls and were hung with brocade draperies. Interspersed between the windows were gold benches and small chairs that no one dared sit upon. Fantastical creations also adorned the wall.

The lower wall was of sculpted wood, French walnut as finely grained as marble, formed into tumbling cornucopias of fruit and flowers. The royal arms of France were everywhere, surmounted by the initial "F"—for King Francis, who had been Queen Catherine's father-in-law and had built this very gallery to reflect his glory.

Kate caught a glimpse of a painting of an elephant and she longed to stop to examine it closer. The whole scene created a song in her mind, a tumble of notes, an elaborate, elegant, lighthearted tune that hid a world of swirling danger beneath, and she wanted more than anything to write it down, to not forget it. But she stumbled a bit over the hem of her new skirt and was abruptly reminded where she was and what she was meant to be doing: watching the French court and learning what they really thought and intended toward Queen Elizabeth.

Amelia tossed her a glance over her shoulder, her eyes wide. For an instant, Amelia seemed almost frightened, yet she quickly covered that flash of fear with her usual careless smile. Kate smoothed her skirt and folded her hands carefully in front of her, staring straight ahead.

At the far end of the room, an enormous tapestry covered the wall, a scene of a royal procession in some ancient city, all gold-edged flowers and prancing horses. A small raised dais sat before it, and on a high-backed gilded chair waited a small child, dressed grandly in dark blue velvet edged in sapphires and pearls, but kicking his velvet shoes with impatience. Queen Mary sat to the other side of the dais, gently smiling in her white gown and veil, whispering to her uncle Guise, who stood behind her.

But it was the woman who sat in the center of the group on the royal dais who captured Kate's attention. In the midst of so much sparkle, she was like a shadow, one that cast its darkness over everything, like the slow-moving encroachment of night.

Kate was sure that could only be Queen Catherine de Medici. She was seated on a gold chair cushioned with black velvet next to her son, her feet on a stool that hid how short she was rumored to be. Her seat was only a little lower than that of the bored-looking boy king, who was now fidgeting and tugging at his short satin cloak.

Queen Catherine looked anything but bored. She sat very still and straight, very solemn, yet her gaze was moving, taking in everything in the crowded gallery around her. She wore widow's black, as they said she always had since her husband died, a matte black velvet that reflected no light. A black silk veil fell from her cap. The only color in her garb was from a collar of ermine and a pair of pearl drop earrings.

Just as everyone had said, Queen Catherine was not beautiful, especially seated so near Queen Mary's statuesque, marblelike loveliness. Beneath the gold-trimmed edge of her cap, Queen Catherine's face was round and double chinned, with a long Medici nose and protruding dark eyes. Beneath her veil, the hair that was visible—parted severely and drawn straight back—was a pale brown.

Yet those eyes seemed to glow with a force of intelligence and curiosity she couldn't suppress. Her hand, adorned only with a wedding ring and a small emerald on her little finger, tapped impatiently on the arm of her chair, as if she couldn't bear to be so still. As if at any moment a surfeit of energy would make her leap from her chair and fly out of the room.

Even though they looked nothing alike and many years separated them, Queen Catherine reminded Kate of Queen Elizabeth. There was that watchful wariness, that energy, that spark to be doing things.

Queen Catherine's dark eyes lit on each individual face as they approached her, her gaze sharp and intent as if she memorized them. Kate felt the cold touch of unease. She knew that no matter what happened here in France, she would do well to stay far beneath the Queen Mother's notice—if that was possible.

Sir Henry led his wife and niece forward, and they made their low bows. Everyone else in the English group hurried to follow their lead.

Rob held out his arm to Kate to help her rise from her curtsy, and she glanced up at him. He, too, looked most fascinated by the two queens, by the grand stage they had set up for their audience.

"Sir Henry, you are welcome back to our court," Queen Catherine said, her voice low, almost rough, still touched faintly with the sound of her native Florence beneath the smooth French words. "I fear you will find things very different here now than when you were last in residence. We are in sad days indeed."

"I am honored to be in France again, Your Grace," Sir Henry said. "Queen Elizabeth sends her deepest condolences and best wishes for God's grace on your kingdom."

"Your queen is most kind," Queen Catherine said, her fingers still tapping at the chair. Her gaze flitted over everyone else. "I see you have brought newcomers with you as well."

"I have, Your Grace, with Queen Elizabeth's compliments." Sir Henry quickly introduced them all. "And this is Mistress Haywood and Master Cartman, who have entertained Queen Elizabeth at her own court, and who she hopes might brighten your own days a bit while they are here."

Rob offered his arm again to escort Kate forward. Kate still felt that cold uncertainty and hoped she would not tremble, would not give away even a hint of nervousness. She had been at court too long for that. She forced her back to stay very straight, and smiled as she curtsied again.

As she rose, she found that disconcerting, bottomless-dark gaze of Queen Catherine directly on her.

"You must be the musician my daughter-in-law has told us about," Queen Catherine said. "She said she enjoyed your English songs very much."

Kate glanced at Queen Mary, who gave her an encouraging smile. "I am very glad my music pleased Queen Mary, Your Grace."

"I also enjoy music very much, as well as plays and masques. The troubles of life can be heavy indeed, but a song can carry us out of them for a moment," Queen Catherine said. "We can use such brightness here to remind us of God's true blessings in this world as well as his trials. You will play for us?"

"Of course, Your Grace. Whenever you wish. I would be honored."

Queen Catherine smiled, and it transformed her plain, round face into something transcendentally intelligent. Like her daughter-in-law, she had the trick of drawing a person close, of making her feel she was the most important person even in a crowd.

It was a dangerous trick indeed.

"Excellent! I have a troupe of players from Florence here now. I am sure you would be interested in meeting them. I look forward to hearing how your style of song differs from theirs. And now I do find myself in need of a walk. We have all sat here too long, and I see the sun is out at last."

As if her burning energy could no longer be contained, Queen Catherine pushed herself to her feet. She took the fidgety boy king's hand and led him beside her down the steps of the dais. Everyone fell into line quickly behind her, and Sir Henry led Kate and the others into another bow. She held on to Rob's arm and dipped into her lowest curtsy.

Queen Catherine's ladies moved past, including Celeste Renard. She nodded and winked at Amelia, who laughed in return. Kate noticed that the ladies were indeed an exceptionally pretty group, all much younger than the Queen Mother and clad in low-cut satin gowns and jeweled headdresses.

The large party made its way down the sweeping double stone staircase into the garden. The day was cold, the wind biting, with a touch of ice as it swept through cloaks, but the sun had indeed come out and beamed down on them with a pale yellowish light. It danced over the white marble statues of classical gods and goddesses that lined the pathway, making them appear to move along with the richly dressed courtiers who passed between them in their furs and velvets. In the distance there was a large glass-still pond with an elegant marble pavilion on its far shore, and for an instant Kate wondered if it was a beautiful illusion.

"Mademoiselle Haywood!" Queen Catherine suddenly called.

For a moment, Kate was sure she had not heard right, until everyone turned to stare at her. Surprised and even a bit frightened, she froze for an instant, until Rob gave her a little push. She hurried to the front of the procession, where the queen walked with her son, and hastily curtsied.

"Y-your Grace," she said, out of breath.

"Monsieur Charles Throckmorton tells me that, as well as music, you have an interest in the alchemical arts," Queen Catherine said. "That you are acquainted with the famous Dr. Dee. Is this true?"

For a moment, Kate was almost too nervous to speak. Queen Catherine had an indomitable reputation, even in England. But when Kate looked into her dark eyes, she saw only the light of interest and intelligence.

"I have met Dr. Dee, yes, Your Grace. Queen Elizabeth relies on his wisdom a great deal. He is a learned and interesting man, though I fear I am not knowledgeable about such sciences myself."

"They do say Queen Elizabeth relies greatly on his good counsel, and I have read some of his writings on the rules of seismography. I would like to know more about him and about the work being done in England." Queen Catherine lifted her hand, and two men in her train hurried to her side. They were both older gentlemen, with the dark eyes and hair of Italians, but one was clad in the somber black of a scholar and one in a blue velvet doublet. "This is my own astrologer and perfumer, Signor Ruggieri, and my personal physician, Dr. Folie. They have assisted me in my studies for many years. Mademoiselle Haywood knows Queen Elizabeth's Dr. Dee, messieurs."

The man in the doublet took Kate's hand and bowed over it. "Fascinating, mademoiselle. I am Dr. Folie, and have learned much from your Monsieur Dee's writings."

Signor Ruggieri said nothing but gave her a small sketch of a bow. She could smell a strange cologne emanating from the folds of his black robe, like oranges and jasmine underlaid with something rougher, more raw.

"Perhaps you would join us in my chamber some evening, Mademoiselle Haywood, when we conduct one of our séances," Queen Catherine said. "You may learn much of interest. Monarchs must be educated and kind as well as ruthless, don't you think? It is all of one pattern."

Interest? That was undoubtedly true. Even in England, there was much talk of Queen Catherine's studies in the science of alchemy, of her powers and the rituals she had brought with her from Italy. It was a bit frightening to think of, true, but also intriguing. Kate could not believe this bit of good fortune. "I would be honored, Your Grace."

"Mademoiselle Renard will show you the way," Queen Catherine said. She gave Kate a small nod and continued on her walk, her astrologer, doctor, and ladies falling in behind her, so she was soon lost to sight.

Celeste gave Kate a smile as she strolled past, but when Queen Catherine was out of sight, she leaned close and whispered, "You must be very careful of Signor Ruggieri, Mademoiselle Haywood."

"The perfumer?"

"*Oui.* But then, I am sure you already know to be on your guard with everyone. Not everyone is as they seem."

Kate nodded. Aye, she did know that—all too well.

# CHAPTER TWELVE

The corridor in the far wing of the palace was quiet as Kate made her way to her chamber. It was late; the evening had gone on long, with card games, wine, and sweet delicacies in Queen Catherine's rooms, and Kate had been asked to play her English songs again, even as the Barnetts retired early. She felt weary, her mind heavy, but she felt she had learned much about French manners, French relationships.

The only light was from a few torches flickering in the shadows. The air was cold. A sound like a low, harsh sob echoed between the bare walls, and Kate thought of tales of restless ghosts roaming palace halls, touching mortals with their icy fingers. She shivered and hurried her steps toward her own door.

But it was not a spirit who was crying—unless it was a spirit who could also blow its nose and sigh. At the end of the corridor, just beyond Kate's chamber, there was a small alcove with a window set in the wall. It was half concealed by a velvet drape, yet Kate glimpsed the embroidered hem of a pale satin gown, the toe of a velvet slipper. Another sob shivered through the air.

Kate worried that someone was ill. "Hello?" she called our carefully. "May I help?"

There was a sudden, surprised rustling, and a pale face peeked around the edge of the drape. It was Amelia Wrightsman who cried there in private. "Oh, Mistress Haywood! You did startle me. I thought everyone was abed by now. I didn't want to wake my aunt, so I came here."

Kate hurried to Amelia's side. "Are you ill? Should I fetch Mistress Berry and her possets?"

Amelia frowned. "Nay, not her. I am not ill. I just needed a quiet moment."

"Oh," Kate said, embarrassed that she had intruded. Quiet moments were few and precious in palaces. She started to turn away. "I am sorry. I shall just—"

"Do stay for a moment, Mistress Haywood! Unless you are very tired and must seek your bed. It's not as comforting being alone as I thought it would be."

Kate studied Mistress Wrightsman's face. She looked very different from when she was laughing and dancing in company. Her eyes were reddened with crying, and she seemed younger, unsure of herself. Just as Kate so often felt. "Of course I can stay." She sat down next to Amelia on the narrow window seat and arranged her skirts around her. "Fontainebleau is beautiful, but also rather cold and lonely, I have found."

Amelia gave a wry laugh and wiped at her eyes. Her lacy handkerchief wafted the scent of her violet perfume. "Crowded palaces are the loneliest places of all, I think."

"Mayhap you are right. I've found I can always lose myself in music. It can feel like an entirely different world, even in a banquet hall filled with people."

Amelia sighed. "I do envy you such an escape." She wiped at her eyes again, and her shoulders seemed to stiffen, as if she found her armor and wrapped it around herself. "Tell me, Mistress Haywood. Have you ever been in love?"

Kate laughed in surprise at the sudden change. "I—I am not sure." She thought of Rob leaning close to her as they studied a piece of music, the thrill that shivered through her at his nearness. And she thought of Anthony, the steady, warm touch of his hand on hers, the feeling of safety she had in his presence. "Maybe."

Amelia laughed. "If you truly had been, you would be sure. You are fortunate, Mistress Haywood, not to know its pain. You should always guard your heart most carefully."

Kate studied her closely. Amelia looked fierce but also frightened. Kate thought of Queen Elizabeth and Robert Dudley, Catherine Grey and Lord Hertford, her father living without her mother for so many years— all the love affairs that ended in sorrow. "I have much work to do. There is no time to worry about love."

Amelia nodded. "Work, yes. That is what we must do. The only way to escape." She gave her eyes another dab with her perfumed handkerchief and smiled a brilliant, shimmering smile that Kate could see now had always been part of that armor. She wished she could learn it for herself, but she also wished she could somehow help Amelia in her sadness.

Would her own future, after years at royal courts, be like this—false smiles and secrets?

"Work is our own to claim," Amelia said. "Men are merely trouble."

*All men?* Kate hoped that was not true. "Even though you have so very many suitors?"

"Do I?" Amelia murmured. "Suitors, admirers. They are mostly useless. Unless one finds the right one, which is most unlikely."

She suddenly rose to her feet and smoothed her golden hair beneath her pearl-edged headdress. "Thank you for listening to my ramblings, Mistress Haywood. I am sure you have many things to do with your evening hours."

"I always like to talk to people. They are constantly fascinating, like a poem waiting to be set to music."

Amelia's smile flickered. "You are so kind, Mistress Haywood. I seldom meet anyone with even a morsel of kindness left in their souls after life at court."

Kate swallowed hard. Sadly, she knew what Amelia meant, for she saw it herself too often. A desire to serve the queen, to serve England, became twisted and selfish. She thought again of that quiet, respectable attorney's house that would one day be Anthony's. "What is the use of our courtly work, then, if not to help others when we can?"

Amelia looked startled, but then she laughed. "I am

sure my aunt and uncle would quite agree with you, Mistress Haywood! As long as the people being helped are their own family. More for someone else means less for them. But never mind that; there are surely more serious matters to worry about now. Are you coming to Queen Catherine's garden festivities tomorrow night?"

Kate found herself once again dizzy at Amelia's changes of topic. She did remember Lady Barnett mentioning a garden party, to be held near the decorative pond so Queen Catherine could show off some of her new work on the pavilion there. "Aye. But will it not be rather cold in the gardens?"

"Not for Queen Catherine! She loves to display her grand creations here at Fontainebleau, to show it is her palace now. It should be a most entertaining evening."

"I will be there."

"Good. Then I shall see you there. Good night, Mistress Haywood."

Before Kate could answer, could ask if Mistress Wrightsman was sure she was well now after crying, Amelia rushed away in a rustle of satin and whiff of violet perfume. Kate found herself alone in the silence.

Kate shivered as a draft from one of the windows swept around her. It was too cold to stay in that stone alcove all alone, pondering the changeable nature of Amelia Wrightsman and her friends. She was tired and had much to think about. She turned back toward her own chamber but found she couldn't seek her bed quite yet. Mistress Berry waited outside her door, pacing back and forth.

"Mistress Berry," she called as she hurried closer. "May I assist you with something? Is Lady Barnett ill?"

Mistress Berry swung around to face her. For an instant she looked almost worried, but that was quickly banished. Just as Amelia's smile could cover any flicker of her true thoughts, so could Mistress Berry's placidity. "Not at all, Mistress Haywood. I was putting away some of my books before I retired, and I remembered you said on the ship that you would like to learn more of my herbal work. I thought you might like to borrow this."

She held out a slim volume, and as Kate took it she saw it was well used and bound in worn green leather. The crackling pages were filled with sketches of plants, recipes for household cures. "Thank you, Mistress Berry. This will be most helpful. But it looks as if you use it a great deal."

Mistress Berry smiled. "Indeed I have, so much that I have it memorized. Others should learn from it now. Keep it as long as you like."

"Then I thank you. Have Lady Barnett and Mistress Wrightsman learned from it as well?"

"My cousins? Nay, it takes too long to read a recipe when one can employ a stillroom maid for such things." She studied Kate carefully. "You seem rather more self-sufficient."

*Self-sufficient.* Kate sighed. She would have to be that now, wouldn't she? Her father, her only family, was gone, and she was adrift in a strange country.

Except for Rob. He was there at Fontainebleau with

her. Surely Amelia was not entirely correct; not every man was useless.

"I look forward to reading it, Mistress Berry," she said.

"Of course. I fear I am keeping you from your rest." Mistress Berry nodded and turned to walk away. She paused for a moment and glanced back at Kate. "Was that Mistress Wrightsman I saw leaving this corridor?"

"We met on the way to retire and talked about the evening for a moment," Kate said.

"Of course. Strange that she would be so far from her own chamber now."

"Fontainebleau is rather confusing."

"True. Confusing indeed. I do hope that you don't believe everything you are told here, Mistress Haywood."

With that, Mistress Berry hurried on her way. And Kate opened her own door to find a fire crackling in the small grate. She sat down beside it to study the herbal and go over all she had heard that night.

# CHAPTER THIRTEEN

Kate had never seen anything like the gardens at Fontainebleau before, all lit up for Queen Catherine's party. For an instant, as they stepped out from beneath the covered terrace landing from the gallery to the *jardin anglais*, she was so dazzled that she froze in her tracks, causing the ladies behind her to bump into her. She stood in awe of the artful jumble that was such a contrast to the usual careful symmetry of English gardens, and the ladies giggled over her English manners.

Kate had to laugh at herself, too, for she felt like the smallest mouse from the countryside, gawking at the lavishness of royalty. Yet surely the gardens were meant to dazzle in just such a way. Even a hardened, lifelong courtier would be arrested by just such a display.

Arrested—and distracted from any conflicts and woes that beset the reign of the new young king and his warring factions.

Brigit Berry came to her side, and Kate turned to see

the older lady smiling wryly as she studied the lavish garden scene.

"Beautiful, is it not?" Mistress Berry said as she smoothed the white ruffled trim of her black sleeves. She wore her usual serviceable garments, which made her stand out amid the shining satins and lustrous furs of the others.

"I have never seen anything like it," Kate answered truthfully.

"Of course you have not," Mistress Berry said. "We are in a world apart here, are we not? None can judge us by everyday rules now."

"Hurry along, Brigit!" Lady Barnett called from the pathway ahead. She was arm in arm with two of Queen Catherine's ladies, laughing with them. Amelia was nowhere to be seen.

Brigit nodded and followed her kinswoman as Lady Barnett and her friends vanished through a thick stand of pine trees toward the carp pond, where the party was to be held. The darkness of the night was gathering fast, a thick, heavy blue-black curtain, with only the swirl of stars overhead and the flickering lanterns to light their way. The pale fur of the ladies' cloaks made them look like ghosts as they drifted between the trees, appearing and disappearing again.

Kate followed them, drawing her hood up over her hair. It was a cold night but very still, no wind brushing through the trees. Everything had a glasslike, frozen quality to it. Even the laughter that hung in the air seemed to belong to spirits. She shivered and had the sudden feeling that she certainly didn't want to be caught alone in those dark shadows.

She hurried down the path, following the sound of voices as they grew louder and were joined by the strains of music, a melancholy, sweet song she had never heard before. She found herself by the edge of the pond, which looked like a fine flat sheet of Venetian glass under the light of the hundreds of lanterns.

It was exactly like the scenes Queen Elizabeth wished to conjure through her royal masquerades—otherworldly in its beauty. On the far side of the water stood a octagonal pale marble pavilion, its windows glowing with amber light. On its steps Kate glimpsed a small figure in black: the Queen Mother surrounded by her beautiful ladies in white, her hand raised as if to summon people into her fairy realm.

To get to the pavilion, boats festooned with wreaths of greenery and fluttering ribbons waited to ferry everyone across. Kate saw Toby Ridley help Amelia into one as she laughed at something he said to her. She wore white-figured brocade with his black velvet cloak draped carelessly over her shoulders. He looked up into her face with eagerness written large in his expression.

Lady Barnett and Brigit were already gone, and Kate couldn't see anyone else she knew nearby. She studied the faces of the gentlemen, hoping to find Rob, but he was nowhere among them.

"How much coin do you think was spent on this nuisance?" someone behind her grumbled.

She glanced back to see two Guise kinsmen waiting for a boat, their faces scowling above the lace collars of their finery.

"The Queen Mother should listen to the advice of the duc," the other one answered. "Instead she gives too much to these Huguenots, and look where that has gotten us!"

"She should heed King Philip's example," said the first one. "Just as the duc has. The Spanish know how to deal with heretics."

"Mistress Haywood?" she heard Charles Throckmorton call, and she turned away from the discontented Guise. She stood on tiptoe to see over the shoulders of the people gathered in front of her and glimpsed him waving at her.

"Pardon, messieurs," she murmured, squeezing through the crowd. She smelled wine and strong perfumes as she tried to make her way through the press, felt elbows catch her in the side. She stumbled, and instinctively held out her hand to catch herself.

She found herself clutching at a smooth satin sleeve, and a strong hand set her upright again. She glanced up, muttering apologies, and found herself looking up into the eyes of Jacques d'Emours, Amelia's erstwhile lover. He gave her an abrupt nod, his blue eyes icy, before he let her go. He *was* handsome with those unusual eyes—Kate would give Amelia that—but so very distant and cold, she wondered he did not freeze everyone around him. Perhaps he was one of the Guise angry about Queen Catherine's "lenient" behavior?

She spun away and stumbled out of the crowd at the edge of the pond. Charles was there to find her and caught her arm to lead her to one of the boats. She sank down onto the velvet cushions of the narrow seat with a relieved sigh.

As they pushed out onto the water, leaving the crowd behind, the music grew louder. It seemed to be rising from the depths of the pond itself, as if sung by mermaids, and Kate was enchanted by the sound. She couldn't help herself and leaned over to peer into the dark waves. A sudden splash made her fall back with a startled laugh.

A large boat shaped like a golden chariot floated past, and she saw that was where the music came from. A man dressed as Neptune in filmy blue and green draperies, with a golden crown and trident, sat high up in the prow of the boat while nymphs in thin white silk fluttered around him, singing.

Smaller boats followed, each one shaped like a gilded seashell and steered by mermaids in green satin with flowing waves of hair, each of them adding their own clear, high voice to the song.

Kate was amazed. "I have not seen such a thing in England."

Charles gave her a weary-looking smile. "Not even by the queen's ardent suitors, each of them seeking to impress her more than any other?"

Kate laughed, and remembered the classical tableaux of the Earl of Arundel at Nonsuch, the whimsical gifts of Robert Dudley, the gilded and painted coaches of Eric of Sweden. "I have seen much that amazes from them, aye, but no sea pageants such as this."

"I am sure once word of entertainments of this sort make their way back to England, as they are designed to do, you will see many like it. Probably you will even be asked to arrange one, once everyone knows you have seen the French court and its splendors in person."

Kate watched a gilded sea horse float past. She lowered her voice to ask, "How are such things possible? Is the court not still in mourning for Queen Mary's husband? Yet Queen Catherine speaks of hunts and parties at her play dairy . . ." Not to mention the financial troubles and religious squabbles that led to so much despair, so many burned homes and deaths. Not that money meant a great deal to courtly splendor—Queen Elizabeth had inherited an empty treasury from her sister, which made it more important than ever that the English court look splendid.

For France, the pinnacle of European culture, surely that was even more important. The turmoil that bubbled beneath the surface had to be kept hidden.

"Queen Catherine has a kingdom to build on the shoulders of a ten-year-old boy," Charles answered. "She stands between the Guise and the Huguenots, neither of whom will give up power easily. She must keep the peace now at all costs, and distractions can be one way to help with such a task."

Kate nodded. Surely distractions would paint a

rosy picture of Paris for other monarchs as well. "And where does Queen Mary fit in all of this?"

"Queen Mary? She does not. Queen Catherine will not countenance the Duc de Guise's proposal that Mary wed her brother-in-law King Charles. Lord James Stewart will lose power if his sister returns to Scotland, and the grand marriage scheme to Don Carlos of Spain looks less and less likely," Charles said. "My uncle says she should stay here and live comfortably on her French estates, but she does not seem like the quiet, comfortable sort, does she?"

Kate frowned, wondering again what Elizabeth really wanted from her Scottish cousin. What Kate herself should encourage here in France. She had written down all she had seen and heard thus far at Queen Catherine's court and carefully coded it, but she could make little sense yet of what was real and important and what was mere courtly subterfuge.

Their boat bumped against the shore, and one of Neptune's acolytes in white-and-gold classical draperies leaped forward to help her alight. The crowd made their way from the boats, twisting up the pathway to the pavilion, while tritons at either side blew their shell horns. Charles vanished into the gathering, and Kate looked about in confusion.

One of the tritons, in white chiton and golden half mask, caught her arm and spun her in a circle. At first her heart leaped with startled fear, as it had on the ship. She instinctively raised her hand to slap him, but then she recognized the bright blue eyes sparkling from behind the mask, the mischievous smile. Even though his short golden hair was covered by a curled, blue-tinted wig, it was undoubtedly Rob.

"What are you doing?" she whispered.

He laughed merrily. "I am to take a role tonight, fair Kate. Signorina Isabella arranged it."

"Signorina Isabella?" Kate remembered the woman who was singing for Queen Catherine, her bright red hair, her eyes that seemed to see everything.

"Aye. I am learning some of the Italian techniques to take to our plays in England. You must meet with these actors more—they are fascinating."

"Rob, I think . . ." Before she could say anything else, Rob quickly kissed her hand and whirled away into the crowd of tritons. "We must be careful of everyone here," she whispered. Dizzy, Kate made her way with the rest of the partygoers into the pavilions. They all lined up to make their bows to Queen Catherine and slipped past her into yet another room of the fairy world.

The domed ceiling high above their heads was painted with goddesses in white and red, with swans flying among them, touched with sparkling edges of gold leaf. The stone walls between the golden glass windows were hung with tapestries whose matching gold threads caught the torchlight and sparkled. At the far end, a red velvet-draped dais waited with gilded chairs and footstools.

A cluster of shepherdesses dressed in clouds of pink-

and-white silk with beribboned crooks danced in the center of the room to a lively tune of tambours and flutes. Just as on the water, Kate could see no source for the music; it seemed to ring out as if by magic. Shepherds passed around trays of silver goblets to laughing court-iers in brocades and velvets, the air warm after the cold night beyond, the rich scents of jasmine and rose lull-ing them closer to the festivities.

She glimpsed Amelia nearby, giggling with two of Queen Mary's ladies. The last time Kate saw her she had been tearful, but now her cheeks were bright red, her usually perfectly dressed hair escaping from its pearl pins as she waved her hands and her laughter grew louder. She seemed to forget she held a goblet, for some of the wine spilled scarlet droplets onto her pale brocade sleeve.

Amelia laughed and wiped at the wine with the sil-ver fur muff she held on her other arm. A diamond brooch nestled in the fur sparkled, and Kate noticed it was a lion—a badge of the Guise family. She glanced across the room and caught a glimpse of Monsieur d'Emours looking like a god himself in white and gold. He seemed to be looking at Amelia, watching her laugh, but he quickly vanished into the crowd.

She felt a touch on her arm and turned to find Celeste Renard standing behind her. Celeste's bright hair was bound up with a chain of bloodred rubies, but her gown was a somber dove gray, and her smile was smaller than usual.

"It seems our friend Mademoiselle Wrightsman has been much enjoying Queen Catherine's fine wine of Burgundy," Celeste said.

Kate nodded cautiously, unsure about Celeste. She and Amelia had always appeared to be good friends, but friendship here at Fontainebleau, like so many other things, was illusory. "I am sure it cannot be an easy thing for her to encounter Monsieur d'Emours at every turn."

"So you have heard of their famous *amour* and the duel that ended it?" Celeste said. A page in Queen Catherine's blue-and-gold livery passed by with a tray laden with more silver and gold goblets, and Celeste took two.

She handed one to Kate, and Kate automatically took a sip. It was indeed a very delicious wine, rich, complex, but beneath lay a heavy taste of spice. Over the braided silver rim, she caught a glimpse of Queen Catherine's perfumer and astrologer, Signor Ruggieri, across the room with Monsieur d'Emours and other Guise retainers.

"Has not everyone heard of the duel?" Kate said. "It seems to be a very romantic tale."

"Romantic?" Celeste said with a scoffing laugh. "Monsieur d'Emours is only in love with his own estates, his position. They say he cannot maintain his château. If the Guise fall here at court, so will he. It was folly to bring such scandalous attention on himself now."

Kate studied Monsieur d'Emours. He listened to the other men but said nothing himself, giving away nothing by the marble expression on his handsome face. She glanced back to the laughing Amelia, who had turned away from her former lover and held out her hand to Toby instead. "Then surely he must have some passion for her, to have behaved so?"

Celeste shrugged. "The d'Emours name is an old one, filled with a history of courtiers who have behaved far worse. Perhaps he thought that would protect him. But times have changed greatly in France."

"Then what of the other man in the duel?" Kate asked.

"Monsieur Mamou?" Celeste said. "He went back to his own estate in the Languedoc and has not been seen at court since, which is probably most sensible of him. He is kin to Montmorency, the Guises' great rival, and it is surely best to see which way the wind is blowing before he returns. He danced with Amelia a few times and seemed to admire her, of course. Most men do. But to lose his senses in such a way? Very odd. Everyone knows the limits of how far a courtly flirtation can go."

Did they? From what Kate had seen, both at Fontainebleau and in England, courtly flirtations flamed into destructive passions much too often. "Then why a duel, if neither man cared so very much for Mistress Wrightsman?"

Celeste gave a small catlike smile. "That, *chère* Mademoiselle Haywood, is certainly the question. I have heard that perhaps Monsieur Mamou, far from pursuing Amelia, had been casting aspersions on Jacques's family. A d'Emours would not stand for any scandal on his name."

"Scandal? What sort of scandal?"

Celeste gave an elaborate shrug. "I do not know. His mother was most pious, they say, but his father something of a rogue. Not that such a thing is very unusual."

A sudden blast of horns filled the domed chamber, echoing off the stone walls. It was unlike anything Kate had heard before. The shepherdesses melted away, and a procession of Lord James Stewart's Scots attendants appeared, led by two pipers.

Queen Mary followed on her brother's arm. She wore white again, a filmy silk with sheer sleeves trimmed with dark fur, and beamed with pleasure at the music. In her sunlike presence, it seemed as if Fontainebleau could not be a dark place, not filled with shadows that changed with every passing moment. Queen Mary seemed to trail laughter in her wake, even in the midst of her mourning.

Yet Kate had seen many times that light could conceal even more than could darkness.

She stopped near one of the half-open windows and peered outside at the cold night beyond. Most of the partygoers were inside watching the dancing now, but a few people moved through the flickering torchlight outside, their laughter a faint echo on the wind.

But one of those people was not laughing. Kate glimpsed Amelia's golden hair and pale satin gown. She stood facing a taller man, her hands curled into fists. She seemed to shout something, words Kate couldn't catch. Amelia tried to turn and leave, but the man caught her arm and spun her back to face him.

Kate saw that it was Monsieur d'Emours, his expression blank and tight. He did not seem as angry as Amelia did, but he did not let her go. Kate started to go to her just as Amelia jerked her arm free and laughed up into his face.

Before Kate could do anything, Amelia vanished into the night, leaving d'Emours to stare after her. Their argument had been brief yet obviously intense. A burst of pipe music caught her attention, and when she looked back outside, d'Emours too had vanished.

"What do you think of France, then, Kate?" Rob asked as they strolled across the marble terrace that looked out over the night-dark gardens. The party had ended an hour before, but Kate found she didn't yet want to retire, and Rob felt the same.

She studied the view before them. Many of the lanterns strung through the trees to light the way to the pavilion had gone out and most of the revelers had escaped the cold night to find their own firesides, but there still seemed to be a sort of magic hovering over the gardens, like a mist caught on the branches, a trace of laughter fading into the sky.

"There is certainly great beauty here," she said. "So much art and music, I am dizzy with it all! Fontainebleau itself is lovely beyond compare. Yet I do prefer England."

"Why is that?" Rob asked. "Because of Queen Elizabeth?"

"Because of the queen, of course. And other English

things." She thought of the queens here at Fontaine-bleau. Queen Mary, with her beauty and charm, her feminine delicacy, the way she seemed to want only to laugh and work at her embroidery and shied away from authority. And Queen Catherine, the very opposite, so strong and sure. They were certainly potential formidable foes for Queen Elizabeth, depending on which way the French winds blew.

Yet could they not be formidable allies, a bulwark against the cold ambitions of men like the Guise?

That vision she sometimes had of a comfortable London hearth with Anthony, a life with no queens and no Guise-like families, shimmered. She pushed it away. "Also," she added, "because France seems so very old. Tired, mayhap. England seems new."

"New?" Rob said with a laugh. "A country that has been there for centuries?"

Kate laughed, too. "So it has. But so very much has changed with the Tudors, with Queen Elizabeth. There is a new freedom, yes?"

"And Queen Mary? She is also of Tudor blood. Do you think she could bring such a newness to Scot-land, if she returned?"

"Queen Mary is charming indeed. I have never been to Scotland, but they say it is rather a rough place. I can't imagine she would find much of France there."

"I am sure she would find gallants eager to serve her wherever she went, even to the wilds of Scotland," Rob said, a wry tone to his voice.

Surprised, Kate glanced up at him. "Do you still

not like Queen Mary, Rob?" That was most strange—Rob always liked ladies, especially pretty ones.

He smiled down at her, but it looked too much, too theatrical. "I like her as well as any man here. She is, as you say, charming, and most beautiful. But as a queen . . ."

"Mistress Haywood! Thank the stars—there you are. I need your help."

She turned to see Lady Barnett rushing toward them, closely followed by Celeste Renard and two maidservants. Lady Barnett looked as if she had been preparing to retire, for her hair was loose, her silver satin sleeves removed and a knitted shawl wrapped around her shoulders, slipping away even as Brigit ran after her, trying to fix it. Her eyes were wide and frantic.

"Oh, Mistress Haywood, Master Cartman! I am so glad to have found you," Lady Barnett cried. "Have you seen Amelia?"

"Mistress Wrightsman?" Kate said, trying to remember the party and the last time she had seen Amelia, which had been during the dancing. "Nay, not since just after the party."

Lady Barnett glanced back at Celeste. Mademoiselle Renard was still dressed in her fine purple silk gown, her hair caught up in its ruby bandeau, not a strand out of place.

"Has she not returned to your rooms at all, Lady Barnett?" Rob asked gently.

Lady Barnett shook her head. "She returned to the

château with me, but then she said she had left her fur muff at the pavilion and went to retrieve it."

"I offered to go with her," Celeste said. "But she said she would not keep me from my bed, that it would only take her a moment to fetch it herself, as she knew where it was."

"Yet that was long ago!" Lady Barnett wailed. "And no one has seen her. Henry is playing cards with Sir Nicholas, and I dare not disturb him. He would just say she is being frivolous and flighty again."

Kate exchanged a worried look with Rob. Amelia might seem frivolous, true, but Kate knew that truly she was not. Also, she had been arguing with the chilly Monsieur d'Emours.

"Shall we go see if she is at the pavilion, Lady Barnett?" Rob asked.

"Oh, would you?" Lady Barnett said with a relieved sigh. "Celeste and I will search with some of Queen Mary's ladies—she has many friends there—and Brigit can ask the servants."

"Of course, Lady Barnett," Kate said, giving her a reassuring smile, even though she herself felt distinctly uneasy. It was true that Amelia had many friends—and Fontainebleau was a vast place. She surely had just gone off to play cards or to hear some music or to chase a lady-in-waiting's dog around the gardens.

She followed Rob down the steps and into the *jardin anglais* that led to the pond. It was silent and dark, lit by only a few of the more stubborn lanterns in the trees.

They said nothing as they made their way along the pathway to the pavilion. The night had grown colder, every small noise louder in the frost, the bare tree branches clicking in the wind. At the edge of the pond the abandoned boats bobbed at their moorings, their festive wreaths wilting and ribbons trailing in the water. There was no one there at all.

Yet there was still a light glowing in one of the pavilion windows, flickering on the water.

"Should we go look in there?" Rob said. "If she has a rendezvous with someone . . ."

"With a suitor, you mean?"

Rob gave a wry laugh. "I am sure they would not wish to be interrupted."

Kate nodded. Amelia's romantic life was indeed complicated, but her behavior the past few days had been puzzling. One moment so merry and laughing; the next fearful, sad. "She should know her aunt is looking for her, at least, before Lady Barnett alarms more people in the household. They have been through such scandal before. I do think . . ."

Her attention was suddenly caught by a pale flash against the dark shore of the pond, the water lapping against the reeds. She hurried over to examine it, and found it was Amelia's silver fox-fur muff.

Shivering with a new foreboding, she knelt down and turned it over, half fearing she'd spot blood marring the beautiful fur, but it was only water staining the fine edges. Surely Amelia had dropped it in the confusion of leaving the boats and then became distracted when she came back to look for it.

Then Kate noticed something else. There was a tear where the diamond brooch of the Guise badge had been. The shimmering jewels were gone now.

She stood and studied the pavilion across the water. "Perhaps we *should* look for Amelia there."

Rob gave a grim nod. He untied the nearest boat and helped Kate climb onto its narrow seat, its soft cushions now gone. He pushed them away from the shore, and for a moment there was only the sound of the oars cutting through the waters.

Kate studied the scene around them, so different now than it had been at the party, so empty and haunted. She and Rob seemed all alone in the dark, cold world, even though a palace full of people was just beyond the trees. Kate slid closer to his reassuring warmth on the narrow seat, and he reached out to give her hand a small squeeze.

Her breath caught in her throat, almost choking her, when she saw something pale break the shadowy ripples of the water. "Rob, over there!"

He rowed toward it in silence. Kate leaned over the edge of the boat and gave a choked cry as she realized it was exactly as she feared.

Reaching out, she grabbed a handful of Amelia Wrightsman's white brocade skirt, now buoyant with trapped air. It was what had kept her afloat, facedown in the dark waves. She tried to drag Amelia closer, but she was too heavy, and Kate herself almost toppled into the pond.

"Help me," she sobbed, half hoping this was just a nightmare, even as she knew it was much too real.

"Nay, my love, let me," Rob said softly. "You steady the oars, and don't look."

Kate nodded, trying to hold back her tears. They would help no one now, and she had to keep a cool head. As he leaned over the side of the boat, she held the oars and studied the shore. There was no one there at all, no clue as to how Amelia had ended up where she was.

Kate glanced back as Rob pulled the body from the pond and laid it gently in the bottom of the boat. Water flooded Kate's boots and the hem of her skirt. Before Rob covered Amelia with his cloak, Kate glimpsed her face. It was as white as ice in the moonlight, her lilac-hued lips parted and her eyes wide-open, staring at the night sky. Her hair was loose and tangled with leaves, matted with dried blood at the back, and her fine gown was torn away from the shoulder.

There was that perfect stillness, that utter absence, that Kate remembered all too well from seeing death before. She remembered Amelia laughing and dancing, her frantic, frivolous energy only a few hours before.

And the tears when she warned Kate against trusting love.

Swallowing back the bitter rush of tears, Kate looked away, back toward the pavilion. The light flickered in the window and a shadow passed in front of it before it suddenly went out.

"I think there is someone there!" she cried.

Rob took back the oars and quickly steered them

toward the small island. By the time they ran into the pavilion, they found it completely empty, aside from the smear of a dark stain on the marble steps. Yet there was still one torch lit in its iron wall sconce, flickering from the wind that rushed through an open window. The tapestries stirred, and dried leaves brushed across the bare floor.

Kate ran to peer out the open window, yet she could see nothing outside except the empty water and the waning moonlight. It was as if Amelia had already become a ghost.

# CHAPTER FOURTEEN

"How could this have happened to Amelia? Everyone admires her! She never hurt anyone at all," Lady Barnett wailed. She sat huddled by the fire in the Barnetts' small sitting room. It had been only about an hour since Rob had carried Amelia's body back to the palace, but a large pile of crumpled handkerchiefs lay in Lady Barnett's lap. Her face, free of the fashionable cosmetics she usually wore, looked worn and lined with grief, her eyes wide with shock.

Mistress Berry, who stood at Lady Barnett's shoulder with a bottle of smelling salts, handed her another square of linen. "I am quite sure it was an accident, Jane. Amelia had consumed a great deal of wine tonight. She probably tripped and hit her head and then fell into the water."

Sir Henry, who sat beside his wife but never offered her a consoling touch, nodded. His bearded face beneath his white nightcap was grim. "I fear that must have been what happened."

Kate glanced at Queen Catherine's doctor, Monsieur Folie, who had joined Rob, the Barnetts, Mistress Berry, and her in the room. He had been roused to look at the body, which had been placed in one of the cold underground storage rooms beneath the kitchens, and had then joined the Barnetts. He wore his fine fur-trimmed night robe and a linen cap, but he did not look as if he had just been roused from his bed. He looked most thoughtful, even interested, and Kate wondered what he had found.

Sir Nicholas Throckmorton had been sent for and had not yet arrived. Kate thought of his general exasperation toward women, from Queen Mary on down, and the way he insisted their foolish behavior made his work in France so much more difficult. What would he say about Amelia Wrightsman turning up so inconveniently dead in the royal pond? Would it even be important enough to make him leave his rooms at such a cold, dark hour?

Perhaps Brigit Berry was correct, Kate thought, and Amelia had only met with a terrible accident. Amelia *had* been full of merriment that night, dancing and drinking wine, but her mirth had been frantic, her laughter edged. An accident of this sort made sense, but more than that, it would create one less difficulty in a royal court that was already overflowing with complications.

Yet something kept tugging at her mind, telling her it was not that simple. The light. The shadow. There was something she could not quite catch hold of, her mind too fuzzy with tiredness and sadness.

She shivered as she remembered Amelia's blank eyes, the dried blood matting her hair. Rob put his arm around her shoulders, pulling her closer to him, and she was glad she had someone to lean on. That she was not completely alone in this strange country, surrounded by people she barely knew and all their secrets. So very many secrets.

"What would my sister say?" Lady Barnett whispered. "I promised I would keep her daughter safe."

Mistress Berry silently handed her the bottle of smelling salts.

The door suddenly opened and Sir Nicholas appeared there, hastily dressed in mismatched hose and doublet, his hair tangled. Charles was behind him, grim-faced but still dressed in his fine black velvet from the party. Beside him was Toby Ridley. Poor Master Ridley was anything but composed, clad only in his night robe, his eyes feverish in his white face. Charles tried to hold him back, but he surged forward.

"Where is she?" he shouted. "I must see her!"

Sir Nicholas gave him a narrow-eyed glare full of disdain, but it was Sir Henry who answered, surprisingly gently. "She has been taken to a suitable place and treated with great decency. Please, Master Ridley, do sit down here with us."

"I will not!" Toby cried. Kate could see he was beyond reason, crazed with grief. Another emotion, too, lay beneath the surface, but Kate couldn't make out what it was. Charles took his arm in a firm grasp and whispered something in his ear as he led him toward the fire. Toby at first stiffened, as if he would snatch his arm away from his friend and fight him, run away, but then he crumpled like a piece of cloth in the winter wind. He suddenly looked very young, devastated. Charles helped him sit down on a stool, and Mistress Berry poured him a goblet of wine.

"Now it only remains to find out what really happened," Sir Henry said.

"We will have to do it quickly, then, or at least agree on a plausible tale," Sir Nicholas said. "For Queen Mary is on her way here as we speak."

"Queen Mary?" Sir Henry cried, leaping from his seat. "What can she know of this sad event already, at such an hour?" He shot an accusing glance at Queen Catherine's doctor, who merely shrugged.

Sir Nicholas shook his head with a scowl. "One of these infernal ladies-in-waiting, I am sure. They have nothing better to do than prowl the corridors at all hours, hunting for gossip to carry back to the queen."

"But what could be her interest?" Sir Henry growled. "My wife's niece was just an English visitor, and a silly, insignificant one at that."

Kate, too, was rather surprised to hear that Queen Mary herself was on her way to the Barnetts' rooms before dawn. Yet she could not agree that Amelia was only an insignificant visitor, not with her involvement with a kinsman to the Guise.

"Queen Mary was very fond of Amelia—you know that, Henry. The queen is a kind lady who takes much interest in her friends." Lady Barnett sniffled. "Everyone was Amelia's friend."

The door opened again without so much as a knock, and Queen Mary swept in, followed by several ladies, including Celeste. Queen Mary was not yet dressed in her courtly garments and wore only a deep-coral-colored velvet gown trimmed with sable, her auburn hair tumbling over her shoulders. She looked even more beautiful in this simple gown than in her queenly robes, but the usual welcoming smile on her face was absent, replaced by a white marblelike coldness.

"I have heard of what happened to my friend Mademoiselle Wrightsman," Queen Mary said, each word clipped and steely. Her amber gaze flickered over the company, touching each person as if to memorize his or her expression, and landed on Queen Catherine's doctor. Her eyes narrowed. "You have seen her, I presume, Dr. Folie? What news of her are you carrying back to my mother-in-law?"

Dr. Folie bowed low, his own expression hidden by his cap. "I fear I have not yet had time for a proper examination, Your Majesty."

"Then you must *make* time immediately," Queen Mary snapped. "I have many enemies creeping around me now that I have lost my husband and am unprotected. Mademoiselle Wrightsman was known to be my friend. What if they attacked her because of that?"

"Your Majesty," Sir Nicholas said soothingly. Kate

remembered how even he was charmed by Queen Mary's feminine delicacy, though he was careful not to approach her too closely now. "We are certain Mistress Wrightsman was merely the victim of a sad accident."

Mary's hands clenched into fists, and Kate could see how much she looked like Queen Elizabeth—right before Elizabeth threw something at someone's head. "How can that be, Sir Nicholas? Why would she be at the pavilion when everyone else was gone? Surely she was lured there! Perhaps they thought she had information about me or my family. Perhaps they . . ."

She suddenly whirled around to face Toby Ridley, who still sat crumpled on his stool, seemingly oblivious to everything around him. She pointed one slender white finger at him, and he looked up, startled.

Kate had the unpleasant sensation she was trapped in a scene of a play and could not get out. Mary had Elizabeth's Tudor genius for setting a tableau, for the drama of every moment, but it was not so amusing in real life as it was on the stage.

"You pursued her, I know," Queen Mary said. "And she sent you away again and again. Everyone knows this, Monsieur Ridley. Perhaps you killed her because of this."

Toby's eyes widened in horror. "I cared about Amelia, 'tis true enough. I would never have hurt her!"

Mary would not relent. "Mayhap you were caught in a great fit of passion—or mayhap you are in the pay of my cousin, or people who would seek to discredit me in her eyes. I know you English are always watching,

watching. Waiting to send foul lies back to your queen, to ruin the friendship that should be between us."

Sir Nicholas and Sir Henry exchanged alarmed glances, as if this was what they had feared all along here at Fontainebleau. A rupture between the two cousin queens.

"I would never do such a thing," Toby cried.

"Your Majesty," Sir Henry said soothingly, or at least what Kate assumed he *thought* was soothing. It sounded more as if he were trying to back away from a mad dog. "I am honored you consider my niece a friend, and truly we will do all in our power to have justice for her. She met with an accident—"

"Accident!" Queen Mary shouted. "I am no fool, Sir Henry. I have been a queen since I was a week old, and even then your England tried to destroy me and my mother. Now *pauvre* Amelia has paid the price. Either you find who did this, or I will. Even my own cousin's servants must pay the price for such an evil."

She whirled around and left the chamber as she had entered it, like a storm rumbling across the sky. Celeste gave Toby a quick, pained glance and Kate a sympathetic smile, and followed the queen. The door slammed behind them. The royal doctor also swiftly took his leave, and the room fell into a heavy silence.

Toby broke down into audible sobs, and at Sir Nicholas's urging, Charles led him away. Mistress Berry mixed some herbs into a goblet of wine and handed it to Lady Barnett, who was sniffling into her handkerchief.

Rob led Kate from the room, slipping out while the Barnetts were distracted. "Shall I see you to your chamber?" he asked. "I am supposed to meet Thomas."

Kate shook her head. "I will be well enough. Thank you, Rob." She felt too confused, too restless, to be alone in her room, yet when Rob walked away, she wasn't sure where to go next. Where to look for answers. She longed for a moment alone to think.

"Mistress Haywood," Sir Nicholas called, "will you walk with us for a moment?"

Kate glanced back to find Sir Nicholas and Charles coming up the stairs behind her. Gray-faced and solemn, they both looked as weary as she felt. She longed for her bed, but she knew it would still be long before sleep could find her. She nodded and followed them into an empty corridor.

"What think you of this sad business tonight?" Sir Nicholas asked.

Kate was rather surprised he'd asked her—a mere female—her opinion of anything. But, then again, he was facing a serious complication, one where as many watching eyes and listening ears as possible would be an asset. "Mistress Wrightsman was kind to me," she said carefully. "And Lady Barnett seems most grief-stricken."

"It could be a dangerous thing for Queen Elizabeth," Sir Nicholas snapped.

"Toby is one of the queen's own emissaries," Charles said. "If it was thought he killed one of Queen Mary's friends . . ."

"Charles says that a lady can go places where we cannot," Sir Nicholas said, with great reluctance in his tone. "Queen Mary would be more unguarded with a woman."

"Queen Catherine as well," Charles added.

Sir Nicholas gave a snort. "Nay, never Queen Catherine. She is never unguarded, perhaps not even in her sleep. But you could be of much assistance to us in this dire situation, Mistress Haywood."

Kate nodded. She was not as known as the Throckmortons; people were not as careful in what they said around her, and she was trained to watch and listen closely without being observed. But a woman was dead under suspicious circumstances. Surely everyone would be doubly wary now, and she herself would have to watch her path most carefully. "I could send a message to Queen Mary tomorrow, begging leave to bring some books of music to her."

Sir Nicholas gave a terse nod. "That would be best. Queen Mary does like her frivolities. It is best to distract her now, before her accusations damage our delicate negotiations here."

Kate remembered being shoved against the railing on the ship, the rush of raw fear, and she swallowed hard before she nodded. "I will do my best, Sir Nicholas. I am here to serve Queen Elizabeth however I can."

# CHAPTER FIFTEEN

Early the next morning, knowing she would never be able to truly sleep, Kate sent a note to Queen Mary's rooms, asking if she could bring her some of Queen Elizabeth's favorite songs as a distraction. While she waited for a reply, she dressed and made her way to Lady Barnett's chamber, her lute in one hand and Amelia's fur muff, wrapped carefully in linen, in the other. She thought perhaps Lady Barnett would wish to have it back. Or perhaps she would not, now that it was associated with such sadness.

Mistress Berry had sent a message asking if Kate would play for Lady Barnett, to help soothe her spirits, and Kate found she would welcome the distraction herself. She had snatched only a few moments of sleep after crawling into her borrowed bed. The images of Amelia Wrightsman, her white face and staring eyes, her water-soaked white gown, haunted every dream.

Just before dawn, a vivid nightmare of Amelia rising from the water and pointing an accusing, bloodstained finger at her made her jolt awake, crying out. She couldn't sleep again.

She had stirred up the fire and huddled by its budding warmth as she went over and over all that had happened. She remembered Amelia's laughter on their long journey to France, her charm, the way she drew everyone close to her, especially men like Toby and Monsieur d'Emours. Her anger and sadness in unguarded moments; the secrets she held in her eyes.

To distract herself, Kate opened the herbal book Mistress Berry had loaned her, hoping to lose herself in recipes for syrups and scents. She hoped that in looking at sketches of plants she might remember something else.

By the time the maidservant arrived to bring Kate's morning bread and ale and help her dress, Kate's head whirled with sadness and fury as she tried to make sense of it all. But the maid had chatted about what was happening at court in the next few days, and hunts and masques. And the crowds Kate passed on her way to visit Lady Barnett also seemed to be in a different world than the sad one in which Amelia lay mysteriously dead. There were the same smiles and light words as always. She did not see Monsieur d'Emours and his Guise relations anywhere, nor did she see Lord James and the Scots, or Celeste Renard.

The corridor leading to the Barnetts' apartment, was silent and empty. Kate knocked softly at the door, feeling choked with sadness and uncertainty.

Mistress Berry opened the door. She was as tidy and

neat as always, her graying hair tucked beneath a snow-white cap, in her hand a small tray that held a variety of bottles and pots. An apron covered her black skirts. But her bright blue eyes were rimmed with red and heavy with tiredness.

"Ah, Mistress Haywood, thank you for coming. I know the hour is early, and not one of us here has had an instant of rest." She ushered Kate into the sitting room, which was empty and darkened.

"How fares Lady Barnett?" Kate asked quietly.

"She has calmed a bit after I gave her some of my valerian mixture in a bit of wine, but she won't eat a morsel. Sir Henry left early this morning to confer some more with Sir Nicholas. Perhaps a song could soothe her."

Kate nodded and followed Mistress Berry into the bedchamber. The embroidered velvet draperies were drawn over the windows, leaving only the light from the fireplace. Lady Barnett was a small figure huddled in the middle of the large bed, the coverlets drawn around her. She lay on her side, staring with wide eyes into the fire, one hand clutching at the edge of her pillow.

"Mistress Haywood has come to call on you, Jane," Mistress Berry said, tucking a shawl closer around Lady Barnett's shoulders. "She will play the lute for you—you do so enjoy her songs, I know. She'll stay with you while I fetch some bread and soup for your breakfast."

Lady Barnett slowly turned her head to look at Kate, her pretty blue eyes blank for a moment. She bit her lip and nodded before she aimed her stare back at the flickering flames.

"I will return anon, Mistress Haywood," Mistress Berry whispered. "If she needs it, mix a spoonful of the herbs in that box into some wine for her to sip."

Kate nodded and watched as Mistress Berry swept out of the room, the hem of her black skirts whispering over the rushes of the floor. Kate sat down on the stool across from the bed, tucking the parcel of Amelia's mud-stained muff beneath her and setting her lute on her knees. She started to play a soft, simple tune as she studied Lady Barnett. The woman did not stir or say anything, but her eyes grew damp with tears.

Kate swallowed her own threatening sobs and played on, finding comfort in the oft-repeated notes, the way the music slowly wrapped around her like a warm, familiar touch.

"What did she look like when you found her—my Amelia?" Lady Barnett suddenly asked. She didn't turn away from the fire and her voice sounded distant, impersonal, as if she asked the plot of a masque.

"She looked . . ." Kate shook her head as she remembered Amelia's pale face in the moonlight, her wide-open eyes and purplish lips. Her father had looked peaceful when he died, as if he had fallen asleep and drifted away to be with her mother again, but most of the times she had seen death they did not. Rob's uncle at Hatfield, her friend Mary at Westminster. It had been fearful.

"It is quite all right, Mistress Haywood," Lady Barnett said. She turned her head on the pillow to look at Kate, her expression serious but composed. She looked much like her niece. "I am sure it could not have been tranquil."

Kate's fingers stilled on the lute strings. She took out the linen-wrapped muff and held it out to Lady Barnett. "I found this at the edge of the pond. I know it was Mistress Wrightsman's."

Lady Barnett took it from her and slowly unwrapped it. She gave a small sob and then fell silent, stroking the fur. "I gave her this and a matching hood for New Year's. How she loved it!" She laid it down carefully on the pillow beside hers. "I was never blessed with my own children, so when Amelia came to us when she was a girl, it was as if I had a daughter at last. Her mother, my sister, was taken much too soon, and I saw her in Amelia. Her eyes, her laugh. The way people were just drawn to her."

"I am so very sorry, Lady Barnett," Kate said gently. "I do fear that when I found the muff, the jeweled brooch was gone."

A frown whispered over Lady Barnett's brow. "Brooch?"

Kate wondered if she had imagined the jewel when she saw it with Amelia at the party, but nay, it was clear in her memory. A rampant lion, like the ones on the Guise coat of arms, formed in diamonds. "Where the fur is torn there along the back. I glimpsed it when I arrived at the pavilion last night and Mistress Wrightsman greeted me. It was most lovely."

Lady Barnett turned the muff over and examined the tear. "I do not know what she could have put there. Was it an emblem of some sort? A design?"

Of course Kate remembered what it was. Yet something held her back from telling Lady Barnett. She didn't want to grieve the lady even more by reminding her of her niece's once-scandalous behavior with d'Emours. "I could not tell. Perhaps it was something from the Barnetts?"

Lady Barnett gave a rusty laugh. "Nay, not my husband's family. I was a De la Chose through my grandmother, as was Amelia's mother, but our family has not the money for such a jewel, even if our name is an ancient one indeed. Much older than the Barnetts'." Reminiscing seemed to give her new energy, and she pushed herself up to sit against the pillows. "Our forefathers came to England with William the Conquerer, and our grandmother was also French, an Orieux. I never knew her, though they say she was very beautiful. Like Amelia. She was the reason why we came to the French court in the first place. French families are indeed fond of such devices, though I do not know where Amelia would have found such a thing. No doubt one of her admirers gave it to her. She had so many!"

"Was there one in particular she favored? An imminent betrothal?"

Lady Barnett shrugged. "There were some who had approached my husband, such as Master Ridley, but

Amelia had not made up her mind. She deserved so much, with her beauty and wit. Mayhap even a title!" She suddenly frowned. "Master Ridley seems a good man, but men have been moved to great anger before when ladies turned away their suits."

Kate thought of Queen Mary's accusations, her finger pointed at Toby. "I am sure Master Ridley would not have hurt Mistress Wrightsman. It must have been a terrible accident."

"So my husband says," Lady Barnett spat out. "He says I must be content it was so, for all our sakes. But I see her when I close my eyes. She calls out to me. . . ."

Lady Barnett's face crumpled, and tears spilled from her eyes. Kate quickly laid aside her lute and knelt beside the bed. She took the lady's hand in hers and found it icy-cold.

"If someone did indeed hurt Mistress Wrightsman, they will be found out—I promise," Kate said.

"Nay, my husband is right. France is a dangerous place. No one knows which way their alliances will fall, where fighting will break out next. Without the good-will of Queen Catherine and Queen Mary, England would be in much trouble here. We must call no attention to ourselves, not now. But, oh! My poor Amelia!"

Kate's heart ached for the woman, for her own help-lessness in the face of such deep sadness. "Shall I fetch you some wine, Lady Barnett?"

"It makes me feel so tired, so confused. But if it can make me forget for a moment . . ."

Kate nodded and rose from beside the bed. She had just mixed up the powdered herbal potion from Mistress Berry's box when that lady returned. The sweet scent of the herbs, chamomile, and something darker, greener, just beneath, still lingered in the air, and a few long sips of the concoction did seem to help settle Lady Barnett. Mistress Berry laid her tray of bread and cheese on the bedside table and coaxed Lady Barnett to take a few bites before she fell asleep.

"Did she fare well enough while I was gone?" Mistress Berry asked as she shook out another blanket to lie across the bed.

"Well enough. We talked a bit." Kate thought of Lady Barnett's French family, and Amelia and her suitors. "Did you happen to come to France with Lady Barnett long ago? She mentioned a French grandmother Mistress Wrightsman resembled."

Mistress Berry gave a faint smile and busily rearranged the barely touched breakfast tray. "I did, but my experience as a young lady at the French court was rather different from Jane's. Or Amelia's, I would wager. I had little dowry, and not as much beauty. And that was a very long time ago. I am sure it could have naught to do with last night's sad events."

Could it not? One thing Kate had learned at Elizabeth's court was that the past was always nearby. Old slights and crimes, old loves, they were always lurking, ready to roar back into the present.

There was a knock at the door, and Mistress Berry

opened it to admit a servant in Queen Mary's black-and-white livery.

"Her Majesty Queen Mary asks if Mademoiselle Haywood could attend to her anon," he said with a bow. "And bring her music."

Mistress Berry glanced at Kate with narrowed eyes. "A royal summons, Mistress Haywood. You must attend at once, I am sure."

Kate nodded. She looked to Lady Barnett, who still slept, her dreams seemingly peaceful for the moment. There was naught left she could do there.

She followed the queen's servant out of the room and down the corridor toward the royal apartments, the sweet scent of green herbs clinging to her skirts.

Queen Mary's chambers were in a wing of the château far from the English apartments, and looked out from the windows onto long manicured garden beds and straight graveled pathways dotted with marble statues of gods and goddesses and tiny cupids, their arrows pointed at the gray sky. Behind the thick glass, Kate glimpsed a distant vision of the carp pond and the pavilion at its edge.

It looked placid and peaceful, abandoned, in the wintry light.

The room was crowded with the queen's ladies seated on velvet cushions and low footstools near the fireplaces, their silken skirts spread out around them like flowers. They laughed over their embroidery or books of poetry, dogs scurrying between them, a parrot in its gilded cage by the window chattering and squawking.

Queen Mary herself sat by the farthest fireplace. Her auburn head was bent over an embroidery frame, her own pack of tiny white dogs gathered at her feet, almost invisible against the creamy silk of her gown. She laughed at something the lady beside her had whispered, her heart-shaped face alight.

The atmosphere in the chamber was calm, bright. After the heavy sorrow of Lady Barnett's room, it was most disconcerting.

Queen Mary glanced up and saw Kate hovering in the doorway, uncertain how to proceed. Her smile turned gentle and she held out her hand. "Mademoiselle Haywood. Welcome. Do come and sit over here, where it is warm. I was glad to get your message this morning, and to see that you have brought your lute. We could all use the cheerful distraction of music today, I do think."

There was no trace of last night's icy anger in Queen Mary's smile. She was changeable, as hard to read as her cousin Elizabeth. It made Kate feel even more cautious. She curtsied and made her way to the fireside. A servant quickly brought her a low stool, and another offered her cakes and wine.

As she settled her skirts around her and set about tuning the lute, she studied the four ladies gathered around the queen, each of them delicately pretty and beautifully dressed.

"You have not yet met my dear Maries, Mademoiselle Haywood," Queen Mary said, gesturing to them. "Mary Beaton, Mary Seton, Mary Livingston, and Mary Fleming. They all came to France with me when we were but tiny children, and have stayed faithfully by my side ever since. I do not know what I would do without them, though I feel I could not ask them to leave their lives here and return to Scotland, if that was what I chose."

"Our lives are wherever you may be, Your Majesty!" Mary Seton, the smallest and prettiest of them, cried. "We would follow you anywhere."

"Anywhere," Mary Beaton echoed. "Even to . . ."

She shuddered and bent her head back to her sewing. Kate wondered if she was about to say to Spain, or mayhap to Denmark, Sweden, or Bavaria, all rumored to be suitors for Mary's hand. They probably would follow; Mary's servants seemed just as devoted as Elizabeth's own.

Queen Mary hinted at returning to Scotland, and the presence of Lord James at court seemed to indicate she would do just that. But Mary also clearly loved the elegant, sophisticated, pampered yet deceptive life of France. Surely she would say nothing for certain, and Kate had little enough to write to Queen Elizabeth.

And now there was Amelia's death—and the rumors that Queen Mary had set afloat that the English must have had something to do with it themselves, that it was a bizarre scheme to blame Mary in front of Elizabeth.

Kate had been at royal courts and at Fontainebleau long enough to know the great power gossip had. Even tempered steel could not cut it once it took hold.

"What would Your Majesty like to hear today?" Kate asked.

"Oh, more of your English songs, I think. I do so love them!" Queen Mary said. "I feel as if I could know my cousin through the music. I long for the day when we meet in person. I have so very little family left, and family is the most important thing there is. Don't you think so, Mademoiselle Haywood?"

Kate started playing a lively new chaconne, one of Queen Elizabeth's favorites. It was a piece she had played many times, and she was accustomed to talking as her fingers plucked at the strings faster and faster.

"Family is indeed a fine thing in life, Your Majesty, though I fear I have none left myself," Kate said. The song made her think of her father, and a wave of sadness washed over her.

"None at all?" Mary cried.

"My mother died when I was born, and my father, who was also a court musician, died just before Christmas," Kate said. She kept her head bent low over the neck of her lute and blinked hard to keep back her tears. She knew better than to show anything more than artful, masquerading emotion. "I have no siblings."

"*Pauvre* Mademoiselle Haywood," sighed Mary. Her Maries made sympathetic murmurs. "I, too, lost a parent only months ago, my dearest *maman*. My father died when I was but a week old, of course, but my mother was like both parents to me. She fought to keep my throne safe, even against people like my own cousin." Queen Mary's lips tightened, and she stabbed at her cloth with her needle. "The Scottish lords were most ungrateful to her. What can a land with such rulers be like? Rough and ignorant. We must help them if we can."

"But the people love you! They speak only of you, long for you," Mary Seton said. "My family writes that to me so very often. You would transform Scotland."

Mary looked pensive as she studied an embroidered flower. "Perhaps so. With my cousin Queen Elizabeth's help, of course. As two queens in one isle, we would have to work together. Do you not agree, Mademoiselle Haywood?"

"I am sure you would have much to share, Your Majesty," Kate said carefully. "Queen Elizabeth also wishes greatly to be friends."

Queen Mary gave a small smile. "I am sure of it. I fear it is like my dear *maman* and the treacherous lords around her. There will always be those who wish us ill, who will try to come between us, and people like poor Amelia will fall victim to such vile schemes."

The Maries exchanged alarmed glances, but their faces quickly smoothed out to mild smiles. Kate saw the queen's message. She suspected Elizabeth, but was more than willing to blame evil forces, wrong advice, for any rift—for now.

"But the people, the *true* people, want only peace and amity," Mary continued. "I could bring them such. With

Elizabeth's help. Perhaps you would assure her of that, Mademoiselle Haywood, when you return to England with pages of our French songs in your trunks?"

"I am only a musician, Your Majesty," Kate said, thinking of those same trunks that had recently been searched. "But I will happily pass along any message you care to send with me."

Queen Mary's smile widened, and it was like the sun bursting out from behind rain clouds. *"C'est bon!* Grand matters are better left to men, I always find. Their minds are stronger, more expansive, better suited to such things as battles and treaties. I rely on the advice of my uncles and of Lord James. Yet there are a few things we females understand so well. Small, personal things. Matters of friendship."

Kate nodded. It was the same as what Elizabeth and men like Cecil and Sir Henry Barnett—reluctantly—said. Women were good for some things: small, personal, secret matters. But she wondered if any were quite so good at secrets as Queen Mary herself.

The queen and her ladies went on to whisper about other things—a planned hawking expedition to some Guise lands, a new fashion in dagged sleeves, a shipment of plumes that had arrived from Florence. Kate played more English songs, listening to it all, letting her own thoughts organize and take shape in her mind. She still did not know what Elizabeth truly wanted from Mary, where she wanted the Scots queen to go or stay, so every scrap of information was to be remembered.

Suddenly, the double doors to Queen Mary's chamber opened, and Queen Catherine appeared, preceded by only two pages in her green-and-white livery and followed by her beautiful ladies. Kate glimpsed Celeste peeking past the much shorter queen's black-clad shoulder. Celeste looked pale, dark circles beneath her eyes, as if she had not slept well.

"Maman Queen," Queen Mary said, her tone startled. She quickly set aside her sewing and rose to her feet, making a small, respectful curtsy. Her ladies hastened to do the same. "You honor me with your visit. If I had known you were coming, I would have sent for more wine."

Queen Catherine waved her hand and gave a small, tight smile. "It is of no matter, daughter; I was merely passing and thought to stop and invite you to a small gathering at my little dairy, Mi Voie. We could all use a distraction, *oui*, a bit of merriment in such dark days? That is why I built my little farm. I have made many improvements to the buildings I am sure everyone would enjoy seeing."

"Of course, Maman Queen," Queen Mary said. "As you know, I have often expressed an interest in building a dairy of my own. It would be most healthful."

"I hope you will one day. It does much to make any palace feel like a home." Queen Catherine's shrewd, dark gaze swept over the gathering. It landed on Kate, and suddenly she felt as squirmy as a child. "I hope you are keeping yourself busy at such a sad time, daughter. So many losses now, first the king and now your English friend."

"Mademoiselle Haywood was just showing us some of the English songs," Queen Mary said. "And telling us news of my cousin."

"Is she? I, too, would like to hear the new music of England. It would be interesting to hear how their taste differs from that of the French or the Florentines," Queen Catherine said with a pleasant smile.

Mary glanced at Kate, seemingly uncertain. She did seem younger, much more unsure, around her mother-in-law, though Kate had heard Mary could be rather dismissive of Catherine's lowly origins when she was not nearby.

"Of course you must send for Mademoiselle Haywood to play in your own chamber soon, Queen Maman."

"Why not now?" Queen Catherine said. "We are going for a walk in the gardens while the sun is shining a bit. You should all join us."

"Oh, I fear it would be too cold for me," Queen Mary said quickly. "I have had a fainting spell only this morning."

"Your old trouble again, daughter?" Queen Catherine said, her voice soft and full of concern. But her dark eyes did not change.

Queen Mary nodded, and Kate recalled tales of her ill health that had reached even England—stories of fainting and pains in the side that would not go away. "I am well enough now, but the doctors say I should stay by the fire for the time being."

"You must always follow the doctors' advice, *ma chère*. Shall I send Dr. Folie to you?" Queen Catherine said. "He is most wise, I have found."

"Thank you, Queen Maman," Queen Mary answered with a sweet smile.

Catherine abruptly turned to Kate. "But what of you, Mademoiselle Haywood? Are you also delicate? Or has the harsh English weather made you hardy?"

Kate was startled Queen Catherine would talk to her directly and for an instant did not know what to say. "Nay, Your Majesty, I enjoy a long walk. Especially when the scenery is as beautiful as here at Fontaine-bleau."

"Then perhaps you would join us now," Queen Catherine said. "I am as anxious as my daughter-in-law to hear more of the new English styles."

Kate nodded with a curtsy as Queen Catherine and her ladies departed as swiftly as they had arrived. As Kate moved to follow, Queen Mary suddenly reached out and caught her sleeve.

"Do not forget, Mademoiselle Haywood," she whispered. "We females are best at small intimacies and loyal friendships. We must all rely on one another."

Kate wasn't sure what she meant by such cryptic words, but she had time only to give Queen Mary a startled nod before she heard Celeste Renard call her name. Mary Seton took her lute with a whispered promise to return it to her chamber, and Kate hurried to catch up with Queen Catherine's party as they wound their way out to the terrace.

It had indeed become a sunny day, the sun shimmering on the lines of white marble statues along the flower beds, but it was also a chilly one, with a cold wind whistling between the carefully shaped trees. Kate shivered, for she had left her cloak in her chamber.

Celeste handed her a woolen shawl trimmed with fluffy white fur. "Here, Mademoiselle Haywood, you must take this. I have my cloak."

"Mademoiselle Haywood," the queen called. "Will you tell me more of your queen's Dr. Dee? He sounds like someone whose talents I could use here in France."

Kate thought of the séance she had once observed at Nonsuch Palace, which had been quite chilling. She still preferred the measurable magic of music to the spirits, but she had heard so many rumors that the help of the spirits was what Queen Catherine sought. "I fear I have not seen Dr. Dee at work, Your Majesty. I have only read some of his writings and spoken with him once or twice at Queen Elizabeth's court. I saw one of his apprentices conduct a séance once, which I confess frightened me."

Queen Catherine peered at Kate's face closely with her large dark eyes. Her black veil fluttered in the wind. "It can be most frightening to see the truth hidden beneath our everyday world. But I have always felt that it is better to know the truth. My dear Signor Ruggieri has many gifts, and I value his advice. Perhaps you would join us one evening to hear what he has to say? It might be of interest to your queen." She waved her closest attendants back and started toward the steps to the garden. "Come, walk with me for a moment, if Lady Barnett can spare you."

Kate was most confused by Queen Catherine's request. She glanced at Celeste, who shrugged. Kate could only follow the Queen Mother as they strolled onto the pathway, the rest of the royal attendants following behind. Queen Catherine moved surprisingly fast for such a short lady, her steps quick and graceful, almost gliding.

Kate remembered hearing tales of how Queen Catherine was once an avid rider, galloping to the hunt at her husband's side. It was the only time she could be alone with King Henri without the royal mistress, Diane de Poitiers, with them.

Now Madame de Poitiers was exiled, and Queen Catherine had taken charge of the kingdom. She no longer rode to the hunt, but followed in a chariot, her eye on everything around her. They said she knew all.

Did she even know what had happened to Amelia? It had been her party at the pavilion, after all.

"Do you like the pretty avenue of trees just there, Mademoiselle Haywood?" Queen Catherine asked as she gestured to a line of silvery beech trees leading down the wide pathway away from the terrace. "Do you have such things at your English palaces?"

Kate studied the gardens, so peaceful and quiet in the winter cold. In the summer, she knew they would be bursting with emerald green life. The shores of the pond would be concealed by flowers and the marble pavilion hidden from view. "Most of Queen Elizabeth's gardens are smaller, Your Majesty, and more compact. I am sure everyone would agree that the gardens here at Fontainebleau are beyond any compare. They are so lovely now—I can only imagine how they must be in summer."

Queen Catherine gave a satisfied little nod. "Gardening is one of my great pleasures. But it was my father-in-law, the great King Francis, who first planted those trees for his first wife, Queen Claude. Neither of them ever saw their full flower, but he knew how it would one day be. He knew the great importance of beauty in all its forms. He was willing to have patience to make his court perfect in every way."

The queen glanced back over her shoulder, and Kate wondered if she studied the palace or her ladies, who waited several steps away. Both of them were indeed beautiful, the pale stones of the palace in the winter light, the windows sparkling like diamonds, the ladies tall and elegant in their satin and furs, whispering together. Celeste watched the queen, her hand raised to shade her eyes from the light.

"Before my father-in-law's time there were not many ladies at court," Queen Catherine said. "Yet King Francis saw women could be a great adornment to a civilized palace, could bring color and laughter and interest, refinement. He even had his own attendants, his *petite bande*, as he called them, who rode with him and danced for him at balls. They were of much use to him in so many ways."

Kate nodded. She could see what Queen Catherine was telling her, perhaps what Queen Mary had been trying to say as well. Ladies could be as lethal at court as men, or even more so, with wounding words and whispers rather than swords. Queen Catherine had spies everywhere, and no enemy would be allowed to pass. France had powers England could not match—yet. "I see, Your Majesty."

Queen Catherine gave her a small, tight-lipped smile. "I believe you do see, mademoiselle. I think my father-in-law was disappointed I was no beauty when I first arrived from Florence, a frightened little fourteen-year-old. Yet we soon found we could learn much from each other, and he became my greatest friend. They say your Queen Elizabeth, though she is but a woman herself, does not care greatly for the friendship of other females."

Kate bit her lip. Elizabeth *did* have ladies she trusted: Kat Ashley, who was like her mother; her cousin Catherine Knollys; Robert Dudley's sister, Mary Sidney. But most of her ladies were merely for show in the rooms of the court. Would Kate herself be so trusted if she had not grown up at the Tudor palaces or had not proven to be the queen's secret Boleyn cousin? "Queen Elizabeth does have many ladies waiting on her and is most fond of those she has known a long time."

"And she keeps a lady as her favorite musician. Most unusual. She would certainly do well to always remember the power we women can have, which is even greater for being hidden sometimes." She looked back to her own chattering attendants. "I fear poor Mademoiselle Wrightsman has reminded us of that."

Before Kate could say anything, Queen Catherine walked onward, summoning her ladies to follow with a wave of her hand.

Celeste caught Kate's arm and walked with her as they let the rest of the queen's attendants hurry ahead. "Queen Catherine seems to like you, Mademoiselle Haywood. Everyone likes you."

Kate shook her head, baffled by the twists and turns of the French court. "Does she indeed? I cannot read her at all."

Celeste laughed. "No one can. It is one of her great powers. We have much to learn from her. What did she speak of to you?"

"Trees," Kate murmured.

Celeste gave her a puzzled glance. "Trees?"

"Aye. She said her father-in-law planted this row, yet knew he would never see them in their full glory. But beauty rewards patience. Or something of the sort."

"How odd. Did it have something to do with music? Or mayhap with suitors? You must have many." Celeste strolled onward, pointing out different spaces that would be filled with flowers in the summer, and Kate went with her in silence. Yet she wondered about Celeste and about Queen Catherine's beautiful ladies. Her own *petite bande*, watching where she could not?

"Mistress Haywood! Mademoiselle Renard!" Claude Domville called. He was playing at a game of boules with a few other gentlemen in a lane of trees, but left them to greet Kate and Celeste on the pathway. He looked rather pale under the shadow of his beard, and he wore a black band around the sleeve of his slate gray doublet. "I am glad to see you here today. I have not been able to get a message to Toby this morning and have had no news. They say he might have quarreled with Amelia before she died, that he has been sequestered in his chamber. I hope that is not true. How fares Lady Barnett?"

"She is sleeping now but is quite grief-stricken. Master Ridley is confined to his chamber, he was so crazed from the loss."

"Ah, but Toby was surely not the only man caught by Amelia's fair charms," Claude said in a dark tone. He waved toward the boules players. One of them was Jacques d'Emours, clad in black, his face shaded by the brim of a velvet hat. A diamond pin flashed on its crown, but Kate could not see its design. "Many shall mourn her passing."

"Perhaps one in particular?" Celeste said sharply.

Claude's jaw tightened. "D'Emours, you mean? I know he fought a duel for her once, but . . ."

"A duel would mean naught to a man such as that," Celeste said, walking on so quickly, her hem caught on the gravel underfoot. "No Guise would ever let their heart rule their head."

"Ah, but what of a Guise in name only?" Claude said with a small, sly grin.

Celeste whirled around to face him. "You mean that

old tale? I do not like the man, but surely that is mere gossip. It has been whispered over and over, but none dare say it to his face. Or to the Duc de Guise."

Kate's curiosity, that dark little thing that so often led her where it should not, rose inside her and she could not help but ask, "What old tale?"

Celeste and Claude exchanged a long glance, and Claude shrugged. "For many years there was a little rumor."

"A foolish rumor," Celeste muttered.

"But an interesting one," Claude answered. "D'Emours is kin to the Guise through his mother, who died years ago but was a most proud, fierce lady. She had no other children and was very ambitious for her son."

"As he is for himself," Celeste said. "There were a few whispers he was to be promoted to a marshal before young King Henri died, and young King Francis liked him as well. Until he was sent away for the sad business with Amelia."

"And now he has returned to court," Kate said. "Does he still hope for such a post?" Could Amelia's death have wiped away the old, scandalous past? Or mayhap he hoped it would?

"The Guise would do anything to put their allies in any court positions now," Claude said. "Even one with a questionable past and a bad temper."

"His temper is no worse than that of any other young courtier," Celeste said. "Though these days, a cool head would serve everyone better. Queen Catherine never loses her calm."

"But his past—the old rumor?" Kate said, her curiosity still burning. "What was it?"

"There were whispers that his Guise mother might not have been his *true* mother," Claude said. "She left court after she announced she was *enceinte* and went far away to a house in Normandy, where no one saw her for many months. When she returned to Paris, she had a healthy, strong son. A blond son—when she and her husband were both dark."

"Was that all there was?" Kate asked. She thought of her own mother, Eleanor Haywood, who had been the daughter of an Italian musician and Thomas Boleyn, though none knew that—except for tiny rumors, now grown still and quiet. "Surely many babies are born thus. If the father claimed him . . ."

"They say there was a maidservant who went around declaring she saw a village midwife deliver a covered basket to the back door of Madame d'Emours's country retreat in the middle of the night," Claude said. He seemed to relish relating old gossip, or mayhap just discrediting Jacques d'Emours. "The next day there was a baby."

"To whom did the maid tell this tale?" Kate asked.

"Someone who must have court connections, for the tale did spread. But the maid herself vanished," Claude said.

"It is like a story from some overwrought Italian play," Celeste scoffed. "And an old, dull one. I think he *should* be sent away from court, but for his own foolish actions, not for old gossip."

Claude shrugged. "You usually do not seem to mind a bit of gossip, Mademoiselle Renard."

Celeste laughed. "Of course I like gossip. Without it, we would be lost here at court. Yet we must also learn to tell the true from the false. And now I should return to Queen Catherine. You have heard about Queen Mary's proposed hawking expedition tomorrow? She thinks some brisk exercise will bring forgetfulness, if her health permits."

"I have heard of it. I'll be there. Perhaps Lady Barnett could be persuaded to go riding, too."

"I do hope so, the poor lady. I shall see you there, Mistress Haywood!" Celeste gave an airy wave and drifted toward the palace on a cloud of satin. Claude quickly made his excuses and followed her.

When Kate found herself alone, she studied the sparkling palace. Lady Barnett's grief waited around every corner there, and Kate's thoughts could not be organized into anything resembling a recognizable pattern. Something was tugging at her memory, but she could not draw it forth.

She left the crowded pathways and made her way through the thick pine trees to the edge of the pond. It looked so very different during the day, with the boats gone and the pavilion merely a stone building. Its pale shadow was reflected in the water, wavering until it cracked and broke before re-forming again.

She wasn't sure exactly what she was looking for, so she went back to the spot where she had found Amelia's fur muff with its missing diamond brooch. The mud was churned there, but she could see nothing of the brooch or anything of Amelia's. Only a tiny scrap of vellum that could have been torn from anything.

Sighing with frustration, Kate brushed the dirt from her hands and turned back toward the palace. A page met her at the door of her room, bearing a message from Queen Catherine's physician, Dr. Folie. *I am sorry to distress a lady thus, mademoiselle,* the note read, *but Her Majesty suggested you might be of some assistance to me in my work today. . . .*

# CHAPTER SIXTEEN

Kate followed Dr. Folie down a winding flight of stone steps that led down to one of the storage chambers deep beneath Fontainebleau's kitchens. The air was even colder there than it was outside, with a damp, clammy quality that made her shiver as she followed the flickering torch the doctor held high.

She wanted to turn and run back up the stairs to the light above, to the bustle and noise of the kitchen as they prepared for the palace's large banquet, but she knew she had to keep going down and down. If something foul had indeed befallen Amelia, something beyond a tragic accident, Kate felt she owed it to the lady to find out what it was.

And if it had something to do with Queen Elizabeth's own enemies there in France.

There was also that wretched spark of curiosity, that deep desire to know how and why that would never quite leave her.

"Are you prone to swooning, Mademoiselle Haywood?" the doctor asked.

"Not very often," Kate answered, and he gave a snorting laugh.

Dr. Folie ushered her into the arched doorway and into the room, which was completely dark until he used his torch to light others in the heavy iron frames affixed to the stone walls. Kate didn't know if she preferred the unknown darkness over the sight that greeted her.

The chamber was usually used for storing vegetables and preserved fruits, or mayhap for game caught in Fontainebleau's forest and hung on the dangling hooks overhead. But today it housed a dark wood casket propped on two tables beside the rough stone wall. Under the unpleasant musty dampness, she smelled a hint of violet perfume.

Kate swallowed against the cold, tight knot in her throat and hurried after the doctor as he made his way across the room.

"They are to bury her in the Protestant churchyard at St. Sebastian's tomorrow, but the Queen Mother bade me to examine her first, due to the sad circumstances she was found in," Dr. Folie said, sliding his torch into a sconce. "You found her yourself, did you not, mademoiselle?"

"I did, Dr. Folie. Her aunt was worried that she had not returned to their chambers, and sent me to look for her."

"And how did she appear to you then?"

Kate didn't want to remember that sight, but she closed her eyes and made herself recall every detail. The floating white skirts in the dark water, Amelia's purple lips and staring eyes. "She was in the water, facedown, borne up by her skirts. Her eyes were open, but there was no expression of fear on her face. I have heard drowning can be a peaceful death. I pray it was so for her."

Dr. Folie nodded, his expression only bland and pleasant, as if they discussed the weather. "I think, though, that she may not have drowned."

"What do you mean?"

"If you will look with me, mademoiselle," he answered, and slid back the lid of the coffin. The carpenters' tools were on a table nearby, including thick nails, but it had not been sealed shut yet.

Kate braced herself and peeked inside. She had seen such things before, of course. Only months ago she had watched her own father be closed away from her forever. Yet she could never entirely accustom herself to it.

It was not a hideous sight. Amelia had been dressed in a gray velvet gown with black sleeves and quilted underskirt, her golden hair brushed over her shoulders and crowned with a wreath of greenery and herbs. She held more herbs in her folded hands, the sweet scent of them covering the hint of damp decay beneath. If it was not for the grayish pallor of her skin, the complete absence of the flirtatious laughter and frantic sparkle, she could almost have been sleeping.

"The wound on the back of her head bled very little," the doctor said. He carefully lifted Amelia's head to show Kate the gash just at the nape of her neck, now stitched together. "And when I made a closer examination, the water in her lungs appeared to be new. She must have been dead, or dying, when she fell into the pond."

Kate bit back a cry and gave a small nod. She remembered the small dark smear on the steps of the pavilion, which could very well have been blood. "You are an—an anatomist, Dr. Folie?"

He gave her a rueful smile. "I learned much in my apprenticeship in Florence, mademoiselle. Artists there as well as physicians and apothecaries need to know much of the body in order to decipher its mysteries."

She made herself study Amelia's pale face closer. Could she have been pushed into the sharp, stony edges of the pavilion steps? Mayhap hit on the head and then shoved into the cold water? She shivered as she remembered the panic of being knocked over-board on the ship. "What mysteries have you discovered from Mademoiselle Wrightsman?"

"Not as many as I would like. But as I said, I would certainly wager she did not drown. If I had to craft a tale for her last moments, I would say perhaps she grew dizzy, fainted, hit her head as she fell into the water."

"What would have made her so faint, then? She was young and healthy. I have heard nothing of any illness or fever here in France."

The doctor shrugged. "Even the young can be seized with all manner of afflictions. Queen Mary, for example, is a most energetic lady, but she is often laid low with dizzy spells and pains in her side. Only a few months ago, she fainted in church and had to be revived with a quantity of wine from the altar. There were hopes she was carrying a little prince, but, alas, it was not so."

"Was Mademoiselle Wrightsman with child?" Kate said, thinking of Amelia's suitors, men like Toby and Jacques d'Emours, men who would even duel for her.

"*Non.* Nor did it appear she had eaten a great deal before her death, or had smallpox or the sweat. But there was this."

Dr. Folie lifted Amelia's arm and drew away the frilled edge of her sleeve. Her wrist was reddened, blistered, the spots red against the icy pallor of her skin.

"A burn?" she asked, puzzled.

"Perhaps. I could not say for sure." He hesitated for a moment. "Have you ever been to Italy, mademoiselle? Queen Catherine says you seem most educated in the ways of the world. In Italy they do know much of herbal remedies—and more harmful concoctions."

*Harmful concoctions?* "This is the first time I have been away from England, Doctor."

Kate looked down at Amelia, now resting peacefully again, her eyes closed forever. She knew Amelia had many admirers, some of whom had already expressed their jealous natures, and Amelia herself was most changeable in her tempers. Could this be a crime of passion? A romantic quarrel?

Or something more?

Kate suddenly noticed some marks on Amelia's

neck, above the high frill of her gown. "What is this, Doctor?"

Dr. Folie peered closer. "Most strange. It almost looks like the mark on her arm, but I do not see how it could have gotten there. You *are* a most unusual lady, mademoiselle, as the queen said."

Kate did not like the idea of Queen Catherine talking about her, knowing much about her. But she remembered the ladies of the queen, her eyes everywhere, and Kate knew she had to be much more careful. "I fear I am not unusual at all. I am very ordinary."

He shook his heads. "Most ladies would faint at such sights."

"I have seen worse, Doctor." And she knew she could not afford to be swoonish, not if she were going to help Queen Elizabeth.

She took one more look at Amelia's face and silently promised to do all she could to discover what had really happened on that night-dark pond. Then she stepped back to let the doctor slide the coffin lid back into place.

Emerging from the underground chamber into the sunlit corridors of the palace was startling. A group of ladies-in-waiting rushed past in rustling satin gowns, giggling over a planned hawking party with Queen Mary, and one of them called to her as they passed. "You will come, too, will you not, Mademoiselle Haywood? We do so enjoy your English songs, and they cheer Queen Mary to no end."

Kate smiled and agreed that she would go, but she

was barely aware of all the bright humanity that swirled past her. She wanted to get to her room to wash, as if the warm water and scented soap might brush away the memory of poor Amelia in her coffin.

There was something so strange about her death, something she could not yet quite decipher. But she would. She had to, for Amelia's sake. And for Queen Elizabeth.

She hurried back to her chamber and took out Mistress Berry's herbal, which she had been reading to try to distract herself earlier. The distraction had not worked, but she was sure she remembered something interesting, something that hovered just outside her memory. She flicked through the pages she had already read, scanning the properties of various kitchen plants and herbs, the sketches of leaves and flowers.

Finally she found what she sought among a section of recipes for beauty creams and potions. *Atropa belladonna*, a plant native to central Europe, much prized by ladies to use as an eye wash, which would dilate their pupils and give them a wide, gleaming appearance. It could also be used to treat pain or menstrual difficulties, but much care had to be used, as only a drop too much would cause delirium, fainting, and death.

Kate closed her eyes and remembered Amelia as she had been at the party, so frantically merry, her cheeks flushed. Could she have taken something, perhaps in her wine? Or mayhap she had used the drops for her eyes and had given herself too many that night. She was fond of beauty treatments, perfumes, and lotions, Kate knew.

She needed to talk to more of Amelia's friends—and learn more about her enemies, too. Queen Mary's hawking expedition would be the perfect time to study all the courtiers.

# CHAPTER SEVENTEEN

Queen Mary's hawking party was just gathering in the Fountain Courtyard when Kate hurried to join them. Amelia Wrightsman had been buried only that morning, and Kate had stood in the churchyard with Lady Barnett and Mistress Berry as they said farewell to their kinswoman on that cold, bright, still day.

Now Lady Barnett had retired to her chamber, watched over by Mistress Berry and that lady's possets to comfort her. Kate wanted to ask Mistress Berry about the belladonna—if Amelia had ever used it—but there was not even a moment alone. She would have to find out later.

The laughter of the hawking party was jarring after such a somber morning. The chatter of everyone as they found their horses and the servants brought out the hooded birds, the excitement and anticipation that seemed to hang in the air seeming so ordinary and strange. Even in the coldness of death, there was life, and she had to think of her own place, her own queen, and what she had to do at Fontainebleau.

Kate watched, still feeling strangely distant from the scene as Lord James Stewart lifted Queen Mary into her saddle. Shockingly, she rode astride, dressed in men's doeskin breeches and a velvet doublet, her auburn hair tucked beneath a plumed cap. Kate found herself envying the practicality of the garb, and she wondered if she could bring the style to England somehow.

Queen Mary was surrounded by her Maries and other courtiers. She laughed at their jokes and reached out her gauntlet-clad arm for the falconer to hand her the bird. It was a pretty little peregrine, its bells jingling merrily in the breeze.

Charles Throckmorton hurried to join Kate, offering his arm to escort her to her waiting horse. It was the same placid mare she had ridden to Fontainebleau, saddled with Kate's own sidesaddle, and she was glad of the horse's quiet docility, even as it reminded her of the burned-out farm they had encountered on their journey, the sadness that had clung over everything, just as it did today. The beauty of the palace felt emptier than ever.

"How does Master Ridley fare today?" she asked Charles quietly as she settled her skirts over her saddle. Toby had not gone to the churchyard. No one had, except the Barnetts, Mistress Berry, and Sir Nicholas, in his official role as ambassador. Celeste Renard was the only French courtier who came, and stood quietly beside the grave in a black veil. For a lady who seemed to gather friends wherever she went, as Amelia had, it seemed most odd, and Kate couldn't help but think of

Queen Mary's accusations—that Amelia had been murdered in a plot against a royal throne.

"He is distraught, I fear," Charles said. "He cared for Mistress Wrightsman very much, even though she was not worthy of him. Losing her, along with his fears of being accused of harming her, have laid him most low."

Kate nodded, fussing with her reins as she tried to gather her thoughts. Charles voiced her fears of the sad situation. "I am sure he was the last person who would have wanted to hurt her. But there is no shortage of secrets that seemed to surround her here in France."

Charles frowned. "Have you heard something about her death?"

Kate sighed in frustration. "Nay, nothing as of yet. As you say, she had many friends and also suitors. But with courtly friends surely come enemies."

A servant brought Charles's horse to him, and he swung himself up into the saddle. "Suitors, aye. And she was too blind and giddy to see or care how she broke poor Toby's heart."

Kate thought of Toby's wild grief over Amelia's death. But was it only grief?

Before she could answer, there was a series of horn blasts, sharp and shrill, and Queen Mary spurred her horse into a gallop out of the courtyard and toward the forest. Everyone else raced to follow, and the huntsman led them into the woods.

It was a cold day but a bright one, crisp and fresh, and even Kate found she forgot the sadness for a moment as they ran into the wind. The crowd spread out on the pathway, and she glimpsed Monsieur d'Emours up ahead. Before he vanished behind his friends, she saw the grim, pale set of his face.

The horses dashed between the trees, leaping over fallen logs and ditches. Kate held too tightly to the reins, praying frantically not to fall off and embarrass herself, but Queen Mary's bright laughter kept everyone's spirits high and reckless around her.

They emerged onto a wide meadow between low, rolling hills beyond the shadow of the forest and in the light. The riders scattered. The hawks were unhooded, and Queen Mary led them into the hunt as she threw her peregrine high into the air. The little bird took flight, soaring into the gathering grayness of the sky and curling in a graceful loop. The day had grown colder as well as dimmer, clouds rolling across the sky, but no one seemed to care.

The peregrine dove out of sight, as if she had caught a glimpse of her prey, and Queen Mary rode off in chase. Kate followed at a much slower pace and found herself riding beside Celeste Renard.

Like Kate, Celeste had changed from her black formal gown and veil into stylish riding garb, in her case, breeches and a doublet like the queen's. She tossed Kate a half smile.

"'Tis good to breathe some fresh air, is it not, Mademoiselle Haywood, after such a sad morning?" Celeste said.

"Indeed it is," Kate agreed. "Sometimes it is hard to think when between stone walls."

"There is much to think about today."

Kate nodded. There was indeed much to think about, and she would love to have someone she could truly discuss everything with—but perhaps Celeste, for all her welcoming friendliness, was not that person. She could talk to Rob, of course, but he was busy with the Italian actors that day. She knew she had to search him out later.

"You should find some French riding clothes," Celeste said. "So much more comfortable."

"I learned to ride sidesaddle, and I fear to change now," Kate answered.

Celeste laughed. "Ah, but gentlemen find a lady in breeches so fascinating!"

"Perhaps a man would—until I toppled from my horse and he had to drag me out of a muddy ditch."

Celeste laughed even harder and turned her horse to follow the queen's path. A burst of excited laughter sent everyone galloping ahead again. Queen Mary's bird had caught a rabbit, and now whirled overhead once more to find new prey.

They rode for a time, gathering more rabbits and small birds as clouds gathered and then blew away again. At midafternoon, as the huntsmen brought in the fruits of the hunt, they all gathered on a hillside for a repast. Blankets were spread on the grass and servants unpacked delicacies from the kitchens and poured wine. Queen Mary seemed in high spirits, laughing with her ladies, and soon they were playing an intricate word game that made everyone laugh even louder as the drink flowed.

Kate, though, could not quite shake away the sadness of that morning in the churchyard, and the merriment seemed to be something she merely studied from a distance. She found a seat under a tree and nibbled at a bit of gingerbread as she examined the countryside around them.

It was indeed a beautiful scene, even as the weather grew colder and grayer. The low hills rolled gently into the dark fringe of the forest, and in the distance she could see the roofs and chimneys of the palace itself, floating white and ethereal on the horizon. In the other direction, she saw another house, painted the palest of pinks and crowned with a gray roof, like a smaller version of the fairy-tale château.

Claude Domville came to sit beside her, offering a goblet of the sweet, pale wine. Kate accepted it with a smile, glad of the company, the distraction from her melancholy. He smiled at her, as light as he usually was, and she wondered if he had any more interesting tales of gossip that might prove useful.

"What do you think of our hunt, Mademoiselle Haywood?" he said. He stretched out on the grass beside her, his head propped on his elbow as he smiled up at her. "Is it like those in England?"

"Somewhat so, of course. Queen Elizabeth, too, much enjoys a day's hunting, and she has a great deal of energy for it," Kate said. "I fear I am only barely able to stay in the saddle. But the fresh air is most bracing."

Claude was quiet for a moment. "Perhaps it is a bit disrespectful, after what happened to Mademoiselle Wrightsman. She was buried this morning, was she not?"

Kate nodded, thinking of the lack of any French courtiers at the churchyard. "Queen Mary declares she was Amelia's friend, but it seems few here really knew her well, so how can it be truly disrespectful? They have been caught in mourning for the king for months, of course, and they want to enjoy themselves for a little while."

"They always want only to enjoy themselves, except for Queen Catherine, who works all the time. All else is frivolity here."

Kate gestured to the house in the distance. "Whose estate is that? It looks most pretty, and rather close to the palace."

Claude scowled. "That is Jacques d'Emours's family château. It has been in their lineage for many generations, a gift to his great-grandfather from the Guise for their long service to that family."

Kate studied the distant chimneys closer, intrigued. The Guise did seem to hover over the court at every moment, even now that everyone said their power was on the wane.

Suddenly, a deafening shout of thunder broke overhead, and cold drops of rain fell onto their heads. Queen Mary and her ladies shrieked and leaped to their feet, running to their horses as servants scrambled to help them.

"It is too far to the palace," Jacques d'Emours shouted, sweeping his feathered hat from his golden head. "Everyone, ride to my house—it is just down the hill!"

Laughter burst out again, for the party was taking a new, unexpected turn, and they all rode for the d'Emours house.

*The d'Emours château is indeed beautiful,* Kate thought as they galloped into the courtyard, not large but a perfect jewel set amid elaborate gardens and marble statues and fountains.

Monsieur d'Emours had ridden fast ahead of the hunting party, and servants were already waiting with linen towels to wipe away the rain and offer pitchers of fresh wine. The house was not as grand as Fontainebleau, of course, but it was very pretty, decorated with painted scenes of gods framed in elaborate white plasterwork, all light and elegant, with gilded ceiling beams far overhead and patterned wooden floors. A fire roared in the great hall, with cushioned chairs and stools already drawn around the hearth.

Queen Mary and her ladies were soon ensconced next to its warmth, sipping at spiced wine, whispering and laughing.

Kate studied Monsieur d'Emours as he calmly directed the servants and saw to the queen's comfort, all cool, capable confidence. This man had once fought a duel for Amelia Wrightsman, the scandal that prompted her departure from France. Everyone seemed to have forgotten the matter, except for a romantic folly to giggle about, and of course such things happened at Elizabeth's court as well. Close quarters in royal palaces and fast-burning passions meant tempers quickly flared. But what did d'Emours himself think of Amelia now? What did he seek from his future? Kate could not read him at all.

She remembered the diamond brooch on Kate's fur muff, her changeable moods when he was around. He did not mourn her as Toby Ridley did, with sobs and anguish, but most people at court were adept at hiding their true emotions. It was baffling.

Kate slipped out of the great hall and found her way to the foot of the winding white marble stairs. She wasn't sure exactly what she was looking for, but some instinct told her that d'Emours must know or feel something about Amelia's death. And she was not likely to find herself in the man's own house again.

She could hear the echo of laughter from the hall, but the rest of the rooms were silent. Surely all the servants were scrambling to provide the royal repast. Kate made her way up a twisting stone flight of stairs lined with tapestries. They were fine work, closely woven and highlighted with silver, yet she could see that the fringe work on the edges had frayed and moths had gotten to some of them. Much of the furniture in the rooms she peeked into were the same fine, heavy carved pieces, but with no cushions or hangings. The only painting she found was a portrait of a lady in a fine red-and-gold gown, her blond hair piled high and bound with pearls, holding a small boy in black by the hand. She wondered if it was Jacques d'Emours and his Guise mother, in more prosperous days.

The chambers were chilly, the fireplace grates empty. She saw nothing that would possibly hold secret papers or letters.

As she turned down another corridor, she heard a burst of laughter echo on the paneled walls and the patter of footsteps coming closer. She glanced down another hallway to see d'Emours speaking to a lady in a black gown, her back to Kate. He was scowling, talking swiftly and quietly, and at an echo from another chamber he looked up. His expression was most fierce.

Kate didn't want to be caught wandering the halls of d'Emours's home. She quickly slipped through the nearest door and closed it behind her. Her heart was pounding, but it was cool and dim in the room, and as her eyes adjusted to the gloom she saw that she was in a chapel.

It was not large, but it was very beautiful. Unlike the rest of the house, it had the air of being well maintained. The gilded altar, crowned with a painted statue of the Virgin Mary, all pale blue, gold, and pink, shimmered in the shadows, with a silver-and-pearl monstrance on one side and a saint's reliquary on the other. Beneath her feet, set in the marble floor, were the gold letters of tombs and monuments to d'Emours ancestors. Kate had seen few places like it in England, where all the altars had been made plain and saints banished, and she was enthralled by the incense-scented hush of it, the quiet peace.

In a tiny side chapel, just beyond the alabaster altar, she came upon a marble tomb gleaming white and bathed in the blue and red light of the stained-glass windows set high in the thick stone wall. It was the effigy of a couple, a bearded man in the long gown and cap of twenty years ago at least, and a lady in a fur-trimmed gown, a book open in her beautifully carved stone hands. The features were the same as those of the woman in the portrait, the lady who held the small child by the hand. Set in fine white stone now, the features were older but still finely carved and elegant.

Kate glimpsed the bronze shine of a memorial tablet set in the wall above the couple, and she leaned closer to study it. In French, the carving read, IN LOVING MEMORY OF MLLE ORIEUX, WITH THANKS FOR HER GREAT GIFT. MAY HER NAME BE WREATHED IN FLOWERS IN HEAVEN.

Orieux—it was an unusual name, one Kate was sure she had heard before. But where? And why would someone not a d'Emours be memorialized in their private chapel?

She glanced back at the marble lady and thought that her stone features concealed as many secrets as the living ones at Fontainebleau. Somehow it felt wrong to be there in that beautiful chapel, alone with this lady. Kate slipped out from the side chapel and tiptoed past the altar toward the château. The door suddenly opened, and she whirled around, her heart pounding, to find Jacques d'Emours standing there, framed in the light from the corridor beyond. His eyes wide, he seemed just as startled to find her there.

Those icy blue eyes narrowed and he stepped slowly, deliberately, into the aisle. Kate glanced past him toward the door, wondering how long it would take her to run for it and make an escape.

"What are you doing in here, mademoiselle?" he demanded.

Kate thought quickly and pulled out an obvious, though rather undignified, answer. "Forgive me, monsieur," she said with a hasty curtsy. "I—I was looking for the privy, and on the way back to the hall, I took a wrong turn and found myself here. I couldn't help but stay for a moment, it is so beautiful."

His harshly handsome face relaxed just a bit at the compliment. "You are the English girl, are you not? The one who plays music?"

"Aye, monsieur. I am Kate Haywood, court musician to Queen Elizabeth."

"Queen Mary praises your work."

"I am glad I can bring her a bit of distraction at a sad time."

His lips quirked in a small, unreadable smile. "A sad time indeed. You knew Mademoiselle Wrightsman, I am sure."

Kate nodded warily. "I traveled with her and the Barnetts to France."

"And what did you think of her?"

Kate wondered why he was asking her about Amelia,

what he hoped to hear. She carefully edged back until she ran into a marble pillar. "She was kind to me."

"Kind?" he said sharply. "When was Amelia kind?" His handsome face twisted in a thunderous expression, and his hand came up in a fist. Kate felt a jolt of fear and fell back a step from his anger. This was a man who fought duels, after all, who seemingly broke Amelia's heart. He could not be trusted.

But he was not a courtier for nothing. His face changed as quickly as if it had been wiped clean, and his hand fell to his side. Abruptly, he turned and gestured toward the beautiful altar. "You must be Protestant like your queen, *non*? What do you think of my family's chapel?"

Kate took in a deep breath and pushed down the urge to flee. "It is beautiful," she answered honestly. "And also welcoming. It has the feeling of being much loved."

He gave her a surprised glance, a smile drifting over his face. "So it has been. D'Emourses have worshipped here for many generations. One ancestor was even declared to be a saint. His relics are behind the altar, just there."

Kate looked back toward the shimmering altar, the silver-and-gold reliquary toward one side. The thought that a saint's bones, however ancient, rested there made her shiver. She was suddenly rather glad for the plainer churches in London; they seemed less haunted.

Or perhaps she was still thinking of Amelia, so newly laid in the ground herself.

"It is most beautiful, especially the Virgin's statue.

I feel as if her eyes could see us, they are so lifelike," Kate said.

"But what is your favorite part of my chapel, mademoiselle?"

Kate was surprised by him again, by his friendly tone. He was not at all what she had expected from the tales of him, from his own demeanor, but she was wary by then of the deceptively lovely face of the French court.

"The small chapel with the pretty red-and-blue windows. It is most beautiful," she said.

"Ah, my parents' burial chapel. It was my mother's favorite as well, which is why she wanted to be laid to rest there. I visit there often."

"I am sorry, monsieur, if you came in here to visit your mother and I am trespassing," Kate said quickly. "I will return to the others and leave you alone."

He just nodded and turned toward the small chapel, as if he had already forgotten she was there. His face looked most solemn and even sad after his raw anger, and Kate couldn't help but wonder what he thought about now. His mother—or Amelia Wrightsman. Or maybe even the mysterious Mademoiselle Orieux.

"Mademoiselle Haywood!" Queen Mary called as Kate slipped back into the great hall after leaving Monsieur d'Emours in the chapel. She had hoped to be unobtrusive, unnoticed, but at the queen's words everyone turned to study her. "It seems we must wait here until the rain stops. Would you play more of my cousin's English songs to pass the time? I have enjoyed them so much."

Kate had time only to nod and take a borrowed lute someone thrust into her hands. She found a low stool near the queen and sat down to begin a song, a lively dance that had once been written by Queen Elizabeth's father, King Henry. It was familiar, and she hoped she would not stumble over it now.

"Is England much like Scotland?" Queen Mary asked abruptly.

"I fear I have never been to Scotland," Kate answered. "I would imagine that, much like England or France, Scotland is very different depending on where one goes. Edinburgh is surely very different from a Highland farm. I have heard it has many beauties."

Queen Mary sighed and glanced at her brother, who seemed to have imbibed much of the delicious wine and now nodded by the fire. "My brother warns me that I would find it very different from France, and my doctors fear my health would suffer in its chilly weather. My father's first wife was a French princess, you know, and she died only weeks after she arrived in Scotland. Yet surely I have inherited my own dear mother's hardier constitution! It was once my home."

"We would all follow you anywhere you went, Your Majesty," Mary Seton reminded her.

Queen Mary smiled at her. She was all ease and friendliness now, tinged with a sort of wistful sadness.

She was very different from the angry woman who had burst into the Barnetts' room after Amelia's death.

"I do cherish your loyalty, my Marie," the queen said. She glanced at her uncle, the Duc de Guise, who prowled by the fireplace. His scarred face looked doubtful. "But I also must think of all of you as I consider what I must do next. I must take more counsel and think matters over most carefully.

"In the meantime, I will listen to your beautiful English songs!"

Kate nodded and kept on playing, half listening to the Maries as they whispered together. She thought of all Queen Mary's possible futures: marriage in a new kingdom, a quieter life in France, taking up her own rule in Scotland. Everyone seemed to have their own ideas of what she should do, and the queen herself kept her own thoughts on the matter most private behind her charming smiles. What did Queen Elizabeth and Cecil really want from her? Kate couldn't help but wonder what she was doing here in France, what she should do next.

# CHAPTER EIGHTEEN

"'All his fair virtues were but candleshine! Speak not of him for fair Ginevra's hand!'"

Kate studied the glittering assembly arranged before her. It seemed the entire court at Fontainebleau had assembled to watch the Queen Mother's troupe perform *Ginevra*, a light romance from Queen Catherine's native Florence, and it was hard to tell which sparkled more—the spectacle on the stage or the courtiers who applauded it.

The play was indeed enthralling, filled with romantic intrigues and beautiful songs. Yet Kate could not quite forget what had happened at the hawking expedition. The d'Emours house, the strange merriment after Amelia's burial. The tablet to Mademoiselle Orieux, whose name she still couldn't quite place. There was so much she did not know about all that had happened ever since she left London. It was as if she groped her way along a darkened corridor, with only tiny flashes of lightning to show what was around her.

Perhaps Cecil and his friend Sir Nicholas *were* hiding

things from her, things that could prove fatal. Amelia Wrightsman was dead, after all, in most suspicious circumstances. Were the Barnetts in danger? Mistress Berry? Kate herself? She shivered as she thought of tumbling over the ship's railing. But no one here at Fontainebleau had been on the ship, had they?

Kate rose from her seat, tiptoed behind the tiered benches that held the rapt audience, and made her way out of the gallery. Sir Nicholas was a most shrewd diplomat; he would not tell her if he had an agent working for him on the ship. Or perhaps there was a double agent he knew nothing about. Kate needed to find out. It was very possible Amelia herself had been a spy for him. There were so many times she hid behind her laughter. Kate would have few other chances to find the palace corridors so empty, as everyone was at the play. But it would not be for long. She had to hurry.

She made her way past the guards at the gallery doors. Rather than go through the large doors to the garden, she turned toward a staircase that led up to the private wings housing courtiers and ambassadors. A few servants hurried past in the flickering light of a few torches and candles, all of them intent on their own errands. They paid her no attention.

Occasionally, a wisp of a word or a quick laugh would float to her from some distant chamber, as if from a ghost.

Kate crept carefully into Sir Nicholas's sitting room, where she had taken him the letters from England. She knew he was watching the play with Charles and the

Barnetts, but Toby had not been seen that day. No one was working in the sitting room, and the moonlight from the window gave her enough illumination to quickly light a candle and study the table where Sir Nicholas usually sat.

It was tidy, with small piles of manuscripts and books, quills and pots of ink, and a carefully locked carved casket.

She took a long carved ivory pin from her hair and slipped the sharp tip into the lock. One of Cecil's intelligencers, an expert picklock, had shown her how to do that, and it had been very useful many times, such as at the Spanish embassy one night in London. She wiggled it around until the mechanism caught and the lock sprang open.

The box was filled with papers, and as she glanced over them she saw what she had hoped to find. Most of them were in code, lists and small sketches that at first seemed to make little sense, until she looked closer.

Code had been one of her favorite lessons in Queen Elizabeth's service. It was like music, the way small ink markings suddenly clicked into place and made some sort of alchemy. Also like the notes, they seemed to stay in her mind until they could be deciphered and fit together once again.

She found the letters she had carried from England, the letters that were in Cecil's own hand. She scanned them, memorizing the lines as quickly as she could, before anyone could return and catch her there. She was careful to leave them exactly where she had found them, replacing the lock before she made her way out into the corridor and hurried toward her own room.

Kate closed and latched her door behind her. Only once she was by her own hearth did she let out her breath. She listened carefully at the door until she was sure there was no one else out there before she went to her small writing table.

She took out her quills, ink, and small code book from their box and closed her eyes, letting the memory of the figures and patterns of the letters come back into her mind. Learning music from the time she could toddle around the house had trained her mind to see things and remember them quickly. Each letter and symbol that seemed to mean nothing had a corresponding letter, and once those were discovered it would click into place.

It was a rather simple transposition cipher, one that she had practiced at Cecil's offices but that would be much harder for someone new to the code to break. The frequency of the letters was the same as in a plain-text letter, but jumbled. She just had to sort them out.

She wrote down what she remembered, the quill scratching quickly over the paper. *YCKKVOTM OTZU*, and so forth. Slowly, she found she could decipher a pattern and match it up to her code book. Much of it was as she expected. Connections to make, messages to deliver, news from the queen's other embassies.

But one of the messages made her catch her breath. *As for Madame Fox and her new cub, they could be of much use indeed, for they are much admired in France, but care must be taken. They are unpredictable and their loyalties are unknown.*

*Madame Fox and her cub.* She thought of all the ladies she had met at Fontainebleau. Perhaps it was Celeste Reynard, with her last name—the fox—and her red hair? It would help explain her changeable nature, her efforts to make friends with Kate. But as far as Kate knew, Celeste had no child. Could the cub possibly be Amelia, the two of them spying together? She knew where she needed to turn for a few answers. She would start with Amelia herself.

Amelia's small chamber had been unoccupied for only a short time, but the smell of dust and disuse seemed to hang in the air along with a hint of Amelia's perfume. For a moment, Kate hovered in the doorway, reluctant to go inside, as if she would disturb the occupant in some way. The quiet sadness seemed enveloping.

But she knew she had to hurry. The corridor where the Barnetts' rooms lay would not be empty for long.

"I am doing this to help her," Kate whispered, and forced herself to step into the chamber and close the door behind her.

She wasn't entirely sure what she was looking for, only that she needed some proof that Amelia was the "fox's cub" to Celeste. That she had some secret work here in France. Work that had perhaps led to her death.

She drew back the window curtain to let a bit of light into the gloomy space. There wasn't room for much there, only a narrow bed with a truckle for the maid, a table lined with Amelia's pots and bottles of beauty potions, and a chair piled with books. There was no clothes chest or jewel case, which Lady Barnett had probably already taken away.

Kate quickly looked through the books. They all seemed to be light works of romantic poetry, tales of handsome knights on quests to rescue fair ladies. There were no letters tucked among the pages, but Kate did find something intriguing in the last book. Some of the letters had been underlined, tiny unreadable symbols sketched above them.

Could it match the code in Throckmorton's letters? Kate quickly committed some of the marks to memory, to compare them later, and stacked the books the way she had found them.

She looked beneath the bed and under the concealment of the mattress. All she discovered there was that the servants at Fontainebleau were not as careful about dusting as Queen Elizabeth's own attendants. Elizabeth was most fastidious about the cleanliness of her palaces and her person.

*Nor would Elizabeth approve of Amelia's lack of tidiness,* Kate thought as she studied the toilette table. The silver lids were not secure on pots of pearl powder and cochineal lip stains, and some of the face cream had leaked out of its bottle. Combs and hairpins and ribbons were scattered everywhere.

Kate carefully sniffed the cream, which had a hint of lemon balm, and reached for a crystal perfume bottle. It smelled of violets, of course, as Amelia always did, yet there was something slightly bitter just beneath the sweetness. She held it up to the light and saw there wasn't much of the oil left. What there was had turned a strange yellowish color, almost like a sticky piece of amber.

Kate thought of the mark on Amelia's wrist, and Dr. Florie's words about the Italians and their poisons. Amelia had probably not drowned, but was pushed into the water after being befuddled somehow. Kate had thought perhaps it was in the wine she drank that night, but what if it was something else? She knew from reading the herbal book that it was easy enough to distill poisons from leaves and berries or to use too much of a harmful substance that was originally meant to help. What poisons could get in through a person's skin, or even by sniffing?

She heard a voice outside, a maid calling in French to someone else, and she knew she wouldn't be alone in Amelia's room for long. She carefully wrapped the bottle in a handkerchief and tucked it into the purse fastened at her sash. As she turned away, she glimpsed a small portrait tucked among the ribbons on the table, an oval of ivory framed in gold. Something about the lady's painted eyes—a bright, clear blue—caught her attention.

She picked it up and studied the delicate features, the high, lacy collar on her black velvet gown, the golden curls that escaped her white cap. She looked very much like Amelia dressed in the fashions of a generation ago. Kate turned it over and saw written on the back, *Dear Mama, Ly E. Orieux DeLC Wrightsman.*

*Of course—Orieux!* Kate felt foolish for forgetting. That was the maiden name of Lady Barnett's grandmother, so presumably of Amelia's mother as well. It was an unusual name. Why would one of that family be memorialized in a French chapel?

There was another burst of laughter outside, and Kate quickly replaced the portrait on the table before she slipped out of the room. She thought she heard something around the corner, but the corridor seemed empty as she hurried away. She had to find Dr. Folie.

The doctor sniffed carefully at the perfume bottle, scowling as he held it up and examined it. "You think there was something put into this potion, then?"

"I don't know," Kate answered. "I have only just begun a small study of herbs. It doesn't smell quite right, though, and you did say the mark on her wrist might have been from some caustic substance. She would have put the perfume on her arm and neck, surely."

"It has been known to happen, *oui*," the doctor murmured. He went to his stone table beneath the window and carefully dabbed a drop of the perfume on a cloth. "But there is so little of this left, it is hard to tell. What do you suspect?"

"I was reading of belladonna."

"Ah, yes, easy to procure in a royal court. Alas, vanity reigns here. It is a pretty plant when in flower and has its uses, but ladies think if one drop makes them beautiful, three will do more. Alas for them."

"I read it can cause disorientation."

"And then hallucinations. But she could not have been given too much at once; it would be noticeable. Very clever to put it in something she uses every day. Was the perfume a gift?"

A gift from Monsieur d'Emours? Or another admirer? "I can try to find out."

"Very good, mademoiselle. I will see if I can conduct some tests here. You are very clever, bringing me another puzzle! It has been dull here in recent weeks."

Kate nodded and left him to his tests. *A bit of dullness would surely be a wonderful thing,* she thought, *compared to murders and secrets.* Where could she find out about Amelia's perfume? Perhaps Lady Barnett or Mistress Berry would know, especially with the knowledge of herbal potions she had. Or maybe Celeste, whose motives had to be worked out now, would know who had given Amelia such gifts.

Outside her chamber door, she was surprised to find a footman waiting. "A letter arrived for you, Mademoiselle Haywood, and Sir Henry Barnett said to bring it to you right away. He also said you must begin to pack, for he wishes to depart Fontainebleau as soon as he can."

"*Merci,*" Kate answered. If Sir Henry insisted on leaving soon, she would not have much time for her inquiries. She waited until she was alone in her chamber to open the letter, and saw it was not familiar handwriting. The signature at the bottom read *T. Overbury.*

Master Overbury—Anthony's old school friend who now served an English bishop's retinue in Paris. She had written to him when she first arrived, sending on a note from Anthony and asking him her own questions, hoping he had heard of some of the French courtiers in his position in Paris. She read his short note eagerly.

*Mistress Haywood, I send my greetings and thank-you for the word that my old friend Master Elias is in good health. Tell him I hope to have an ale with him at the Rose and Crown soon, for these Frenchies cannot make a fine beer, though their wine is enjoyable! I hope you are faring well at Fontainebleau. My master as well as everyone in Paris wishes they were there. But I hope you are wary. There was much talk here a few months ago of a duel between a man named d'Emours and someone who was not his social equal. There have been questions of his opponent's loyalty to France, for he has many English friends, though I can say nothing for certain. I will ask and keep my ears open . . .*

Kate remembered that d'Emours's opponent, presumably another of Amelia's admirers, was named Mamou, and he had not been seen at court since the fight. Where was he? Could he also be a spy?

Or could he have sent Amelia gifts, begging her not to forget him?

# CHAPTER NINETEEN

"I don't like this, Kate. You are putting yourself in danger again," Rob said with a scowl. He held tightly to her hand as they walked the empty garden pathways in the early, pinkish morning light. Kate had confided in him what she suspected, or most of it anyway.

"If Mistress Wrightsman was spying for France, Queen Elizabeth must know," Kate answered. "And even if she was, her murderer cannot go unpunished."

Rob still looked most doubtful, but Kate knew he would help her, as he had in the past. He shared her curiosity, if nothing else.

"So, whom do you suspect?" he asked.

Kate sighed. "There are many choices. First, perhaps someone thought Amelia was telling secrets to her lover, Monsieur d'Emours—or more likely he thought she was telling *his* secrets. He depends on the Guise, after all, and they would not like to find out he had an affair with an English spy. Or perhaps he was still jealous over Monsieur Mamou and that duel, or one of

Amelia's other admirers, though he did not seem to be the overly possessive sort. Amelia was changeable—it is very likely he feared she would become angry with him again and cast doubt on his loyalty to the Guise. Or it could have been one of those other suitors."

"Most murders are committed to cover secrets, 'tis true," Rob said. "And your theory makes much sense. But d'Emours was nowhere at the pavilion the night we found poor Mistress Wrightsman."

"How do you know? I saw him at the banquet." And after—with Amelia.

"Signorina Isabella, the actress, was boasting he was having an, er, late supper with her. She was showing the others in her troupe the gifts he bought her."

The pretty Italian actress? Kate had thought she was interested in Rob, but it was true d'Emours would have more riches to bestow. "Did he give her a Guise badge in diamonds?"

"Nay, ruby earrings."

Kate sighed. That was one easy clue vanished. But surely a man like d'Emours would know how to hire an assassin if needed. "And she was sure he was with her all night after the banquet?"

"Aye. I doubt she would forget if he slipped out of her chamber for an hour in the midst of their rendez-vous."

Kate had to laugh. "I suppose not. Perhaps he had an accomplice, then, one who found Amelia at the pavilion."

"Perhaps. Who could it be?"

"Another lover of his? A servant? A hired assassin?

There are rumors that many of those reside here at the French court. I have heard such tales of Queen Catherine's Italian perfumer, Signor Ruggieri." She thought of the liquid left in Amelia's perfume bottles and shivered. She needed to visit Dr. Folie again.

"What of Mistress Wrightsman's other suitors? Or mayhap jealous ladies whose husbands or lovers looked at her once too often."

Kate nodded. That meant the whole court could possibly be suspect.

"There is also Master Ridley, who has already fallen under suspicion," Rob said.

Kate did not like to think that of friendly, kindhearted Toby. But Rob was right: Jealousy caused many otherwise sane people to behave most irrationally. "Perhaps. He did care for her greatly, I think. Yet he does not seem the angry, bad-tempered sort."

"Would one of his friends have become angry on his behalf? Charles Throckmorton, for instance."

"Charles has a cool head, but if he feared Amelia was somehow jeopardizing his uncle's work here, he might have done something about it. He didn't seem to like Amelia very much."

"And what of her own family? The Barnetts? Sir Henry is friends with Sir Nicholas Throckmorton."

Kate shook her head. "Jane Barnett was very fond of her niece, and I do not think she would be strong enough to kill her, anyway."

"Unless she was poisoned and weakened first, as you said."

Kate thought of Lady Barnett's tales of her youth, her girlhood in France, her French relations. The Orieux monument in the d'Emours chapel. "I still think Lady Barnett would not have hurt her niece, though I suppose it is possible she herself was spying for the French. Sir Henry, he did not care for Amelia and was often most impatient with her, but surely he would not jeopardize his position merely to be rid of her. He would be more likely to marry her off and gain some advantage in the process."

"I fear your kind heart does not want to suspect anyone you know, dear Kate."

"'Tis most true," Kate said with a sigh. She had learned in her time at Queen Elizabeth's court that most people were capable of terrible things, given the right motivation, but she didn't like to truly believe it.

"Surely you have seen by now, after the queen's coronation and Nonsuch, that most people in our world are not so tenderhearted as you."

She shook her head. She did not like to remember what had happened the night of the coronation banquet or in the gardens at Nonsuch Palace. And now it was happening again here at Fontainebleau. "So, our choices are the Barnetts, Toby Ridley, Monsieur d'Emours and his agent, another of Amelia's lovers *or* a jealous wife, or an enemy of England who saw some advantage in killing an Englishwoman who is friends with Queen Mary. Surely that could be anyone here at Fontainebleau."

And then there were the letters she had carried to Sir Nicholas, the ones someone had tried to steal on the ship. What had they to do with Amelia, if anything at all?

It made her want to scream with anger and frustration at the puzzle of it all. She had to content herself with kicking out at a nearby rock, which only caused her toes pain.

The sun was rising higher in the sky, casting its meager warmth over the winter gardens, and a few courtiers had emerged for morning walks, their laughter floating back to her. Distant church bells tolled the hour.

Rob squeezed her hand. "I must go now, my Kate. I promised to meet Thomas and show him part of that Italian masque, but I will not be long. Should I escort you back to your chamber?"

Kate glimpsed a lady slipping down the stone stairs of the palace, the fur-lined hood of her cloak falling back to give a glimpse of distinctive red-gold hair. Celeste Renard, Amelia's friend.

"Nay, not now," she told Rob. "I must talk to Mademoiselle Renard for a moment."

Rob leaned back to give her a doubtful glance. "Promise me you will be careful, Kate? These French courtiers can be most changeable."

"More so than English courtiers?" she said with a laugh. "I will be careful—I promise. Meet me after you finish with Thomas?"

"Of course."

Once Kate was alone in the garden, she followed Celeste along the pathway, until Mademoiselle Renard turned and gave her a welcoming smile. Her eyes were red-rimmed, as if she had been crying, but her smile didn't falter. The light gleamed on her fox-red hair. "Mademoiselle Haywood. I hope you are well enough this morning. You have recovered from the shock of finding Amelia like that, I hope? Perhaps the day of hunting helped?"

"I am over the shock, but it is so very sad," Kate answered. "Poor Mistress Wrightsman. But I am sorry for you, too, Mademoiselle Renard, for were you not friends for a long time?"

Celeste gave a little shrug. "Since she was in France last, *oui*. We had much in common."

"Some of the same suitors?"

Celeste laughed. "Of course not. I certainly know better than to come close to men such as Jacques d'Emours. I spent only one night with him once. Amelia was supposed to know better as well. But she forgot our purpose here."

Kate thought that was a most odd choice of words. "Purpose?"

Celeste laughed again. "Oh, come now, Mademoiselle Haywood. You came here with Amelia; you have met with Sir Nicholas. I know that you must know."

Kate thought of the letters to Sir Nicholas, of Queen Catherine's pretty ladies who could go anywhere at court, charm anyone. "You do not work for Queen Catherine." It was not a question.

"*Certainement, non*. I work for Sir William Cecil—as

you do. I have been waiting for Sir Nicholas to send you to see me since Amelia died."

Kate was surprised—and angry with herself for being surprised. She had not expected Cecil to send her into a lion's den half-aware. But she knew deep down that he would indeed, if it kept Queen Elizabeth safe, his first and only purpose. But that was Kate's purpose as well. There was no need to hide things from her.

She swallowed her anger, her sharp feeling of betrayal, and nodded. "Sir William did not tell me all. I saw your name in a coded letter he wrote to Sir Nicholas."

Celeste tsked. "That was most careless of Sir Nicholas to leave such things lying about. Surely we all need to work together now, for the sake of Queen Elizabeth, more than ever. But I am not so surprised. Sir Nicholas thinks we females are incapable of serious thought, of real work beyond our embroidery. He would be dismissive and careless of us, I fear."

"That is indeed most foolish of him," Kate said. It was not a mistake Queen Catherine shared, obviously. Celeste's words rang true, her gaze steady, but Kate was still suspicious.

Celeste smiled like a cat in the cream. "So he is, yet Sir Nicholas is also loyal, and works so closely with Cecil. They will work for Queen Elizabeth to their last breath, if needed. Anything to keep the Catholics away from the English throne."

"As you will, even though you are French?"

"You are still suspicious of me, *naturellement*." Celeste reached into the front of her stiffened brocade bodice and drew out a small tube of parchment. She handed it to Kate, who quickly scanned the tiny, cramped writing. It was in code, the same as on the letters.

"Why?" Kate asked simply. She glanced up to find Celeste watching her, that smile fading away into an expression of perfect stillness.

"My family were Huguenots. When I was a little girl, my parents were killed in a Guise raid on a Protestant church, and my grandmother fled with me to England. We had nothing, but the Renards are an old family and my grandmother had connections from her girlhood waiting on Queen Mary, King Henry's sister who married the French king. Another old lady-in-waiting from those days took us in and was most kind to us. We even went to court with her. I saw how things were in England, so much simpler, so kind, how we did not have to take our lives in our hands to go to church. I loved it there, but I never forgot my parents and what happened to them."

Kate swallowed hard, thinking of how terrible it must have been to lose her parents so young and in such a vile way. "Yet you seem to very French."

Celeste gave a startled laugh. "You are something of an actor yourself, are you not, Mademoiselle Haywood? When my grandmother was dying, she did not know what to do with me. A friend of hers who is now one of Queen Catherine's ladies found me a place with the queen's daughter, Princess Elisabeth, who is now

Queen of Spain. When she left, Queen Catherine herself took me into her household. She always needs pretty ladies to assist her in many ways, especially to find out secrets from gentlemen. She came to trust me, and I admire her in some respects. Yet I knew I could not go on in such a manner forever. I wanted to help England, as it had helped my grandmother and me—and to bring down the Guise however I could."

"And how did you do that?"

"I met Amelia, of course. Cecil and Sir Nicholas remembered my grandmother and me from our time in England, and asked her to seek me out when she came here to France with her aunt and uncle."

Kate's mind raced over all the suspects she had named to Rob—and all she had not deciphered. "You mean Amelia Wrightsman was an intelligencer for Cecil? Not for the French?"

"Of course. You did not think she was really as silly as she behaved?"

Kate shook her head. There had been moments when Amelia's laughter faded and she looked sad and solemn. Once or twice, Kate had even felt Amelia wanted to confide in her, something secret no one else knew. "Nay, I suppose not."

"She did have many suitors, important gentlemen here at the French court, and she learned much from them that was of use to Sir William. But I fear she lost her reason over Jacques d'Emours."

"Was she spying on him, then?"

"I thought she was. *Surely,* I thought, *that was all it*

could *be*. She seemed so clever to find out more from him. He has such close links to the Guise. I myself was his lover for a time, but not long. I thought that was all it was for Amelia, too. Yet she truly fell in love with him and she could not stay away from him. Passion, you see, Mademoiselle Haywood, is impossible in such a situation as ours. It is often fatal. We must be so careful at every moment."

Kate glanced back toward the palace, as if she could see Rob there, even though he had vanished. "So true indeed. Do you think d'Emours killed Amelia?"

"You do not? I warned her not to meet with him again at the pavilion, but she would not listen to me. Then she was dead."

"Monsieur d'Emours was with Signorina Isabella, the actress, all night," Kate said. "Of course, he could have sent an assassin. Yet I think he cannot be the only one capable of such a deed."

Celeste leaned closer. "Whom else do you suspect?"

Kate quickly told her of the list of suspects she had made with Rob. Celeste nodded thoughtfully at each idea, sometimes whispering, "*Oui*, that could be so."

"I fear I do not know enough of the French court to be sure of anyone else," Kate finished. "The poison that could have made her ill, disoriented her so it was easy to push her into the water, was perhaps in her perfume. Could that have been a gift from d'Emours?"

Celeste pursed her lips in thought. "Perhaps. He did give her some gifts—jewels, furs."

"A diamond brooch in the shape of a Guise badge?"

"I do not know. I never saw such a thing with Amelia. Why would he do that? And her perfume was a distinctive scent, one she wore last time she was in France. I suppose he could have slipped something into it, or hired a maidservant to do it."

But if d'Emours could have, so could anyone else. Kate mentioned that thought to Celeste.

Celeste shook her head. "D'Emours's name has long been plagued by scandal. He wouldn't want more."

"His birth? The duel over Amelia?" Or perhaps the duel had been about his birth, the old story of secrecy and bastardy. That would be worth killing for.

"*Exactement.* The Guise are his patrons, his source of power at court. If he found out about Amelia's work, would he not seek to protect them against her?"

"Or if the Guise found out about the affair with Amelia and Amelia's true work . . ." Kate was not sure why she would doubt d'Emours's guilt. He seemed a cold, ambitious man who had not managed the affair well. He certainly seemed the likely killer. But, like Amelia herself, he was changeable. He could easily have hired an assassin, yet his feelings for Amelia did not seem entirely feigned.

"How shall we discover him for sure?" Kate asked.

"There is only one way. We must confront him before he can find us."

"Really?" Kate exclaimed. "After what happened to Amelia?"

"I am accustomed to danger, Mademoiselle Haywood, as I am sure are you. It is around us every day.

And we have some advantages *pauvre* Amelia did not. We are not blinded with love for d'Emours, nor will we be alone. Your handsome friend Monsieur Cartman? He works with you, too, does he not? I have often seen you whispering together."

Kate nodded. With Rob there, she *would* feel safer, for he was quick-minded with a strong sword arm, though she feared he might lose his cool head too often. Rather against her more prudent side, she found herself curious and, aye, even excited at the thought of drawing d'Emours into confessing to his evil deed. "We could certainly trust Rob to help us."

"*Très bon.* A man with a gift for fighting, even stage fighting, is always most useful."

"Is there also no one else here at Fontainebleau you could call on for help?"

Celeste shook her head. "I trust none of the French; I know too many of their secrets through Queen Catherine. Sir Nicholas and Sir Henry are surely too doubtful to be of help to a mere woman, and I do not trust Monsieur Domville. He is charming, but has some strange friends."

Kate thought of Monsieur Domville, seemingly so eager to show Kate around the French court, friends with everyone. But surely he, too, had connections and alliances. He was kinsman to the Guises' rival Montmorency.

"Then you are right. How shall we do it? It must be soon. Sir Henry sent word we are to leave for England at the first opportunity."

"Tomorrow is Queen Catherine's gathering at her dairy, her Mi Voie. D'Emours will be there. He knows Amelia and I were friends, but I hope he does not yet know I worked with her. I will write him a message telling him I have learned a frightful secret about Amelia's death and that I fear he may be in danger himself. I will say I can only tell him in person and ask him to meet me at the queen's farmhouse. There is a chamber where you and Monsieur Cartman can be concealed while I talk to him."

Kate liked the way Celeste schemed. "Do you think he will confess to you? Or tell you whom he suspects or would cast blame on?"

"I hope he will tell us much indeed. Men, even ones as cold as d'Emours, can be susceptible to a lady's wiles. And you and Monsieur Cartman will be there to hear it all. . . ."

# CHAPTER TWENTY

Kate hoped Celeste would discover all they needed to know very soon. Her nose itched, and she dared not sneeze.

She crouched in the tiny closet, peering through the knothole to the chamber beyond. She was very glad Rob was next to her, his body warm and strong in the tiny space, or she would scream from being shut up in there. He held her hand, and she felt herself grow calmer.

She could see Celeste there, sitting at the round table with a book open before her. It was the same octagonal closet where Queen Catherine had staged her séance, but today the fine tapestries were gone, the crystal stone nowhere to be seen. The window was partially open, letting in the sound of laughter from the courtiers about to depart for the queen's *laiterie*.

"He will surely answer my message soon," Celeste had said. "He can't be away from the rest of the Guise party too long, but I know he cannot resist finding out my purpose in invoking Amelia's name."

Kate prayed she was right, prayed she could truly

trust Celeste Renard. Amelia's death was an injustice that had to be answered, but her legs were becoming cramped from kneeling in the closet. Surely it was easier to be a man, to address wrongs with a sword in a straightforward duel.

Celeste slowly turned a page in her book, and Kate shifted on the cushion beneath her. Her breath sounded too loud in the hot, stuffy space, and she hoped fervently that no one else could hear it except Rob, who sat so close beside her. She wondered at the great fortitude and dedication of Queen Catherine's own spies, and thought of the ways she could carry such methods back to England.

If she lived to see England again, of course.

At last, the door to the chamber opened, and Jacques d'Emours appeared. He looked the very portrait of a fashionable French courtier in his dark blue velvet and satin, his golden hair shining in the sunlight, his short cloak tossed back over his shoulder. It was fashioned with a diamond pin, yet Kate could not see what it was.

He frowned, his face showing nothing but impatience. "What is this about, Celeste? There is no time for idle chatter today."

Celeste looked up at him with a sweet smile. Kate was impressed with her coolness, her stillness. She was also glad she had learned French in her childhood, for they spoke very quickly. "It will not take long, Jacques. I merely wanted to talk with you about Amelia, whom I know we both cared about a great deal. I am sure you wish to find her killer as greatly as all her other friends do."

His frown flickered. "Her killer? You have been reading too much of Queen Catherine's blood-soaked Italian poetry. Amelia drowned, which is indeed very sad, but hardly a theatrical tragedy. She had too much wine that night."

"Did she indeed? Dr. Folie has other ideas—as do Amelia's family members." Celeste slid the book she had been perusing across the table—it was the herbal Mistress Berry had given Kate. What was it doing there? Kate remembered all the warnings she had been given not to trust anyone at all. "You see here? Something was perhaps slipped into her perfume, which weakened her when she was attacked. I am sure it was *meant* to look like an accident."

D'Emours sank down onto the stool opposite Celeste's, watching her carefully, his handsome face giving away nothing. He talked of Celeste's theatricality, but Kate thought he was just as good.

"Why do you think this?" he asked hoarsely. "And why summon *me*? I could do naught to help her before—how can I do so now?"

"That is just the thing: She loved you, and I am sure you cared about her as much as you are able. You would not wish to see someone who hurt her go unpunished. But I fear there are those who would say that *you* are the one who wanted to hurt her."

D'Emours reared back as if he had been hit. "Who says such vile falsehoods?"

"Too many for you to challenge them all to duels, I fear. Everyone knows what occurred between you and

Amelia, and that your Guise allies would help you to be rid of her when she became troublesome." Celeste reached across the table and caught his velvet sleeve as he tried to stand. "Please listen to me, for Amelia's sake. I am in Queen Catherine's household. You know I hear many things there. You must be very careful at the *laiterie*. They are watching you."

"I have nothing to fear," d'Emours said tightly. "Amelia was most foolish beneath her great beauty. She had many lovers—surely any one of them could have hurt her. Perhaps that is why Monsieur Ridley has been confined to his chambers?"

There was the sudden clatter of steps outside their little chamber, a burst of laughter, and Celeste quickly stood up. They would not be alone there for long. "You know as well as I do the English are capable of ruses, no matter how clumsy they prove to be," she said. "But we French are cleverer; we are always better at hiding things. Yet even you cannot hide forever. It seems we cannot talk now. If you wish to know more, meet me at the *laiterie*."

D'Emours looked down at the book for one long, silent moment. Celeste gave him a serene smile, and gracefully swept out of the room in a swirl of green damask. She shut the door softly behind her.

Kate held her breath as she watched d'Emours. He stood as still as one of the marble statues in the garden for a long, tense moment. Suddenly he shouted out an oath and swept the book onto the floor with a crash.

His shoulders heaving, he stared down at the volume, its pages fanned out. His frown returned. He picked up the book and rushed out of the room. The door swung shut behind him, leaving a thick, heavy silence.

Kate waited a few more moments to be sure he would not return. Carefully, she unfolded herself from the cabinet and took Rob's hand as he helped her out. Her legs were shaky for a moment.

"We should hurry," Rob said. "We can't let everyone get ahead of us."

Kate nodded and followed him down the back staircase. She wondered what d'Emours thought of being accused, whom he would summon for assistance—and what he saw in that book that she had missed.

Hopefully it would be only a small matter of time before those questions were truly answered.

By the time Kate and Rob arrived at Queen Catherine's dairy, the Mi Voie, most of the guests were already there. Lady Barnett had decided at the last moment that she would attend the fete after all, hoping for some distraction from her tears, and Mistress Berry at first could not be found to help her dress. Lady Barnett was so unsure of everything, the maidservants were in despair assisting her and sent for Kate.

Mistress Berry at last returned to the Barnetts' chambers, just in time to help Lady Barnett pin her veiled cap to her curled hair and soothe her with another posset.

But after the two ladies set off in one of Queen Mary's own covered carriages, Kate and Rob barely found the last of the carts to carry them to the dairy.

Like the boats at the pond, the carts meant to convey the guests to the rustic party were festooned with wreaths and ribbons and set with striped satin cushions. The ponies that drew them had large velvet bows decorating their bridles, and the drivers wore wide-brimmed hats pinned with greenery. More ribbons fluttered in the trees along the lane leading from the palace grounds to the gates of the dairy.

It was all most whimsical and beautiful, but Kate could take no pleasure in the fine day. She could think only of Amelia's body floating in the cold water of the pond, and Monsieur d'Emours's simmering anger.

"Kate, are you sure you are quite well?" Rob whispered. "You look pale."

She flashed him a small smile. "I only want all this to be over. Poor Amelia . . ."

"Then let me go alone. You have already put yourself in danger too many times over this matter."

"Nay," she murmured. "I must see the end of it now."

He studied her for a long moment, his brow furrowed, his blue eyes dark. "I know you well enough to be sure now I cannot talk you out of it. But you will stay very close to me?"

"Of course."

The cart rolled to a halt in a large cobblestone courtyard. Its raked gravel pathways were crowded with courtiers dressed as shepherds and shepherdesses in pale silks and wide hats, with beribboned crooks and walking sticks. For a moment, Kate was sure they must have been transported into a different world entirely from the gilded formality of the palace. The chimneys and dark gray slate roofs of Fontainebleau could be glimpsed beyond the trees, not really far away at all, yet it all seemed like something in a dream.

Queen Catherine's beloved dairy, her great building pride, the symbol of her nurturing motherhood and care for her adopted French home, had a plain facade of pale stone with slate roofs that mirrored those of the palace, crisscrossed with rough-hewed beams. As she climbed down from the cart, Kate saw a farmhouse before them with a stable and the dairy itself at one end. A wooden fence beyond the stable held back a clutch of fluffy white sheep with black-and-pink ribbons around their necks, peeking out doubtfully at the arriving crowds.

"We should find Celeste," she said as they followed the crowd along a shady allée that led between the farmhouse and the dairy itself. They emerged into a walled garden where maidservants waited to give each guest a little sheep formed of fluffy silver wool. Kate clutched at hers as if for reassurance.

In the summer, surely the garden was a haven of roses climbing over the stone walls amid little nooks of trees and wooden swings. Even in the midst of winter, it was pretty. A dais was at the far end of the garden pathways, draped in great swaths of green and gold satin. The queen's small children capered there, tiny shepherds and shepherdesses declaiming poetry under the strict eye of their mother. "She restored us to our fields and our woods . . . She made us to return to our former pastures," little Princess Marguerite, the loveliest of the royal children, with her ivory complexion, sang. Feathers bobbed in the waves of her dark brown hair.

Queen Catherine sat on a throne in the center of the stage with little King Charles on one side and Queen Mary on the other. She nodded at their pleasant honor of her, smiling.

The Duc de Guise stood behind the queen, whispering in her ear, but d'Emours was nowhere to be seen. Kate went on tiptoe and glimpsed Lady Barnett standing with her husband and Sir Nicholas, her face pale and tearstained under her gossamer veil, but she was smiling as if court life itself had the power to rejuvenate her.

Kate heard a flutter of silvery laughter and spun around to see Celeste hurrying toward her, as light and smiling as if she hadn't just threatened Jacques d'Emours. A gentleman was on each arm, both of them staring at her as if she were a sun goddess. She stepped away from her escorts and leaned in as if to greet Kate with an airy kiss on each cheek. "He has agreed to meet me at the small chamber of the attics in the farmhouse. No one will be there while the royal children are performing. Everyone must be seen by Queen Catherine to exclaim over the charms of her rather toadlike children.

You can hide as you did before, this time beneath the bed. You and Monsieur Cartman should be able to see and hear all from there. You will find the room at the top of the back stairs. It is the only one on that story. Don't be late."

"We certainly will not," Kate murmured as Celeste drew away. She caught a glimpse of fear in Celeste's eyes, a disconcerting flash of uncertainty, before she laughed and strolled on with her admirers.

Rob offered Kate his arm and they made their way slowly around the edges of the garden. There was naught to do for a while but wait. And Kate was not good at waiting. She studied the people around them, Queen Catherine's beautiful ladies, Queen Mary's Maries walking with Lord James Stuart's Scots attendants, giggling with them. It seemed Toby had not appeared, nor had Charles Throckmorton.

The clock above the stables chimed the hour, and Kate realized it was time for the next part of their scheme. She and Rob made their way up a narrow flight of wooden steps to the large attic room at the top of the house, tucked beneath the slate roofs. It was a stuffy room, obviously seldom used. Bundles of wool lined the whitewashed walls, the smell greasy and sharp.

She and Rob found a niche behind the bundles, a small shelter where they could watch the door from the small crack between tufts of wool. *It is as cramped and itchy as the wardrobe, but at least it has a soft place to sit,* Kate thought ruefully as she tucked a pelt beneath her skirt. She held on to the toy sheep the maidservants had handed her and waited for Celeste and d'Emours to arrive.

*Please*, she begged silently. *Let this not be a chase in vain!*

She was glad of Rob beside her. He was large, warm, and strong, and had brought several daggers, one of which now nestled in its holster on her wrist, beneath the folds of her silk sleeve. The smile he flashed her was reassuring, and she leaned back against the wall of wool, stroking the little silver sheep toy.

She couldn't relax for long, however. The door opened, and she shot up to sit straight, peeking between the bundles. It was Celeste, by herself. She leaned against the wall beside their hiding place, watching the door herself. Her fists opened and closed in the folds of her skirts, crumpling handfuls of the rich fabric.

"I got the message to him," she said.

"Are you certain he will come?" Kate whispered back.

"Of course. He won't be able to resist finding out if I have proof he did away with Amelia."

"And do you?" Rob demanded.

Celeste gave a harsh laugh. "*Non*, certainly not. Men like him are not often so careless. But I am sure that between us we can find a way to force the truth out of him."

Kate was not quite so confident. D'Emours seldom let his cool mask slip away, not even in the burial chapel of his parents. She rested her arm, with the weight of its small dagger, against the tiny sheep and held her breath.

They had only a few moments to compose themselves when Kate heard the thud of booted footsteps on the wooden stairs outside, and the door was shoved open with a loud bang that made her jump. Jacques d'Emours appeared there, a pale ray of light in his white satin amid the dark, dank attic. He scowled as he looked at Celeste, who pushed herself away from the wall and strolled into the middle of the room as if she hadn't a care in all the world.

"What is this evidence you spoke of?" he demanded. His tone was icy, his burning anger apparent, as could be expected, but it also contained something Kate would not have expected of him: desperation. She hoped they could hear words of confession before he became violent. He had already dueled once.

"So you do admit you were responsible for Amelia's death?" Celeste said, as if she asked him about the weather.

"What is it you want from me, Celeste? You, of all people, know how I felt about Amelia."

"*Oui*, and that is why I am sure it was you. She wanted to marry you."

"And I her. But she felt the same as I did, that it was not possible. Our situations in life, our religions, would make such a match unthinkable."

"Why?" Celeste cried, her calm, cool tone taking on a sharp edge. Kate tightened her grip on the tiny sheep, ready to leap out if needed. "Because of the Guise? You are indebted to them; everyone knows that. Surely it was become of that, to keep your secrets, that you challenged Mamou?"

"You must stop this now, Celeste," a quiet, low voice said from the doorway. "Jacques was prepared to be a fool for the sake of love, but I will not let him. I saw you creep away from the party, my dear, and I feared you were going somewhere just like this."

Kate gasped at the sound of that familiar voice and reached for Rob's hand. She realized with a sick, cold certainty that she had not been able to put together the whole puzzle of Amelia's death, that she had misjudged the players. For it was Brigit Berry who slipped into the attic room now. Brigit, in her somber black gown and mild smile, moving so quietly. Seeing everything that happened around the Barnetts and their niece. Brigit who owned the herbal.

Brigit, who held a shining dagger lightly in her hand.

Even Celeste looked shocked, frozen in place. Jacques swung around to face Brigit, his cool distance shattered. "*Non!*" he said in a hard, furious tone.

"Madame Berry," Celeste whispered. "What are you doing here? Are you and Jacques lovers?"

Brigit laughed, a chilling sound of merriment. "Of course not! Even a woman who works for a witch like Queen Catherine should know better than that. I am his mother. And who better to look after the best interests of her son? Queen Catherine and I do share that."

Kate's free hand pressed to her mouth to hold back a cry. She thought of all she had missed, and it all clicked into place. The herbs, the quiet looks, the web of family and secrets. Even the bright blue color of their eyes, Brigit's and d'Emours's both the same.

"Tell me you did not do this," Jacques said hoarsely. "Not you, my real mother."

Brigit looked up at him, her eyes wide with surprise, as if she wondered that he would be angry. "I had no choice. She was spying for William Cecil. And you would not, could not, stay away from her. Just like a foolish man, giving up everything for the sake of a pretty, false smile. Just like your father. If the Guise found out about such a connection, you would be utterly finished. You would probably be dead—we have all seen what they do to traitors."

D'Emours had turned completely white. "You did kill her? Your own kinswoman?"

"But you are my son!" Brigit cried. "I gave you up to your natural father and his wife when you were born so you could have a place in the world, an estate, the honor of a fine name. All I had in return was their promise they would remember me. You were just going to throw it all away. She was flaunting that brooch you gave her to all the court; I knew it meant you had gone back to her."

"How did you . . ." he said in a strangled voice.

Brigit smiled—a sweet, terrible sight. "It was so easy. It wouldn't have been necessary at all if I had been able to get those letters from that silly musician girl. I am sure they mentioned Amelia and would have been intercepted. But then I realized that it would be better for her to be gone. She would never cease to make trouble."

Rob's hand tightened on Kate's, as if he knew the sick feeling that flooded through her at those words.

"I had a careful plan," Brigit went on. "A slow-acting, small dose of poison in her perfume. Everyone would think she was merely ill, a sad wasting disease. But it had no time to work, not after I knew you were going back to her. I gave her a larger dose in her wine so she would feel giddy. And I followed her back to the pavilion that night. I sent that Italian whore of an actress to you so none would suspect you. I was only looking after you, as a mother should. That woman was vile, unworthy of you! A horrible creature. A witch. A spy, just like that musician girl. I tried to find the letters I knew she carried from Cecil, letters that could have mentioned you, but I failed in that. I could not fail with Amelia."

She reached out to touch his arm, and he fell back a step with a disgusted cry.

Everything happened quickly then, in a blur of movement. *"Cochon!"* Celeste shouted. She lunged at Brigit and scratched at her eyes, as if in defense of her lost friend. Brigit was startled and stumbled off balance, but she sidestepped Celeste's attack and her dagger arced up into the air. Celeste ducked, tumbling to the dusty wooden floor.

D'Emours caught Brigit around the waist and swung her off her feet. She lashed out at him, kicking and screaming. Rob dashed out from their hiding place, his own dagger drawn, Kate close behind him. She helped Celeste up and they scrambled out of the way of the melee.

"This ends now!" d'Emours shouted. His mother twisted in his grasp, as agile as a feral animal in her fury, her eyes glassy with her desperation. There was no sign of the old, efficient Mistress Berry or the cool Monsieur d'Emours.

"Nay!" Brigit screamed. "I have done all this only for you. How dare you repay me so? You are all I have!"

Her flailing dagger suddenly pierced his shoulder, moving through the white satin of his doublet, which was quickly stained with a scarlet bloom of blood. He let go of her and stared down at his shoulder with stunned disbelief.

Brigit screamed again, an anguished cry of despair. Before anyone could realize what was happening, she spun around and fled, her racing footsteps clattering away down the stairs. Rob took off in pursuit.

D'Emours collapsed to the floor, his hand pressed to his wounded shoulder. Blood seeped between his fingers. Kate and Celeste ran to his side.

"Such fools," Celeste muttered as she tore at the hem of her gown. She wrapped it quickly around the wound.

"Go after her!" he gasped. "She cannot be allowed to escape. She killed Amelia; she will not hesitate to murder someone else."

*Rob.* A cold panic rose in Kate, and she stumbled to

her feet. Celeste looked up at her, wide-eyed. "You go after Monsieur Cartman. I will stay here and call for help. But be very careful."

Kate nodded and spun around to run after Rob. She dashed out of the farmhouse and past a few courtiers who lingered in the courtyard, laughing together, completely unaware of the drama that had just happened above their heads. They called after her in astonishment, but she did not slow down. She glimpsed Rob's golden head vanishing down the allée of trees, toward the pond, and she followed, stopping only to point the guards at the gate toward the farmhouse. They shouted after her, tried to snatch at her sleeve, but she evaded them. She wanted only to catch up to Rob before Brigit had a chance to hurt him as she had d'Emours.

Holding up the heavy hem of her skirt, she followed Rob down the winding path to the pond where Amelia had died. Her fashionable stays were tight and she was out of breath, unable to keep up with him. She thought that Queen Mary was quite right to wear breeches whenever possible. By the time she found him, he was at the muddy banks of the pond and Brigit was nowhere in sight. The pavilion gleamed bright white, reflected in the water, horribly beautiful.

"Where is she?" Kate gasped.

"You should go back, Kate," he cried. "You should be nowhere near her!"

"I sent the guards to find Celeste and d'Emours. I had to find you. What if she hurt you, too?"

"I don't think—" Rob suddenly broke off and pointed out across the water.

Kate saw Brigit there in one of the boats that had been used the night Amelia died. She was pulling on the oars across the water, toward the pavilion. Rob shouted her name but she never slowed down. Halfway across the pond, she stopped, and as calmly as if she stepped from a carriage, she dove over the side into the icy water and vanished from sight.

Rob tore off his doublet and boots, shoving them into Kate's arms even as he waded into the murky water just offshore. Once it was deep enough, he too dove in. Kate watched in cold fear as he swam in quick, smooth strokes, his bright head breaking the greenish waves. He reached the boat bobbing alone and heaved Brigit's body over its side.

By the time he came back to Kate's side, Brigit was dead, a calm smile on her pale lips.

# CHAPTER TWENTY-ONE

"I cannot believe this!" Lady Barnett wailed. "Brigit murdered Amelia? Why?"

Sir Henry sighed. He looked gray-faced and exhausted, as surely they all were, gathered by the fire in the Barnetts' sitting room, untouched goblets of wine on the table. Sir Nicholas had departed once he heard what had happened, gone to write to Cecil and Queen Elizabeth and, thus, in his mind, put it all behind them. Lady Barnett could not cease sobbing, and Kate felt frozen in place by the window. Even the warmth of Rob's hand on her arm could not chase away the cold. Brigit Berry had tried to kill her on the ship—and *had* killed Amelia. She even tried to kill her own son. It was hideous.

But Sir Henry had suddenly become patient. He explained to his wife once more that her kinswoman had once borne a French child out of wedlock and had killed Amelia to try to protect him now.

Lady Barnett shook her head, clearly still most baffled, her world upended. "But I was here with Brigit when we were girls—how could she not tell me this? I gave her a position, a home, for all these years. And she repaid me by taking away my poor, innocent Amelia."

Sir Henry awkwardly patted his wife's hand. His gaze met Kate's over Lady Barnett's bent head, and he nodded a fraction. Lady Barnett did not, could not, know of Amelia's work with Cecil, and now it would never be known. Her confusion and grief were already too great without politics tossed into the stormy mix.

"I will stay with her now," Sir Henry said. "We all need to be ready to depart for England at the first opportunity."

"Of course," Kate murmured. England had never felt so very far away. Whitehall, Elizabeth, Cecil, all the familiar things seemed like something she had known only in a dream. She wanted to run back to it, but at the same time she feared to find it all changed while she was gone.

Or perhaps she was the one who had changed.

She let Rob lead her out of the chamber, Lady Barnett's cries drifting behind them. They made their way down the stairs and through a side door into one of the gardens, a small walled space with trees and marble benches, a quiet haven after the palace.

"Are you quite well, Kate?" Rob asked gently.

She gave him a small smile. "As well as I can be. Poor Amelia. Poor Mistress Berry and Monsieur d'Emours as well, despite their actions. Such a terrible story."

"We will soon be home again," he said. "Kate, I want to say—"

But his words were cut off when they turned a corner of the garden pathway to find Celeste and Toby standing near the stone wall. They were not alone. Queen Mary was with them, her Maries gathered around her. Her pretty face was streaked with tears.

"Ah, Mademoiselle Haywood! Monsieur Cartman!" the queen cried. She waved her white handkerchief to them before pressing it to her eyes again, the very image of grief and shock. "I heard of what you did today, finding the villain who killed my friend Amelia. You are so very brave."

Kate and Rob quickly made their bows and hurried toward the queen, who pressed their hands. "We are most happy that is finished, Your Majesty," Rob said.

"*Alors*, but you must be very brave," Mary Seton said.

"Indeed," said Queen Mary. "I do wish you could stay here with me, for I have much work to do now. But I understand from Monsieur Ridley that you are all going back to England. We will miss you so very much."

Kate glanced at Toby. He also bowed to the queen, his usually open, merry face pale and somber. It seemed Queen Mary did not remember coldly accusing Toby of killing Amelia, but surely he would not forget.

"I have enjoyed a glimpse of the beauties of Fontainebleau, Your Majesty," Kate said. "Yet I confess I will be glad to be at my own home."

Queen Mary smiled sadly. "Home is always the best place to be, *n'est-ce pas*? I have decided, after all of this, that I too must find my true place. I must return to

Scotland, where I can keep my friends safe. I am sure my own people will be like my family now that I do not have my mother or my husband, and will welcome me. You will tell this to my cousin Elizabeth?"

Kate was surprised that Queen Mary had so suddenly decided to return to Scotland, a country she had not seen since she was a child, and confidently expected a loving welcome. But perhaps she *would* find it there. She was, after all, a princess of enormous charm, and had great loyalty to her friends. Kate would certainly tell Elizabeth all she knew, all she had learned and heard, as soon as she returned to London—but she did not know if Elizabeth would greet the news of Mary's return with equanimity or with an angry tantrum.

"I will take all my ladies with me, of course," Queen Mary said. "I only wish I could have offered Amelia a place! But perhaps she would have been like Celeste here, determined to marry and leave me."

Kate glanced at Celeste, who gave her a rueful smile. "You are to be married?"

"To Monsieur Ridley," Queen Mary said, waving her handkerchief at them. "He will take her back to England, I am sure. But I hope you will give my cousin this message. We are family, two queens who shall be neighbors and must be friends. I send Elizabeth only love, as I am sure she does to me, and I hope we will meet very soon. I think we must thrive or fail together."

Queen Mary turned and swept away through the garden gate, her white skirts ghostly in the winter garden. Kate would certainly tell Queen Elizabeth all Mary said, but whether she meant it or not—that was something Cecil and his intelligencers would have to discover.

She smiled at Celeste and Toby, who stood close together but not touching. Celeste smiled and Toby looked distant, as if he were not quite with them. "You are to be married?" Kate said.

"Yes. You must wish us happiness," Celeste answered with a little laugh. "I find I long to see England again, and Toby has been a kind enough friend to offer to help me. We will wed before we leave Fontainebleau."

"I *do* wish you happy, indeed," Kate said. She kissed Celeste's cool cheek and touched Toby's arm. He gave her a smile, and she hoped she glimpsed his old happiness somewhere beneath the grief. Somewhere that Celeste could help him find again.

"I am sure we will see each other often in England," Celeste said. "I shall need friends in my new home."

"Any friend of Celeste shall have to be brave indeed," Toby said. "And you have certainly proven yourself to be that, Mistress Haywood."

Kate waved at them as they followed Queen Mary out of the garden. She was not at all sure Toby was right. She did not *feel* brave, merely sad and homesick. Rob took her hand, and she glanced up at him. He smiled at her, and she turned to move away. He caught her hand.

"So, there is to be a wedding before we leave," he said.

"Aye. One happy thing, I hope."

"Perhaps we could make it a double wedding? Two couples in the church doorstep?"

Kate was shocked at his words. She turned back to him, half-sure he would be grinning, that it would be a jest. But he watched her intently, his sky blue eyes shaded by the brim of his velvet cap. "Are—are you asking me to marry you, Rob?"

"I am sure it can't be a complete surprise, Kate. I hope I have shown you my feelings. This time in France has only made me see things even more clearly. I love you, and I want to keep you safe. Lord Hunsdon's patronage is ensured, and I am sure I could make us a home. I know I could make you as happy as you make me. We are a fine team, are we not?"

Kate was absolutely certain he *could* make her happy—at least for now. How could any woman not love him? He was so handsome, so daring, so witty. He knew what the love of music and poetry was like to a person's soul, how it became as necessary to life as air and water. Yet he was also restless, moody, with a need for applause that would surely never leave him. He promised her a home, and she longed for just that. A fireside of her own, a family, peace.

Could Rob truly give that, be that? He fed her curious, adventurous side, but with marriage would come children, and children would need security. Elizabeth knew that. She knew the dangers and mysteries of marriage and romance. Seeing what had happened to Amelia Wrightsman made those dangers only starker.

If Kate wanted to stay with the queen, she would have to choose. And she found, now that she stood at the crossroads, she had to listen to herself, trust herself. What life did she want?

She did not yet know. "I do care for you, Rob, so very, very much," she whispered. She went up on tiptoe and softly pressed her lips to his. It was a sweet, warm kiss and made her crave so much more. But she had to think very carefully, for she knew from the moment she truly answered him life would not be the same.

"But I cannot marry you yet," she said. "Not until we return to England and I can speak with Queen Elizabeth."

Rob gently touched her cheek, his eyes so very blue as he studied her face. "Is the queen the only one you must talk to, then?"

Kate swallowed hard. Nay, she also had to talk to Anthony Elias. He was her friend; perhaps he was more. His life and what he could give were the opposite of Rob's. As a lawyer's wife, there would be a home and security. But would it be too quiet? Would she miss the court, the theater?

"I will answer you when we are in England," she said. "You must be certain as well, Rob. Can you be happy as a husband, with only one lady waiting for you? It will be very boring, I fear."

He laughed and raised her hand to his lips for a quick kiss. "If *you* are that lady, Kate, I could never be bored. There would be villains to chase every week."

Kate sighed. "That is what I fear."

They turned back toward the palace, and for a moment Kate was caught by the unearthly beauty of Fontainebleau. Truly, she had never seen anything like it, and she knew she never would again. The white towers, the alleys of giant trees, the shimmering silver roof—it was astounding. But beauty could hide far too much ugliness, and she could not be fooled by its illusions ever again.

As they climbed the winding horseshoe stairs toward the carved doors, a page in Queen Catherine's green-and-white livery came running toward her, a package in his hands.

"Mademoiselle Haywood," he said with a bow. "The Queen Mother sends you this, a parting gift, as she has heard you are to leave for England soon. She said I must give it directly into your hands and no other."

Kate took the parcel from him. It was light and square, wrapped in silk and tied with a ribbon, and she half dreaded opening it. What could Queen Catherine be sending to her? "Tell the queen I send many thanks," she said.

As the servant rushed away, she quickly unwrapped it and found a leather-bound book. She turned it to its cover. Stamped there in gold were the words THE PRINCE BY SIGNOR NICCOLÒ M. She remembered what Queen Catherine had said, that a true monarch must be kind as well as ruthless. That loyalty was all.

She opened the gilt-edge vellum pages and a small note fluttered out. *For your queen, and for you, Mademoi-*

*selle Haywood. If you ever wish to return to France, I know the value of a lady's mind.*

"What does Queen Catherine send you?" Rob asked.

"Nothing," Kate answered. She tucked the book into the purse tied at her kirtle and took Rob's arm to hurry into the palace. She had much work to be done still before they could leave for home. "Merely a small gift for Queen Elizabeth from Fontainebleau."

# AUTHOR'S NOTE

I hope you've enjoyed following Kate to France as much as I have! Fontainebleau is one of the most beautiful palaces in Europe, with a fascinating history, and I enjoyed the chance to spend a little more time there (even if only in my imagination!) at one of its most turbulent times in history.

The 1560s were an incredible period for amazing women, and I had a lot of fun incorporating two of them, Mary, Queen of Scots, and Catherine de Medici (one of my favorite historical figures), into Kate's adventures. Mary Stewart (1542–1587) has, of course, been a figure of much fascination for centuries, the subject of endless stories/movies/plays, and it's easy to see why. She was renowned for her beauty and charm, she was an adventurer at heart (even though those adventures ended in mayhem more often than not), and she died most tragically. She is a counterpoint to her cousin Elizabeth I's great success.

The only surviving child of King James V of Scotland (who died mere days after her birth) and the indomitable Marie de Guise, daughter of one of the most powerful and ruthless families in France, Mary's early childhood was one of much turbulence. Henry VIII's so-called rough wooing, trying via raids and battles to win Mary's hand for his son Prince Edward, drove Queen Marie to arrange a marriage with the three-year-old son of King Henri II of France. In August 1548, Mary was sent to France to be raised as a true French princess, setting sail with a large retinue that included her playmates, the Maries, who would stay with her for many years.

She was a great favorite at the French court, considered to be stylish and charming. She loved hunting and hawking, embroidery, music, and dancing, and mastered several languages (though she was no scholar like Elizabeth). She was very tall (almost six feet) and pretty, with auburn hair, brown-gold eyes, and a famously pale complexion. She married the Dauphin Francis in a lavish ceremony at Notre Dame in 1558.

As the granddaughter of Princess Margaret Tudor, she had a strong claim to the English throne, and her father-in-law did not hesitate to press that claim, ordering that Francis and Mary's arms be quartered with those of England—an action that haunted relations with Elizabeth forever. She became Queen of France much sooner than expected, when King Henri died in a terrible jousting accident on July 10, 1559, leaving his sickly fifteen-year-old son as king. Mary's Guise uncles practically ran the country under King

Francis and Queen Mary, but the reign did not last long. Francis died of an ear infection in December 1560, and Mary's life changed forever.

With her ten-year-old brother-in-law, Charles IX, now king and firmly under the control of his mother, Catherine de Medici, there was no place for Mary to go in France, though she could have chosen to live there in comfortable retirement. Various proposed marriages did not work out, and her adventurous heart led her back to Scotland.

The other powerful woman in France at the time, Catherine de Medici (1519–1589), did not seem at the time of her arrival as a teenage bride to be one who would seize power. A fascinating, complex woman, she was the daughter of Lorenzo de Medici and the French noblewoman Madeleine de la Tour d'Auvergne, and was orphaned as an infant and raised by her uncle the pope, who arranged a stunning marriage with Henri, the second son of the King of France, when she was fourteen. She fell deeply in love with her husband, who was already in love with the beautiful Diane de Poitiers and had no time for his new bride. For ten years, Catherine had no children, was ignored by her husband, and was shunned by the elegant and snobbish French court. There was often talk of sending her back to Florence, but she kept quiet and bided her time. After the death of her husband and of her eldest son, she came into her own power as regent. She sent away the Guise, presided over the royal council, and decided the policy in France for many years. She was a great patron of the arts, such as painting, music, theater, and architecture, as well as food in the Italian style. She was also deeply interested in the occult, bringing in astrologers and alchemists to help her decide policy. (Ruggieri was a real figure.)

Unfortunately, even though she herself did not seem to have strong religious feelings and tried to run the middle line between the Catholics and Protestants of France, she failed to realize the high passions and hatreds that had been simmering for years, and soon France was launched into the thirty years of the Wars of Religion.

Sir Nicholas Throckmorton (1515/16–1571) was also a real historical figure. He was a staunch Protestant, imprisoned for a time under Queen Mary Tudor for possible involvement in Wyatt's Rebellion. Under Queen Elizabeth, and with the support of his friend William Cecil, he rose quickly at court. From May 1559 to April 1564, he was ambassador to France, where he got to know Queen Mary quite well. He grudgingly admired her for her charm and her seeming helpless femininity, even as he was exasperated by her evasions in the matter of the Treaty of Edinburgh (which she never ratified). In 1565 he was sent as ambassador to Scotland, where he tried and failed to stop the disastrous Darnley marriage. (Interesting historical tidbits: His daughter Elizabeth, "Bess," went on to marry Sir Walter Raleigh, and his widow, Anne Carew, married

Adrian Stokes, who had also been the second husband of Frances Brandon Grey, Duchess of Suffolk.)

One real-life aspect of sixteenth-century Fontaine-bleau I loved using in the story was Queen Catherine's dairy. I've visited the Petit Trianon at Versailles and loved seeing the still-working gardens (growing pumpkins last time I was there) and the items like Sèvres china milk buckets, but I didn't know that Marie Antoinette was far from the first queen to build her own rustic retreat. Last year I read Meredith Martin's fascinating book *Dairy Queens: The Politics of Pastoral Architecture from Catherine de' Medici to Marie-Antoinette*, and learned more about this facet of royal life in France. Mi Voie ("midway"), Catherine's dairy, has long been demolished and its location is hard to find in the grounds at Fontainebleau, but the queen put a great deal of work and interest into it during her life. It was designed and decorated by many of the same artists who worked on the château. On February 13, 1564, she hosted an elaborate banquet there before embarking on a long royal tour with young King Charles, and I stole a few of the aspects of this party for my own story (just a few years early!).

I also came to feel like Fontainebleau itself was a character in Kate's story. It's an amazingly beautiful place, and the corridors, richly decorated chambers, and exquisite gardens seem to be full of ghosts! The king's gallery, where Kate meets Queen Catherine for the first time, the pond with its stone summerhouse, and the towers and staircases are all still there, just waiting for new stories. . . . These are just a few of the sources I used for the historical background of *Murder at Fontainebleau.* Please visit my Web site, amandacarmack. com, for more information and Tudor sources.

**For Mary, Queen of Scots:**

Jane Dunn, *Elizabeth and Mary: Cousins, Rivals, Queens* (2003).

Antonia Fraser, *Mary Queen of Scots* (1969).

Roderick Graham, *The Life of Mary: Queen of Scots: An Accidental Tragedy* (2009).

John Guy, *Queen of Scots: The True Life of Mary Stewart* (2004).

James Mackay, *In My End Is My Beginning: A Life of Mary Queen of Scots* (1999).

Alison Plowden, *Two Queens in One Isle* (1984).

Susan Watkins, *Mary Queen of Scots* (2001).


**For Catherine de Medici:**

Leonie Frieda, *Catherine de Medici: Renaissance Queen of France* (2003).

Robert J. Knecht, *Catherine de' Medici* (1998).

Princess Michael of Kent, *The Serpent and the Moon* (2004).


**For sixteenth-century France:**

Frederic J. Baumgartner, *France in the Sixteenth Century* (1995).

Vincent Droguet, *Fontainebleau: The House of Kings* (2002).

Robert J. Knecht, *The French Renaissance Court* (2008).

Henry D. Sedgwick, *The House of Guise* (1938).